The Burgundy Briefcase

To Jane,
I hope you enjoy this
journey of discovery.
Best wishes,
Roberta Burton
4/24/15

Roberta Burton

Published by:
Southern Yellow Pine (SYP) Publishing
4351 Natural Bridge Rd.
Tallahassee, FL 32305

www.syppublishing.com

This is a work of fiction. Names, characters, places, and events that occur either are the products of the author's imagination or are used fictitiously. Any resemblance to actual persons, places, or events is purely co-incidental.

The contents and opinions expressed in this book do not necessarily reflect the views and opinions of Southern Yellow Pine Publishing, nor does the mention of brands or trade names constitute endorsement.

ISBN-10: 1940869315 Trade Paperback
ISBN-13: 978-1-940869-31-5 Trade Paperback
ISBN-13: 978-1-940869-29-2 ePub

Cover Design by Elizabeth Babski, Babski Creative Studios
Author's Photo by Riko Carrion
Forgive You, Charles Wilkinson ©1995. Used with permission of the author.

Printed in the United States of America
First SYP Publishing Edition

Feb. 2015

Praise for the Author

Tantalizingly close to achieving her lifelong goal, the protagonist must confront the ghosts of her past, which threaten to stand in her way. Burton skillfully puts the reader in a front-row seat for the trip. Intense, insightful, and well done.

Darryl Bollinger, author of *The Medicine Game, A Case of Revenge, and The Pill Game*

You'll cheer for Lee on every step of her determined, late-in-life pursuit of a Ph. D. in clinical psychology. You are certain she will be able to help others through therapy, but will her newfound skills help her recover from the loss of the love of her life and escape from an abusive relationship? A fascinating story you won't want to miss!

Donna Meredith, author of *The Glass Madonna, The Color of Lies, and Wet Work*

The Burgundy Briefcase by Roberta Burton is a moving account of survival, growth, and hard-won personal and professional victory. Readers willing to peel away the many onion layers of Lee's story will attain a core of hope and humanity.

Rhett DeVane, author of *Suicide Supper Club, Mama's Comfort Food, and Cathead Crazy*

Dedication

To all the men in my life who made this story possible.

And

In memory of Mitchell L. Burton who taught me acceptance.

Acknowledgements

The old adage "it takes a community to raise a child" applies to writing a book. I wish to thank my community:

To my family for supporting me in my writing and for accepting me for who I am and not who they wish me to be. I will not name you, for I'm sure I am an embarrassment at times.

To my editors: Adrian Fogelin, Heather Whitaker, and Gina Edwards, editors extraordinaire. You each contributed in different ways. Without you, this book would not be a reality. To my artists: Elizabeth Babski, you designed a cover that exceeded my wildest dreams. And to Evan Staley, you created the perfect trailer for my story.

The members of the writers' group of the Osher Lifelong Learning Institute (OLLI) have been a part of this journey and have always encouraged me in this endeavor. You know who you are. My Tallahassee Writers Association critique group: Michele Moncure, James Noble, and Jack Pittman, who continue to guide and nudge, often pushing me into being a better writer. The Fiction Among Friends retreat group who kept me focused on writing for an entire week. Twice. My online Just Jane's critique group: Judy Goodman and Paulette Lein, for providing sage advice during the times we met. The What? Writers writing group: Kim Poole, Brooke Harrison, Janeen Price, Bonnie Armstrong, and Darryl Bollinger, along with our leader Heather Whitaker, for their generosity in making my story better.

My beta readers: Susan Allen, Darryl Bollinger, Riko Carrion, Rhett DeVane, Donna G., Donna Meredith, Jenny Crowley, Lee Heffner, and Charles Wilkinson, the latter of whom also generously gave me permission to use his poem, "Forgive Me."

A special thank you to: Rhett DeVane, you have been a part of this process almost from the beginning. You graciously allowed me to interrupt your writing to get feedback on mine. You provided encouragement and sage advice amidst fits of laughter. Darryl

Bollinger, you not only encouraged and prodded me to finish the manuscript but also kept me laughing through this process. Without you both, I could easily have crossed the line into insanity. Yeah, I know it's still questionable.

To all my teachers along the way without whom I would never have the learned the lessons I needed to write this book.

My heartfelt thanks to all of you.

Prologue

There comes a pivotal moment when one's life will be forever changed. This was such a moment for Lee Lindsey.

Sylva, North Carolina, April 22, 1991

You ducked into the coma just in time, didn't you, Alex? I crawl into bed with you. Then, the Lindseys descend. Your mother parks on the chair beside the bed, your father at the foot. I clutch your arm like my favorite childhood teddy bear while your mother brags about your brother's exploits, and your father grunts agreement.

My heart cries as I remember your whisper at the door of your brother's home. "You are about to meet my parents' only child." From your coma, I know you hear your mother, and my heart cracks. I feel your chest muscles tighten as she bows her head and lets it rest near your groin. I cringe. The odor of rubbing alcohol seeps under the door. "He doesn't want your head there."

She sits up. Your body relaxes. The mind-body-spirit workshop I took two weeks ago awakens my awareness of minute changes in your muscles. You already know that, don't you?

The hospice nurse enters and takes your vital signs. Your dad reads a newspaper he found discarded in the waiting room. Your mother clicks on the bedside lamp, and afternoon settles into evening. She sits in silence, hands folded in her lap. Are you as grateful for her silence as I am?

Almost midnight. Suddenly, you sit straight up and look at your father. I recognize the pain on your face from the times we've talked about the way your parents see you. I look at your mother. "He wants to hear that you love him."

Your arm muscles relax.

"We love you," her voice tight. She rushes from the room.

Your father stares over the top of the newspaper. "Of course we love you." The paper falls to the floor. With a grunt, he follows your mother. You drop down like you sat up.

I ache at your pain brought on by their disconnection. I grasp your hand and squeeze. *I* love you. I will always love you. I run my fingers down the side of your face.

Your mother returns with a nurse. "...then-he-sat-up-and-looked-from-me-to-his-father-have-you-ever-heard-of-such-a-thing?" Her arms flail about as fast and wildly as her speech. She stops for a breath.

The nurse looks you over like some specimen. "I've heard of it. But never seen it."

Your mother, as if realizing why she summoned the nurse, "He needs pain medication. Now." Can you hear the nagging in her voice?

"He's in a coma," the nurse says. "He's in no pain." Your stomach tightens.

How does she know what you can feel? Your muscles tremble. Beginning of the shakes? "He's a recovering alcoholic." I clutch your hand. "He's been on Oxycontin for over a month. Could he be going through withdrawal?" I struggle to remember how the various bodily systems work. "Couldn't this be an autonomic response?"

The nurse pauses and checks your chart. "I'll call the doctor and see what he thinks." A few moments later, she returns and gives you an injection. She pats your hand. "This should help." Your muscles relax.

I jolt awake to the commotion of a shift change in the hall. My in-laws stand at the door staring at me.

"Lee, we're going down to the cafeteria to get something to eat. Want anything?"

The idea of any food, except sugar, nauseates me. "Large coffee. Black. And anything sugary. The sweeter, the better."

Halfway through my gooey pastry, the hospice social worker arrives. She walks straight to you without even a glance at me as I stand on the other side of the tray table with my coffee and food. She leans over and says something to you. I can't hear. You breathe in. Out. In. Out. In. Out. You pause.

Just like you to increase the drama. An unexpected chuckle threatens to strangle me. I cough. At least you didn't die last week, on Good Friday. Knowing you, you'd expect me to wait until Sunday to see if you'd rise from the dead. I cover my mouth and bite my lower lip as if stifling a yawn. Is that a hint of a smile on your face? Are you laughing with me?

You breathe in.

I didn't give you cancer. Partly, you did this to yourself. I can forgive you your years of smoking and drinking. I'm not so forgiving that you're ready to go. Blood rushes to my face and my heart beats faster.

I'm not ready to forgive the spread of Agent Orange in a war that took away my idealism. Body bags on the news brought to the dinner table every night will do that.

Whatever the cause of your cancer, our years together won't be a lifetime for me, just you.

I take five slow, deep breaths. My jaw relaxes.

I eat the overly sweet crème-filled doughnut. Knowing how you hate crumbs in the bed, I'll finish it before I sit with you. Ah, you're taking another breath. I'll wait until the social worker leaves before I go to you.

I stare at the sugary remnants on the cafeteria plate. During these final weeks, we have bared our souls and said everything we needed to say. I felt as if my skin peeled away and exposed my heart. Yet, you never turned away.

I watch and wait. You breathe in just the way you always do. You're in control and have everyone's attention while I subsist on sugar. I won't let myself feel. Not in front of other people.

What is the social worker saying to you? Her with her accusing looks in my direction.

You breathe out.

You don't breathe in. Another pause?

No breath in.

You look so peaceful. No more pain. No more agony. I know you're still here with me.

It's as if everyone in the waiting room simultaneously understands that you are dead. Friends and family come in and make stiff or tearful goodbyes, then retreat.

Time to call your brother? No, your best friend will do it; he's in the hallway. He promised to call friends and co-workers. Will your brother inform your daughters? He said he would. My love, you continue to make life easier for me, even in death. I have to call my family.

The nurse's aide arrives to prepare your body. "I will do it," as I place a protective hand on the sheet.

She snatches the sheet from my hand and off your body, leaving you naked. I grab the sheet. How disrespectful. You would hate this. I cover you. I begin to wash you. I wash your face and neck, moving from your arms to your torso. I stand so she can't watch. I cover your top half. I uncover and wash your legs and feet. Together, we turn you over.

As we roll you onto your stomach, I see it. A decubitus ulcer. One I'd not noticed. Didn't know about. Bright red. The color of raw hamburger. A cavern of bone and meat. Oozing yellow pus. You never mentioned it.

Had I walled myself off so effectively that my whole being said, *I don't know and I don't want to know?* Was this detachment? Survival? No trips into the danger zone of the psyche for me. I simply hadn't paid attention.

Guilt arrives, carrying its own bag.

Chapter 1

Tallahassee, Florida, January 1999

"Lee Lindsey?" My attorney. "Your closing is set for one o'clock tomorrow in Crawfordville. Can you make it?"

Suddenly, my heart accelerates, and my lips curl upward into a wide grin. Of course I can make it. "Yes," my voice is higher in pitch than normal. I've long dreamed of owning a house at the beach, and tomorrow I will. Finally, I'll have a place to get away from the drudgery of schoolwork. She and I work out the details, and I hang up. Dancing around the room, I chant, "Tomorrow we're going to have a beach house. A beach house. A beach house." Two pairs of eyes peep around the corner—Yin and Yang my black and white Japanese bobtail cats.

Soft, silky, and squishy, Yin has her principles—she would never deign to appear in need of love and attention, a trait I know all too well. Smaller than Yin, Yang, the stronger of the two, is muscular with coarse fur. Even though I had to be convinced to take these two as kittens, I can't imagine my life without them.

I return to my editing of the Theory of Therapy paper, the first of the four hoops through which I have to jump to earn a doctorate in marriage and family therapy at Florida State University. I pick up the remaining pages and begin reading them aloud, the best way for me to pick up any errors and awkward sentence structure.

I'm finishing up when Frank calls. "Hi. It's just me, Frank Islip, here." I should know his voice by now, and he should know I know. He *is* the man I've been seeing for the last fourteen months. "Just touching base."

"The attorney called. The closing is tomorrow afternoon in Crawfordville."

"Going to be in Apalach. How about I meet you at the house after the closing?"

We set up an approximate time, and then Frank says, "Know you're busy, so I'll let you go. See you tomorrow."

The next morning, I complete my editing and begin practicing for my defense. I drop off the tape and required hard copies of the paper to my committee members before I drive to Crawfordville for my appointment. Because it's a cash transaction, I'm there no longer than ten minutes.

Afterwards, I drive to Alligator Point to meet Frank. The sun is high and shines warmly in a cerulean sky sprinkled with powder-puff clouds: one of those January days that entice you into believing spring is here.

I offer up gratitude to Alex who, eight years ago, left me enough insurance money to pay for graduate school and my dream house. To Frank for saying, "Cosmetically, it's a mess. Structurally, it's sound. We can fix it. If you don't buy it, I will." And, to my friend Vinnie who offered me my dream.

Frank is waiting when I pull up in front of the house. He hops out of the state's park service truck. "Welcome home," accompanied by a tight hug and a wide grin.

"I've been imagining the stairs moved to the side rather than straight on." I grin. Subtle. Beautiful. Welcoming.

"Easy enough to do." He looks at the yard. "But harder to imagine with all the yard junk."

To my house-gratitude list, I add Vinnie's former girlfriend and the woman responsible for the helter-skelter cabinets and carpeting that clutter the front lawn. I turn to view Alligator Harbor, the quiet part of the Gulf of Mexico across the street from my home. "Yeah, but thanks to the ex-girlfriend, Joy, we're standing here."

Months before, when Joy had shown me the house, I'd seen evidence of her destruction and now have visions of her yanking up the carpet and heaving it out the door in an explosive rage. "All men are evil! See these light fixtures? Breasts!" The woman seems to traipse along the borderline of psychosis. It looks like she's crossed it. The breast-pink paint can is another indication of her disturbed thinking.

Frank rests his hand on my shoulder, and I breathe in the pleasure of this moment before we go inside. Once there, we open all the doors and windows to air out the house. We move to the side deck with the front view of Alligator Harbor and the rear view of the Gulf of Mexico across Alligator Road. This land juts out into a section of the Gulf of Mexico that I thought was a bay, but I discovered at the closing that it is known as Alligator Harbor. We lean over the back rail, watching waves lazily break on shore. I close my eyes to take in the salt air. Frank slides a finger along my cheek. When I gaze into his eyes, they soften. I am home.

With a sigh, Frank lets go. "Better get to work."

I help him load the tossed carpet and pad into the back of the pickup. We store the cabinets in the living room. Thank the gods for the several weeks of no rain.

With the front yard cleared, we move inside with notebooks and pencils. Frank measures the kitchen and appliances. I write the dimensions on my paper. He measures again. "Measure twice, cut once." With his tape, he gathers the dimensions of every room and draws a floor plan. As he goes from room-to-room, he calls out what needs attention: "Kilz," to cover the girlfriend-slopped paint, "two coats flat, two coats trim, and material to repair and repaint ceiling, carpet, and pads." I have a second page where he gives me a list with the amount of paint, numbers of screws, and other supplies like paint brushes or drop cloths that are not on his list.

By four o'clock, we have enough information to begin the repairs. Frank puts away his notebook and pencil. "What you say we quit before we get into work traffic?"

"Sounds good." I need to practice for my theory defense. "I have an early day tomorrow."

As we stand by my white Camaro, Frank hugs me and kisses my nose. "I'll make a list of what we need first." He puts out his hand. "Your list."

I hand it to him.

"By the way, I'm seeing the doc tomorrow." In all the house excitement, I'd forgotten that he should soon have a doctor's appointment because he'd missed the one in November. Tomorrow is the earliest he could get.

"How about dinner tomorrow night?" I hope we can celebrate my defense and his good health. We firm up our plans and then we leave for Tallahassee.

As I drive home, something about Frank's doctor's appointment gnaws at me. I'm reminded of the day in November when I saw him and he looked different. A little pale, and his movements were slower. Not anything I could identify.

Through the open windows, birds chirp and I inhale the combined scents of pine trees, fresh air, and death from an animal along the side of the road. My arms and shoulders relax as the energy of the trees surrounds me. Everything in this world is exactly as it should be. Traffic slows and becomes heavier as I pass the two universities. I grip the wheel. The clear blue sky turns dark and ominous as I pass the Tallahassee Mall. Crepe myrtles sway. Large drops of rain splatter against the windshield. Before I turn into my parking space, the sun bursts through the clouds.

I barely make it inside my apartment when two pairs of eyes peep around the corner. I pull off my sunglasses to peer at the cats. "We have a beach house, little ones." Yang tugs at my leg and rolls over. I reach down to rub his tummy. Yin, the aloof one, turns her back.

I glide through the living room towards the office, one of two extra bedrooms. I shut the studio door and block the distraction of an unfinished painting. A relic from Vietnam, a bamboo POW cage. Can't imagine why I choose to dwell on this subject. I suspect it's my way of working through a war that took so much from me: First my idealism. Then my husband.

As I enter my office, I touch the feathers on the medicine stick, a twisted branch with a large crystal encircled by a rawhide string. An eagle's feather attached by a leather thong tops the stick. Narrower leather strings hold beads and other feathers in place. The shaman who created this symbol must have infused it with healing powers. I am drawn to its energy.

I toss the closing papers on the desk, and then realize they'll likely get lost in the mess. I stuff them into an empty cubbyhole above the desk. My cat-shadows follow until I pick them up and hold them to my chest.

I put down the cats and pick up the now worn copy of my theory paper. Yin watches, with the disdain only a cat can express, as she lazes on the desk chair. Yang reclines on the floor underneath her, in exactly the same position. How do they do that?

I stand in front of Yin. I begin reading aloud: "As a phenomenologist, I believe we create meanings for our lives. Our beliefs influence those meanings, which have—"

Yin jumps up and walks across the keyboard leaving a trail of letters on the screen. I turn to face her. Should have shut down the computer this morning. I pick her up and place her on the floor. "Okay, Yin. Tell me what you think." She stares at me.

"What do you mean I'm using highfalutin words to sound smart? This is my field. I'm supposed to sound smart. I do know what I'm talking about." *At least I hope I do.*

She cocks her head and crosses her front paws as if to say, "Pride goeth before a fall."

"Okay. Okay. I'll try to give you my theory of therapy for regal cats." I look at my paper and then at Yin. "So, as a therapist, I want to know what you think when I tell you I love you."

She looks at me as if I've misplaced my sanity—which I probably have, considering I'm lecturing to a cat.

"To put this in cat terms, if your mama told you she loved you while she was feeding you or licking you clean, you'd have a different idea of love than if she told you she loved you and then bit your ear or scratched your nose. Or even walked away." Yin looks around the room as if considering walking away.

"Pay attention, Yin." She turns her head towards me. "If, for example, when as a small child, I was so completely controlled by my family that I had no freedom, I would value my independence above everything."

I lean towards her before I continue. If I can simplify this, maybe I stand a chance tomorrow. "Better yet, remember how your temperature rose every time you went to the vet after your experience in the loud family with the barking dogs, hissing cats, yelling humans, and then in the chaos of the animal shelter? I know it scared you because you run and hide if I raise my voice. So, we'll conclude that you believe if you are yelled at, you will die."

As she twitches her nub of a tail, the beach house pops up, but I must put that thought out of my mind if I'm to pass this defense. "When William James wrote, 'I don't smile because I'm happy; I'm happy because I smile,' he is telling us that we can change our

9

attitude by changing our behavior. In other words, acting *as if* will make it so."

I turn to Yin. "This is important." Her eyes open wide. I bend down, pick her up, and cradle her in my arms.

"You can change being afraid, Sweet Girl, by acting as if you are not afraid." Yang saunters over and nudges my foot. Yin wiggles out of my arms and jumps on the desk. I bend forward and gentle Yang's head.

A thud from above. Then a crash. I jump. Cats disappear. I rush to the den and dial the upstairs neighbors. Laughter greets me. "Knew it was you," says Mrs. McPherson. "Trying to break apart three frozen chickens by smashing them on the kitchen floor. Yeah, we're all alive up here. The noise was that loud in your office?"

My adrenalin continues to pulse when I return to the office and sit in my chair, both legs shaking. It takes a few minutes before the cats return.

Yin jumps up on the desk, paws my face, and looks at me as if suggesting, *go on*. Yang jumps in my lap. Yin creeps to the monitor and stares at the screen.

I want coffee, but refuse to reward myself until I've completely explained my theory to Yin. I know I must act as if I'm confident even though I feel unprepared. I flash back to the many conversations with my sister-in-law while I was getting my master's. "You always think you're going to fail. You never do." That was then. This is now.

I put Yang on the floor and stand up. "Since what you think and what you do are connected," I start to pace, "if you don't feel good and hear a crash upstairs, you're more likely to think you're going to die. If you spend a lot of time thinking you're about to die from fright, you'll get sick. If you are afraid long enough, you'll hack up a hairball. So let's not go there. Okay?" I reach down to pull Yin to me, but she's gone before my hand is halfway there.

I need to put this aside for a while before I completely lose it. I pour a mug of coffee, move into the den, and pick up the Margaret Atwood novel I've been reading before bed each night. I curl up in my favorite chair. A large square one, at least a hundred years old. The wide arms enfold me when I tuck my legs up under. Yin and Yang settle in, one on each side of me, facing the same direction.

An hour later, hunger overtakes me, and I wander into the kitchen for a fast peanut butter sandwich. Gone are the days when I had time to cook after work on the psych unit in North Carolina. Peanut butter is the one staple in the pantry these days.

The next morning, I dress in a professional uniform for my defense, navy suit with white silk blouse and navy pumps. Wish I could ditch the pantyhose, but I know the more I look the part, the better I'll perform.

With morning coffee in hand, I watch Yang chase Yin as they circle round and round the living room, through the dining room, into the kitchen and through the den. They reverse to flash into the office. I gather my notes and stuff them into my monogrammed, burgundy leather briefcase.

I arrive at the clinic with ten minutes to spare. I pour a mug of coffee and find a seat at the conference table. My clinical supervisor Joe Promough, my major professor Simon Dimsley, and another professor, who is officially on sabbatical, but in town, arrive at eight-thirty with their copies of the theory paper and accompanying transcript of a session.

Joe taps the paper and glances up. "The female client, an emergency medical technician, is having a problem with her deputy sheriff boyfriend who is consuming all her free time to the point that she can't visit her mother."

He tilts back in his chair. "Why did you choose this particular session with this particular client?"

"I've watched the client give up one more piece of her independence each time they've come in for a session. After her five previous ones, you can see on the tape that there's a hesitancy in her walk, and she hunches over in the chair."

"Do you see any correlation to your own life?" Simon combs his fingers through his beard.

I take a deep breath. "I see me when I was married to an active alcoholic. I made myself sick trying to get him to stop drinking. I had the if onlys: If only I were more attractive; if only I were more submissive; if only I would lose weight—I was at my perfect weight—he would quit. She's doing her own version of this process."

Joe leans forward. "You say that because they are both in crises-type careers, you suspect they are addicted to the adrenalin rushes which their jobs provide." He leans back with his arms crossed. "Any similarities in your family history?"

I have the feeling he's trying to trip me up. "On the surface, you might not think so. Her father abandoned her and her mother to marry a younger woman. She and her mother are very close." I twirl my ring. "My father was my ally until I was sixteen. I knew he often pleaded my case with my mother even though I never heard it. Mother was more like the deputy sheriff boyfriend."

The third professor glances up from his non-stop writing. "What about your father? Did he abandon you?"

"No…Wait." My heart flutters. "I take that back. I felt abandoned when he attempted suicide. I never trusted that he would be there for me after that. I never trusted my mother to protect me after she had me hide behind the sofa from the Fuller Brush man. I was three."

I lean my forearms on the table and clasp my hands. "So yes, I guess he did abandon me. At least in my mind."

I catch Simon giving Joe a look and a just-noticeable nod.

Thinking what does that look mean? Will they think I'm unaware of how my family history affects my judgment? Will I get kicked out of the program if they don't like my answers? I tell myself to breathe.

"What happened with the Fuller Brush man that caused you to lose trust in your mother?"

I go back to that day in my first house. "Mother opened all the windows," allowing the stench of old arguments, fears, and bitter thoughts to escape, from winter's enclosure, into the fresh spring air. "She hummed Strauss's 'Blue Danube' while she washed the windows. I chattered to my doll. The Oriental rug hung on the clothesline to be beaten and brought in later when the floors carried the scent of Johnson's paste wax."

I flinch. "All of a sudden, she grabbed me, her hand over my mouth, and pulled me behind the sofa, sitting in the middle of the living room. When I turned to look at her, her index finger covered her lips. 'Shhh,' she whispered."

Joe shuffles his papers. He nods.

"Knock. Knock. Knock." The Spic and Span that Momma used on the walls left its perfume in the room. "We held our breaths. The deep brown horsehair covering the sofa tickled my nose." Off to the side, in Daddy's chair, lay the soft, beige linen-like fabric slipcovers.

They'd cover the sofa and the chair before the sun hid behind the mountain.

"The doorbell rang." We waited, as silent and still as the air before a summer storm. "I looked at Momma. She frowned as she put her finger to her mouth once more. The storm door opened and closed." Fear sucked energy from the room. Silence. "Footsteps left the porch. We waited." I take a breath.

"Momma peered around and over the back of the sofa. She whispered that we could get up and that I'd have to talk quietly."

Simon tugs on his beard and shoots a look at Joe.

"When I asked why we hid, she told me the knocker was the Fuller Brush man and she didn't want to buy anything from him that day."

Joe's smile is quizzical. "Why did that experience cause you to lose trust in your mother?"

"I thought that she was afraid and that's why she hid. If she had to hide from someone who had been in our house before, then how could she protect me from someone who might really harm me? Remember, this is the logic of a three-year-old." I take a deep breath.

"And you still remember it?"

I let out my breath. "Like yesterday."

Simon turns a page and points to the paper. He clears his throat, "Do you really believe you can change by acting *as if*?"

"Nineteen years in twelve-step meetings have taught me the truth of the slogan. Not only in my own life, but in watching a number of alcoholics get sober." I sit back in my chair.

The next thirty-five minutes are spent debating my theories of adrenalin addiction, whether a smile can change a mood from sad to happy, and the merits of a positive attitude and its effect on real-life outcomes.

At last, Joe points to the door. "Go get some coffee, and we'll call you back when we make our decision."

Chapter 2

I take my half-full mug and microwave it. I can hardly believe I enjoyed the defense. To think I was so stressed that I had to practice on the cats. Hope all my other hoops are as easy.

Joe smiles when he summons me back. "You passed, Lee. You'd have heard sooner if you'd bribed us with muffins like your cohort did."

I return the laughter as each of my professors congratulates me. Simon says, "Your next assignment is to write your critical review paper." He hands me a bound book, a dissertation. "Have you narrowed your topic?"

"I want to study female abusers." There's an intake of breaths.

Simon's mouth sets in a straight line. "You can't do that."

"Why not?" I put my elbows on the conference table. "I've worked with enough couples to know it happens. So many recovery stories are about wives who have abused their husbands in retaliation for the drunk's abuse."

I move my ring from one hand to the other. "When I worked in a naval hospital, one of the most serious burn cases came from an abused wife who waited for her spouse to pass out. And then," I pause, "poured a frying pan full of boiling oil on him."

There is a collective gasp, and then Simon hands me a recent dissertation. "Read chapter two," he crosses his arms over his chest, "and use it as your guide for the critical review paper." The second of the four hoops, it is a review of the literature in my chosen topic.

I take the dissertation and head to the library. Since I have a few hours left in my day, I might as well begin my research. I flip to chapter two and begin to read. I don't care about adolescent-boy behavior that was measured through psych tests. This subject has been done to death, while there is absolutely nothing on female abusers. Shit, just find twenty studies and write them up. Get it done. As Errol, my cohort and best work-friend, keeps reminding me, my main objective is to get the doctorate. We've helped each other maintain focus from day one.

I met Errol the first week of classes at a get-acquainted party for the marriage and family graduate students hosted by the program director. I noticed his snowy hair and his eyes, the color of a pale blue sky, when he walked in the door. Less than five minutes later, he sauntered over. "Hi, Errol Harper." He put out his hand. "Here to study traumatology."

He didn't give me a chance to respond.

"Came in January. Mid-term. From Alaska. Was an EMT there? What's your deal?"

"Short version: married times three, trophy wife times two, widow times one."

We soon determined we lived within a mile of each other. From that moment, we became inseparable in our professional lives. When I mentioned my recovery, he puffed out his chest. "Been sober five years. You?"

"In recovery for fifteen."

"There's a good Saturday meeting for joint recovery programs. You should try it." Funny, how the past four years since that night, I've never seen him there.

Before the evening was over, I knew that Errol, the program director, and Simon somebody were all alcoholics who had a meeting somewhere on campus. He'd even mentioned something about Simon's son refusing to speak to his father over some lawsuit, not something I needed to know. So much for program anonymity.

The week after I re-injured my coccyx—the first accident occurred when I was fifteen and slammed my coccyx on the terrazzo kitchen floor, climbing the door frame—Errol took me to school and brought me home each day until I could manipulate my clutch without agony.

At the library, I continue my online search until I find that I'd have an easier time doing this at home. Since it's just now ten, I drive back across town.

A half-mile from my apartment, I stop at a nearby mall and go straight to a local bookstore to pick up a new journal to replace my nearly full one. My progress through graduate school, coupled with my relationship with Frank, requires something special. I spy a small Chinese-red volume, covered in silk, tucked away on a high shelf. I celebrate my beautiful journal with a new, ruby-red Schaeffer fountain pen which flows effortlessly over the satiny paper. The relationship between pen and paper is important. Together, they marry my thoughts.

When I pull into the parking area in front of my apartment building, the McPhersons from upstairs have again taken three spaces to park two cars. Why can't they get it together? Something must be going on with them besides breaking up frozen chickens. When their household is in chaos, their parking is in disarray. So far, I've been dead-on accurate with that observation. I smile, thinking about writing a dissertation on personal conflict and parking habits.

Excitement about passing my defense flows through me as I walk from the car to the mailbox. The oily pavement sizzles as water evaporates from a recent morning rain. The sky, now cobalt, is dappled with wisps of white. I inhale deeply, drawing in the cleansed air.

Freshly mown grass sparkles like diamonds. A family of finches nests in the package portion of the no-longer-used mailboxes. A baby chick peeks out of the nest when I pass on my way to the front door.

Unless I'm at Florida State, walking or running around Lake Ella and observing the animal life or embarking on some other form of exercise, my habitat is my apartment, where I am most comfortable when left alone to think and to analyze the world from a distance. Mostly by thinking or talking to the cats.

Although I've overheard my cohorts and colleagues describe me as outgoing, I'm introverted and non-intrusive. While that can be a problem in my personal life, it's an advantage in my professional one because I'm non-threatening to clients. Still, when necessary, I can be blunt and plain-spoken. I don't couch my observations in niceties.

Once I decided to use Alex's insurance money to get a Ph.D., my motivation for helping others find their way to mental, physical, and spiritual health was so strong that I had no doubt I would succeed. After all, it is my life's purpose.

My confidence in my new journey was affirmed the day before I left the mountains of North Carolina. I'd scheduled a massage from a Native American woman who lived so far back in the woods that I had to drive over two creek beds to get to her two-room cabin, filled with handmade amulets and dream catchers.

A new medicine stick, with a large crystal encircled in a rawhide string, stood in the corner of the massage room. It drew me to itself. After the massage, when I'd dressed and walked into the front room, the therapist, whom I'd swear was a shaman, repeated the words of White Eagle, a well-known Indian spirit guide: "You will succeed. Period. There will be barriers and roadblocks along the way. Don't let them stop you. You will get your degree."

Once I'd taken that in, I pointed to the medicine stick. "I love this. Can I buy it?" The energy feels as if he made it just for me.

"An old Indian back up in the hills made this to sell," she said. "I'm glad you want it. It will serve you well."

Little did I know when I drove down the mountain, my muscles like mush and my energy pulsating in a slow, steady rhythm, just how White Eagle's message would soon be punctuated. Passing my house, packed for the move to Florida, I continued up the hill to my neighbor's to spend the night. I insisted on cooking. Cooking in her French-blue and white kitchen where the sun streamed in the window over the sink, spotlighting the pot of violets on the sill, was like entering another world.

With the gas fire on high, I dropped chopped vegetables into the wok. The floppy sleeve of my sweater caught fire. I acted automatically as I quickly patted out the fire. Without a visible sign of the burn, my friend's gasp of acknowledgement and the smell of scorched cotton rejected the idea that the entire experience was a product of an active imagination. I took the incident as a sign that I really would walk through fire to get my degree. But I wouldn't be burned.

By choice, I'm an apartment dweller, even though a lack of apartments in North Carolina forced me to own houses. A beach house is the exception. I want to be able to feel the sand on my feet without taking an elevator. Today, I can.

Now as I enter my apartment, I drop my shoes in the marble entryway. Yin and Yang run out to greet me. Yang rolls over on his back to have his stomach tickled. Yin, on the cool white marble, turns her back. "You punishing me for leaving, little girl?" My stockinged feet glide on the hardwood floors into the family room where I drop my briefcase on the floor by the antique chair. I call and leave Frank a message that I passed.

I go online and start researching domestic violence and adolescent boys. This is so much easier than researching in the library. I can download to the computer or print out what I need, but this subject holds no appeal. None. Zip. It has already been done to death. I don't want to use someone else's data either. I find five studies that look like they'll work. I print them out.

I need to get up and move. After all, as Errol often reminds me, the objective is to get the doctorate. I walk out to the mailbox and check my mail. Mostly junk. Before I can enter the apartment, the catty-corner upstairs neighbor pokes her head out the door. "I watch that man from my kitchen window. When you aren't looking, he stares at you with such devotion in his eyes. He adores you. I wish my husband would look at me like that."

I had no idea. "The one with white hair or the one who comes over more often?"

"You don't know?" She moves to the landing. "The one who drives the old blue van."

Frank. I didn't know. "Thank you for telling me." I need to think about this. Later.

I make half a peanut butter sandwich and pour a cup of coffee. I take them into the den along with one of the studies I printed. I try to read. Can't concentrate. Now that I'm not pressed to perform for school, I'm excited about the house. I think about how I want it to look when we've finished, how we'll enjoy the large side deck with the view that the jutting piece of land provides into the gulf, sleeping and waking to the sound of waves hitting shore.

Yang jumps up on the footstool and puts a paw on my leg. Glad for the interruption, I put down the journal article. "Thank you for keeping your claws in, my little man." I pull him into my lap and rub his head. Yin jumps into my lap, too. They no longer fit so comfortably. It seems like yesterday that they curled up together in the bowl on the table. They've outgrown the bowl and now my lap's getting too small. After I pet each animal, I sit down to work on the critical review paper. I pull out the four-hundred-page dissertation. Talk about overkill.

Hours with the perception of *weeks* later, before I'm completely numb with boredom, I leave the dratted dissertation behind and move into the kitchen to prepare dinner. I pull out a portion of the batch of *arroz con pollo* I froze last week. I place it in a pan and turn it on low. By the time Frank arrives, it will be heated through.

I retire to the large pillow on the den floor and grasp the new journal, still in the bag. I rub my fingers across its silk cover and then pull it out. My new pen skates flawlessly across the page as I write my name, address, and phone number on the first page, then start my entry:

> January 21, 1999
>
> The neighbor told me that Frank adores me. Is that true? If so, what do I want to do about it? Maybe he is safe to love. Another decision for the think-about-later file to be added to my burgundy briefcase.

I put down the pen. I can't seem to get over the feeling that something is wrong with Frank. What's precipitating this? I remember that day back in November when I saw Frank on the St. Mark's trail. He was leaving town the next day, and as he turned to walk away, I was struck with the feeling he had something seriously wrong with him. He didn't look right. His coloring was off and he walked like an old man, not the vital runner he usually is. I ran after him. "What did the doctor say when you had your appointment yesterday?"

His jaw tightened as it does when he holds in anger. "Missed my appointment. Apparently, I was scheduled for last week, not this week. Can't get another one until January."

Well, journaling was an exercise in futility. At least I know the source of my unease.

In order to get my mind off Frank, I treat myself to an hour of reading from my novel before it's time to prepare dinner. I curl up in my antique chair and settle in with a cup of coffee. My two feline companions soon join me, one on each side, facing the same direction. Do they have some internal guidance system that allows them to move as one?

When the alarm rings, I check on dinner. I stir the pot, no frozen chunks here. I set the table and prepare the salad. I open a bottle of chilled chardonnay to let it breathe, and then return it to the refrigerator.

Before Frank arrives, I jump into the shower and throw on a sweatshirt and yoga pants. Comfort is everything if I'm to keep my stress level low.

When Frank knocks thirty minutes late, I open the door to a bear hug. Once he's inside, I ask.

"Doc felt a nodule, but all my blood tests were normal." His eye tics. "Wants to do a biopsy because of the family history. Scheduled it early morning on Monday."

This takes me back to Alex's biopsy. I steel myself not to react. "I have a mid-morning meeting scheduled. Want me to take you in?"

He turns towards me and grins. "That would be great."

"I should be out of my meeting by the time you're ready to go." I move to the kitchen. I breathe to calm my shaky hands, and then put the rolls in the preheated oven.

"How was your defense?" He asks through the open doorway.

"I was surprised at how easy it was. The committee seemed more interested in my views than in trying to trip me up." My neck tightens. "Simon assigned me the longest, most boring dissertation to study before I begin the paper that is to be a chapter in my dissertation. I spent much of the afternoon mind-numbing myself into oblivion."

Frank laughs. "Hmm. Mind-numbing without drugs." His face muscles relax. "That's a new experience."

The timer goes off, and I return to the kitchen to take out the rolls and to serve dinner. I pour Frank his usual half red wine, half water, over ice. He takes it from me and sits down at the table. "Smells good in here."

I pour my chardonnay and then return to the dining room to clink glasses with Frank. "To a good outcome on the biopsy." I clink his.

He clinks mine. "And to a job well done."

I lean over and kiss the top of his head before serving dinner. Our conversation is light. I'm sure the biopsy will indicate the nodule is benign. Frank seems to be of the same opinion. We don't discuss it.

I've learned to let him bring up whatever bothers him when he's ready. It is not my business unless he wishes to make it so.

When Frank leaves, his comment "I've got an early day tomorrow," is the only indication that the news has affected him. I know he must be concerned because his grandfather died of prostate cancer.

Since I have a nine o'clock research meeting on campus, I clean up the kitchen and make it an early night by reading in bed. Tomorrow, I'll think about the critical review paper. I want it done by the end of the semester. How will I get it done by then? Worrying about it now won't make it happen. A good night's sleep will be more effective.

The following morning, the ringing phone startles me awake. Daylight has arrived so quickly that I feel like I stepped out of a time machine. My book falls off my chest as I reach for my phone. Six forty-five. Must be Errol. No one else calls me that early.

"You sound like you've been on a three-day toot," Errol booms. "Did I wake you up?"

"Yes, I was sound asleep. Haven't had coffee yet."

"Bet you didn't eat dinner last night."

"Actually, I did. Frank came over and we celebrated passing my defense."

"Called to tell you I'll pick you up for research group. Bring you some of my chicken soup. Just made it. Good for what ails ya."

Oh, he wants to share his soup. How thoughtful. Or it's a bribe.

Why would he drive across town to pick me up? He must want something. "What time?"

"Be there at eight-fifteen."

I hope that whatever Errol wants, it isn't too time consuming. I can't afford to spend a lot of extra time doing his projects if I'm to get this review of the literature paper done by the end of the semester. The last time he enrolled me in one of his schemes, we ended up spending every Friday afternoon doing family therapy for one of the schools. As satisfying as the outcomes were, the therapy hours and progress notes took the entire afternoon.

Promptly at eight-fifteen, Errol arrives carrying a quart jar of warm chicken soup wrapped in newspaper and topped with a red plaid kitchen towel. He sets his package on the counter and gives me a bear hug, then unscrews the lid. "Still warm." The aroma causes my stomach to growl.

I reach for my briefcase. He points to the soup. "Before we do anything, you need to eat. Remember HALT: hungry, angry, lonely, tired. Any one of these states messes with your mind, and you look like more than the hungry-part is going on."

A smile of recognition flits across my face. "You know I was only moving it out of the way," I say, referring to the briefcase. He pulls down a mug and fills it with his chicken soup. "Thanks." I don't tell him I never eat breakfast. I take the first sip. "Ah, just what I need. Of course, the coffee already helped my attitude."

"So, besides hungry and tired, anything going on in the angry and lonely department?"

No need to tell him about Frank, yet, and I for sure don't want to tell him how I feel about being forced to study old data for my dissertation. "I appreciate that you offered to pick me up, but why?"

"Wanted to talk with you about a paper."

I shift away from him, only a fraction. No, not another paper. Maybe he just wants to go over his. I can do that.

He presses his hands together as if he's praying. "Joe wants us to do a journal article comparing Lehmann's theory of marital satisfaction with his theory." Errol uses his please-please-please-just-for-me tone.

He already does so much for me. I'll do his damned paper. Somehow. It is a journal article, which means I don't have an immediate deadline. I sit at the kitchen table with my soup. "The idea is intriguing, but I'm not certain how it can work. My first inclination is that we'll be comparing squash to bananas." I slurp the soup. "If I keep an open mind, I'll see how the two theories are alike and how they differ." Besides, I owe Errol. He's the reason I have two published articles.

He sits across from me. "You know Joe is about promoting Joe."

Yeah, he plans to use Errol to advertise his new book, and I'm supposed to keep Errol sort-of-honest. Joe likes Errol's unusual interpretations, and his creative use of numbers that I can never comprehend. Errol also makes up theories and spins them as the latest.

But he doesn't understand the subtleties of language, like the time he wanted another word for promotion and used propagation because it showed up in his computer's thesaurus. Besides, being a wordaholic, I won't allow Errol to add made-up facts in his articles, at least the ones with my name on them.

"Since Joe's book is coming out next month, will the journal follow a month to six weeks later?" How ethical is it to both his position as editor of the journal and his professorship to expect students to promote his book? Forget it. Making mountains out of molehills again.

"Joe wants to meet with us after research group to talk about the article. Know you still have work to do, and…" Errol pauses, "…when is the closing on the beach house?"

Here it comes. I take a deep breath. "Day before yesterday."

"Why didn't you call and let me know?" He sounds as if I'm withholding from him.

"My attorney didn't tell me until the afternoon before." I take a deep breath. "I was preparing for the theory defense and sandwiched the closing in the middle. I went from the closing to the beach. Frank and I spent several hours at the house, and then I came home and practiced my defense. Yesterday, after the defense, Simon handed me a dissertation and told me to study it for my critical review paper. That's why I looked so bad this morning. I spent way too much time trying to get interested in the assigned dissertation. I was so trapped in the research that I didn't think to let you know. I'm sorry. It never occurred to me to let you know since I don't keep up with the details of your life."

"They'd bore you to death if you did."

I punch him on the arm, "That's why I don't ask. Can't stand boredom."

Within the hour, Errol and I are in the industrial-green department conference room. I sit at the long, mahogany table flanked by eight chairs with dark, nondescript, green leather seat covers. Simon Dimsley, who is both my research professor and my major professor, sits at the head. We students sit on the same side of the table facing a screen.

Simon shows a portion of a taped co-therapy session with Errol and me. On the tape, the middle-aged client-couple talk about their *perfect* relationship going awry—a new experience for them since they moved in together the week before. They had known each other one month and been in couples' therapy for three weeks.

Why is he showing this tape? Developing cookbook therapy is Simon's current interest. How can you prescribe a recipe for a certain kind of therapy? I can see it now: Use this therapy recipe for every depressed male fifteen-year-old, and this one for girls. People aren't all the same. Even though I'm not sure why our co-therapy tape is being shown now, I'm more interested in finding out about the specific comments I couldn't hear than what these people think.

I look around the highly polished table at my fellow students. All eyes are on the screen. The woman says, "He didn't tell me..." The client's lips move, but I hear no sound until the sound returns with, "...about him." What will Frank and I accomplish on the beach house this weekend? What's the best use of my time to get all my research and writing done as well as getting the house ready for occupancy? I can't do all this and a journal article, too, in a timely manner. I tap my pen against my knee.

The large, round wall clock with big numbers, a reminder of elementary school, reads ten-fourteen. Only sixteen more minutes and I can go home and get to work on my review paper. Wrong. There's the meeting with Joe after class.

On the screen, Errol asks the male client, "Have you ever...a partner?"

After the client answers Errol's question, Simon pauses the tape. "What did you hear, Lee?"

Heavy ground fog blurs the view of a camellia bush next to the building. Students passing on the sidewalk become shimmering ghosts where the fog thickens. The air buzzes with electricity. Smells that way, too. Simon stares at me. "What? Oh. A jumbled mess."

The other graduate students look at me as if I'm covered in filth. They shake their heads in rhythm with the ticking clock. Disbelief? Pissed off to have to sit through this? No one except Errol is interested in therapy; their research is in child development.

Why is Errol watching me instead of the other students as each repeats the client's answer? The first student tucks her hair behind her ear, "I...my ex-wife." She untucks the strand. The second student rolls his bulging browns clockwise and then counterclockwise, stops when Simon looks at him, "I...my wife." The third student, repeats the words, and then squishes his butt back and forth on the chair. If he were a cat, I'd take him to the vet for worming.

I hear their words, but can't remember their answers five seconds later. Simon gets up, walks to the board, and writes. "I physically abused my ex-wife." Simon rewinds the tape and replays that portion of the session. Where did the taste of chocolate and peppermint come from? My stomach growls. That's what happens when I eat in the morning.

"That time, did you hear, 'I physically...my ex-wife'?" Simon looks directly at me, his voice a low growl.

My voice reverberates as if through sloshing water in my ears. "No."

Simon points to the sentence on the board, "Read this aloud, please."

"I. Physically. Abused. My. Ex-Wife."

Once more Simon plays the tape. "Did you hear the client speak those words?" A chair squeaks as someone's weight shifts.

Again, I shake my head, no. A memory floods back: I was in North Carolina watching a John Bradshaw tape borrowed from the treatment center where I worked. I'd kept it over the weekend, and each time I played it, I couldn't get past the first five minutes. Without further thought, I chalked the experience up to a faulty tape.

Now, because of my training, I know selective hearing or blind spot is a physiological gap in the brain. When we hear or see something that goes against a core belief, the gap happens. I'd never heard of this phenomenon until someone told me not to worry about what I say, because if my words would do damage, that person would be unable to hear them. See it all the time in friends and clients. In Errol, too.

Simon interrupts, "What's going on?"

I shrug. "Selective hearing? Blind spot? Still can't hear it." My frustration grows until a headache bullies its way into my awareness.

Gardenias. Where does the sweetness of gardenias come from? They remind me of my mother, the ostrich, who buried her head in the sand and heard only what her belief system allowed. She placed fresh gardenias in my bedroom when they bloomed each Tampa spring.

"One finger pointing out leaves three pointing back at you," something often repeated in recovery meetings. Perhaps I should pay more attention to my accusations and assess my own thoughts. If I can catch them. Behaviors too.

Ah, the clock reads ten twenty-nine. The students gather their things and class ends without further discussion or question. I'll hear no more about blind spots. Thank the gods Simon didn't ask about this tape yesterday. We'd have been in there all day. Maybe not, blind spots are a common occurrence.

Errol and I walk out of the building and amble over to the clinic where we're scheduled to meet with Joe. Errol keeps bringing up my inability to hear the client's words even though we both know Simon won't follow up. "Come on, Errol. Everyone has selective hearing. Didn't you notice it with your kids?"

He slows his pace. "Yeah, but they outgrew it. My hearing's not selective, just physically reduced in one ear. Vietnam."

"Even so, you hear what you want to hear." Why am I trying to explain something that he refuses to hear? He's such a dork. "Think of it as your blind spot. Joe always talks about them."

"How so?" A motorcycle roars past.

"When we role play for our domestic violence couples, the issues you bring up are usually about miscommunication." I stumble on a root.

Errol grabs my elbow and prevents a fall.

"Thanks."

He stops. He turns toward me with his hands on his hips. "Example. Just give me an example of my so-called blind spot."

"Remember the time I role-played your wife, and you accused me of making a date with the guy across the street?" Doesn't he know how obvious his mistrust of his wife is to others? Of course not. Blind spot.

"Big deal." He lets go of my elbow. "Just role play."

You think? "Why did you choose that topic rather than money or sex?" We walk through the rear parking lot of the clinic. "Come on, we both know your question wasn't about me, your friend. It was about you and your mistrust of your partner."

Errol pulls open the clinic door, as I add, "It's also a physical reaction. People who are able to avoid feeling severe pain are the same people who can turn their attention elsewhere when traumatic events occur."

"You're so—"

Joe steps out of his office as we walk in the back door. "Go on in. Be right back."

Errol enters and walks straight to Joe's desk. He turns over a couple of papers, reads them, and returns each to its original position.

"Well, I won't ask you to check on the cats when I travel. I'd have to lock up my journals and bank statements."

He looks over his shoulder and grins.

When he helped me move into the new apartment and set up the stereo equipment and television, he'd eyed my desk as if it were a magnet drawing him toward some golden content.

He's been a good friend: always available when I need something, even the chicken soup today, but as a colleague, he uses me. I allow it because it works to my advantage. Usually. As his co-author, I have two publications, now possibly another one. However, I'd once observed him taking work from a business colleague and publishing it as his own. When I asked about the original author, Errol insisted that he'd written the paper. Hah, too well written. I told him never to do that to me. So far, he's been straight with me; as far as I know. I don't trust him not to steal my work, which is why I'm careful about allowing him access.

Joe's office is small, located in the rear of the clinic across from a galley kitchen area with a sink, refrigerator, and enough counter space for a coffee pot and an electrical warming pot for those nights when we bring dinner for our practicum groups. As I pass the galley, I eye the coffee pot. Inside the office, papers and books cover the two visitor chairs. Old wood soaked in sloshed coffee and crisis clients' fears scent the room. Joe's desk and chair reside next to the door. I move the contents of one chair to the floor and then check if there's coffee in the pot. Empty.

I return to the office and sit down seconds before Joe gusts in. Errol picks up the phone receiver and replaces it on its base, as if he was ready to make a call, not snooping among the papers. He moves away from the desk but makes no attempt to sit.

While Errol stands, nodding to show how attentive he is, Joe explains what he wants and the time line. He then turns to Errol to discuss ideas for the article. This article sounds a lot more interesting than the critical review paper. Shouldn't be too much of a problem to do either.

Joe hands me a rough draft of his book and tells me which book I'll need for comparison. "Thank you, Lee." I've been dismissed. Knew I should have driven in today.

I draw my shoulders back, "I'm riding with Errol."

Joe looks at Errol and raises his eyebrows, "You go on. I can talk with you later."

On the drive home, before I can ask him about Joe's *later*, Errol glances at me, "Why did you choose family therapy?"

Where did that come from? "I chose this program because of the theory taught. It's most like my twelve-step program: Self-responsibility, family emotional patterns handed down from generations, the idea that no two-person relationship is stable, so we have to create a third person or, in our case, alcoholism as the third leg. Just made sense to me."

He hangs his elbow out the window. "And from what you've said about your family, it'd take a Ph.D. to figure them out."

"Guess so. Because no one in my family talked about, or even acknowledged, family problems, and because I was never allowed to talk about what I saw that didn't match what was being said, I became a therapist. To a family therapist, there are no secrets. All family problems are fodder for the therapy mill."

Oh, my God. No wonder Mother tried to talk me out of this. She wanted to preserve her secrets. "When I hear others say therapists go into the profession to heal themselves, it doesn't ring true for me. My self-healing comes from my recovery program. It was the sexual abuse issues that came up with the women I sponsored that sent me back to school. I thought I had to learn how to deal with them." I'm learning the twelve steps give the best chance of recovery.

"Whatever heals you…."

I turn and look at Errol. "Why did *you* choose to become a marriage and family therapist?"

His hands grip the steering wheel. "I came here to study trauma to help other vets."

Oh yeah. Can't get the trauma degree without the marriage and family degree. The two are definitely intertwined.

Errol pulls up to my apartment. As I undo my seatbelt, he says, "See you Monday."

I laugh, "Not if I see you first." I wave as he drives off.

After I've settled in, Yin walks over to my chair and jumps up. "What do you say, little girl? Without twelve-step recovery, would I become a typical therapist, one who takes on the client's problems, not the one who sends those problems out the door with the client?" She walks away. Either I was wrong about her wanting attention or she wants her litter box changed. Again.

As I pick up the overkill-dissertation, and begin adding to my pad of notes, the phone rings.

"Hey, Babe. It's just me. Frank Islip here." His greeting is fingernails on a blackboard, even though his voice is upbeat and jovial. Good. "Mind if we postpone working on the house until Sunday? The boat friend I met while working in Apalachicola just called. He and his girlfriend just got into town about an hour ago and want me to take them flying tomorrow."

I swallow hard. I'd been looking forward to spending the weekend with him, just the two of us for both days. Now that's not going to happen. I engage my cheerful voice, "Sure. Spend Saturday night here?" Because he usually spends the night before a doctor's appointment, he'll spend Sunday night since his appointment is early Monday morning.

"You bet," he raises his voice an octave. "Call you tomorrow." We talk exactly one-and-a-half minutes.

Chapter 3

On Monday morning, at what feels like-crack-of-dawn o'clock, Frank and I walk into the surgical outpatient center. The attendant says they will call when he's awake. I give him a quick kiss and leave for my eight o'clock class with a sense of déjà vu.

About this time nine years ago, I dropped Alex off for his biopsy, certain of a positive outcome, and went to class. A year later, I was burying him. Still, I have that same certainty now as I walk into my research meeting.

I report on the studies I've found, but the meeting focuses on a student who is readying for her prospectus defense. I listen as she and Simon bat ideas back and forth. I don't know enough to give input.

My mind wanders as I think about Frank and then skips to the work we've begun on the beach house. The meeting is breaking up when my phone rings. "Mr. Islip is ready to be picked up."

When I arrive at outpatient surgery, Frank is awake and ready to go. After he checks out, he says, "I'm starved." He fastens his seat belt. "What you say we go to the airport and clean the plane?"

At least he's not insisting on working on the house, which is more strenuous. "You okay to do that?" I'd think he'd need to rest this afternoon.

"Piece of cake." He grins. "Let's stop by your apartment so you can change clothes first. Then we can pick up burgers on the way."

Frank grabs a banana while I change, and then we take off for the airport.

After lunch, we spend the rest of the day washing and waxing his Piper Cherokee. "My daughter's in Tampa for a couple of days. Thought I'd fly down to see her tomorrow." He moves to the wing where I work. "Be back tomorrow night, most likely. If not, the next day."

I understand his need to see her, and the timing is good for me. I can concentrate on the paper.

"Since I'm working this weekend," he wipes the sweat off his forehead, "was wondering if you'll be available to work on the house Monday or Tuesday?"

Research group. "Sure. Monday all day is good. Tuesday, we'd have to leave at eleven."

He moves to the cabin, which is beyond his reach without a ladder. "How about we stop at one of the home stores on the way back into town and pick up the supplies on our lists? That way we'll have more time to work."

"Great idea. How'd you get so smart?" I flick him with my polishing cloth. "Pass the polish, please."

He hands me the can. "You'll need to pick out the colors you want. The bathrooms and kitchens will need a semi-gloss or satin. Kitchen cabinets shouldn't take more than a gallon." He stops polishing. "Your thoughts?"

"I want to paint the entire interior the same color so the rooms look larger. I'm thinking of the palest yellow to accentuate the sun streaming in the windows." My excitement builds. "Shouldn't take me too long to choose it since I know the color. Want to start painting next week."

"Sure thing."

We stop for the beach house supplies on the way to my apartment. "Think I may have to fill in at Apalach tomorrow," he says. "If I take the beach route, I can drop everything off at the house."

How thoughtful. "That would be great. Maybe I can find time to work on the cabinets over the weekend. Then we can do the painting together next week."

"Good. Need something to keep my mind busy while I wait for the biopsy results. The lab says about a week."

It's the not knowing that's so hard. It must be even harder for Frank.

Errol and I begin our trek from the library to the civic center parking lot when he snatches a paper from the side pocket of my briefcase. "Show me your drawing."

I grab an edge. "Careful." Then I let go. "You'll tear it." Why did I leave the drawing there? It was part of a workshop taken years ago, an anthropological drawing of my birth family.

"Sorry." We stop in the middle of the sidewalk while students swirl around us. Errol shoves the paper in my face and waves it. "You aren't in this family. You've placed yourself above your mother, who is by the way, the largest figure in your picture."

I shrug and flick my hair. "So." I turn to leave.

He grabs my arm and waits until I meet his eyes. "You are superior to your family," his words accusing.

My muscles tense. He has the tendency to make leaps from little evidence. "What do you mean I'm superior?" My tone strident.

Errol waves the paper in my face. "Look at it."

"Hold still if you want me to see." It registers. "Oh...I might need to ponder this."

"Might be a good idea," his tone neutral. His face has a self-satisfied look as he hands back the drawing.

I slip it back into the briefcase and begin to walk again, confused as to how to take what he said. I hope no one thinks I feel superior, definitely not in graduate school where I have to bust butt just to prove I'm good enough to continue.

Errol sets the pace for our trudge up the hill towards our cars. A student whooshes by on skates. We're quiet. I try to wrap my mind around Errol's pronouncement.

He breaks the silence. "Remember when I said you intimidate me?"

I shake my head. "Not really." But I do.

"I based that statement on the fact that your frilly side is emotional, able to express feelings, and yet, you also reason like a man. I've never known a woman who could do both."

"Okay, I get that. What's the other part?"

"You *are* superior. We all know you're brilliant."

He must be kidding. No one has ever told me I'm superior or brilliant.

"Come on, how brilliant am I?"

He rolls his eyes. "You are the lantern that marks the way to the dark corners of the mind."

Was that a snotty remark he made or was he simply being funny? "Been writing poetry these days?"

"As a matter of fact, I have."

I slow my pace. "Seriously, I don't think I'm brilliant. I'm not dumb, but I'm not brilliant. Are you saying I project brilliance or that I project superiority?"

"Not sure. Hadn't thought about it that way until I saw the drawing." He shakes his head. "Thinking about it…thinking about it." He grins. "Nope. Still don't know."

"In the drawing, I wasn't trying to show I was superior, but that I was separate. I didn't feel a part of the family." I slow my pace.

As two students pass us, "Hurry up," says one. Their long hair flies behind them. "We're late."

Errol checks them out and then says, "Why not?"

I shrug. "I don't know."

"How odd. How very, very odd."

We wait at the light on Pensacola. "Come on. Other people must feel that way." I'm jostled as the end-of-class traffic piles up behind me on the curb. "How odd could it be?"

"Only as odd as the sun forgetting to rise in the morning."

The light changes, students swarm around us, but I hesitate. "It is, isn't it?" We cross the street and walk toward our cars. "Don't know how to explain it." I turn towards mine.

He turns back, "Lunch?"

"I should go home and plow through this dissertation section and see how I can match Mr. Overkill's criticisms with my five studies."

"Aw, come on. We can eat at the park. I want to hear more about what you're doing now that you've been denied your topic."

The generous warmth of the sun removes our jackets. The temperature is picnic perfect. The weather promises spring, even though a hard freeze is predicted tomorrow night. I check my phone before I fasten my seat belt. "Hi, Lee. It's just Frank Islip here. Plans have changed. Will be able to see you tonight, but I have to work tomorrow so can't spend the night. Oh, and your stuff is at the beach house." Well, damn, another lesson in flexibility.

On the way to the park, we stop at Errol's favorite deli, where we order sandwiches. "Hey, want to stop by the house after lunch?" He grabs a handful of catsup packages off the counter. "Show you what I've written on our paper."

I stuff a few mayonnaise packets and a bunch of napkins into the white paper bag. These are sloppy sandwiches we've ordered. When we get to the park, Errol sets down our drink cans. While he spreads an old army blanket, I tell him about Frank's call. He raises his eyebrows, "What'd you tell him?"

I place the bag of sandwiches on the blanket. "I didn't." We pull stuff from the bag like two kids. "I'm going to tell him I have a recovery meeting. I feel like I'm being jerked around."

He takes his straw, opens one end, and blows the paper in my face. "Maybe he's floundering about. That's a scary diagnosis for a man. Not death, but impotency. Would be for me."

Even though we seem alike in so many ways, I forget that Frank's reaction would likely be different from mine, even given the same circumstances.

A young father, with his son in a stroller, throws a Frisbee as his golden retriever waits, tail straight up. The dog barrels across our blanket.

I open my drink, and our conversation switches to my frustration about my dissertation topic and one of Errol's clients. Afterwards, we head back to Errol's.

Going into Errol's house always reminds me of my life with Alex. Errol's living room furniture replicates the furniture I bought when I moved from my big house into an apartment when my second husband Todd and I split up. When I see Errol's furniture, I see blue skies and sunshine. On occasion, I'll even hear the *phft, phft, phft* of hot-air balloons, a Saturday morning surprise for Alex and me as we sipped coffee on my balcony in Jacksonville. It was the morning after our first night together.

"Here, take a look." Errol points to the computer screen. "What do you think?"

I quickly read through a couple of pages. "I see where we could make some changes and do a little editing." Really, a lot of editing.

The chair shifts as he rests his weight on the back and peers over my shoulder. "What? Are you messing with my masterpiece?"

"Of course. Don't I always?"

"I know, I know." He reaches toward the computer. "You just want to be the one in charge of the keyboard."

"She who controls the keyboard has the power." I chuckle. "How about emailing this to me?"

Before departing Errol's, I leave Frank a message, "I'm having dinner with one of my friends this evening. Will be home by eight." Now I'm starting to lie. I don't like lying. It never augurs well for me. One lie leads to another lie and then another. Lying is not who I am now.

On the way home, I pick up the book I'll need to compare Joe's theory with this guy's. When I arrive, the cats are nowhere to be found. I pull up Errol's paper and scan through it. More interesting than my stuff. Yin jumps up on the desk and stares at the screen. "Where've you been, little girl?"

Yang enters and meows. I pick him up and scratch his ears. I turn to Yin. "Do you think I have an I'm-superior attitude?"

Yin turns her head towards me, lifts her chin, and turns back to the screen. Was that a takes-one-to-know-one look? "Yes, little girl, I know you're superior to me. Hands down."

I change clothes and hustle my butt to Lake Ella. Maybe I can get my bearings there. Once at the lake, I begin to walk—walking brings clarity. The first mile, I tell myself all the reasons why Errol is wrong. My mother's superiority meant she was never wrong. Never. Never.

Don't believe it? Just ask her. In her eyes, I never did anything right. Didn't she believe my first husband Richard when he blamed our divorce on me? Didn't she call Todd to ask what I'd done to cause the breakup? No wonder I thought I alone had to fix my marriages. Probably why they both failed.

I stop for a moment on the concrete path and watch the ducks. What if Errol is right? I don't need to assume he's right, just accept the possibility. I start walking again, slowly. When do I feel superior? To whom? I made better grades than my brothers all through school. Did I feel superior? I don't think so. Where else?

Richard. Didn't I need to teach him how to manage the silver at a formal dinner? Give him etiquette lessons from Emily Post?

Two crows caw, and I look toward a tree near the bicycle shop. They caw twice again. They sound like they're jeering. A message? Do I jeer?

Then I see Frank at a table near the tree when he wraps his head with a blue sweater, a familiar shade of blue. A woman sits beside him. He ducks his covered face towards her. I don't see anything but the top of her red baseball cap. I pretend I don't see him and walk on. Does he not know that he's called attention to himself? He's like my old dog that used to hide her head under the bed with her butt sticking out. If I can't see you, you can't see me.

I refuse to worry about what Frank is doing. Instead, I file the incident in the think-about-later folder in my briefcase.

I'm more concerned about Errol's accusation. Where else do I act superior? Morally? Richard screwed all those women from the day of our wedding. Even propositioned my friends, as I discovered after the divorce. Hell, I *was* morally superior.

What else? Intellectually. I barely studied and made better grades than Richard. Hmm. Richard had to set the curve in all his economic classes except where advanced math was concerned. I didn't set the curve. Can't compare Todd's intelligence to mine, because our interests were different. Richard's, too. Okay, so I know more than Errol about marriage and family therapy, only because I've lived it for fifteen years through my relationships and my recovery groups and my master's in clinical psychology. This feels like an excuse.

Now, I wonder about Frank and his need to hide. I have to remember that what he does is none of my business. Only my reaction to it is my business. I can't afford to let him live rent-free in my head. As I come around again, he's gone.

The next two weeks seem to rush along in one sense and creep in another. Frank and I have worked on the house, and I have spent several days during the week removing doors and hardware, and then painting cabinets.

Frank has heard nothing from the doctor about the biopsy results. He expresses his frustration. "I don't know what I'd do if I didn't have the renovation to concentrate on."

Yin and Yang greet me as I walk in the door to a ringing phone. Thinking it may be Frank with good news, I pick up without looking at the number. "Vinnie is stalking me." When I hear the familiar female voice, my lips tighten as if someone twists unseen screws at the corners of my mouth. I know I should have checked caller ID. Why would Joy call me now? Did she just find out I bought the beach house? Ever since I met her and Vinnie at a spiritual workshop, she's tried to drag me into their business. Did she see my car at the beach? "I'm sorry, Joy. I can't talk right now."

"Well," she huffs the word. Click.

Is Joy the only person in the world who refuses to enter the twenty-first century? She must keep that old-fashioned phone just so she can slam it down and have it go click.

I lie on the floor and let Yin settle on my stomach and Yang tug at my hair. When the phone rings, I let the machine pick up.

"It's just me. Frank Islip here."

The cats scurry away as I grab the phone.

"Hi, Lee. It's just me, Frank Islip."

My heart skips a beat. Will this be the good news for which I wait?

Chapter 4

"Just heard from the doc." His usual upbeat tone slides down an octave.

"Oh." My stomach clenches. I tighten my grip on the phone. My legs are heavy as I move from the office computer to the den. I pull up my feet and hug my knees with my free arm as I curl into a ball in my antique friend, the chair from my parents' house.

I look up at the watercolor, a large, close-up of a white azalea, surrounded by negative-space leaves. I concentrate on the painting's vivid vermillion dropped into a water-splotched background of Grumbacher's Academy thalo and cobalt blues.

"Got the biopsy results." Frank takes a deep breath and blows it out. "Positive. Cancer." His voice trails off.

The clock reads three forty-seven. My spacious three-bedroom apartment shrinks to a box with no windows.

I take a deep breath. My heart thuds against my ribs.

I plunge into another time. Another phone call. Another cancer diagnosis. This one fatal. I'm standing in the office of Western Carolina University's psych department, using the secretary's phone to call my husband. Her plants grow in the streaming sun, healthy and green.

"Cancer. Larynx." Alex's voice, barely audible.

My sun crashes cold. My stomach retches. Below, students walk by the window laughing and talking. For them, it is a normal day.

Someone calls out, "Good night." A door slams. I reach over to pluck a dead leaf. How can I live without him?

"You still there?" Frank's voice breaks.

I let out my breath. "Oh, Frank, I'm so sorry. Are you all right? Is there anything I can do?" I calculate how much time I have left in the day. Doesn't matter. I'm not likely to get any work done. "Come for dinner?" I'll find something to cook, quick and easy.

Concern creeps into his voice. "Don't you have a presentation to prepare for?"

"You're more important than my presentation."

Yin and Yang, slink from underneath the entertainment center. I crook the phone on my shoulder. "See you at seven?" as I reach down to scratch Yang's ears.

"Anything you want me to bring?"

"Just your charming self."

"You got it. See you at seven."

When I hang up, I sit, stunned.

It's been four years since I moved from the mountains of North Carolina to Tallahassee. Here, with a tenacity bordering on vengeance, I pursue a doctorate in marriage and family therapy. I must get that degree regardless of personal expense. My sense of self rides on this degree. What would I be doing right now if I'd not heard the news? Working on that boring critical review paper.

After all these years, I thought I'd gotten over my guilt about dropping Alex off at the hospital late Friday and not showing up until visiting hours on Sunday. Will I ever forget the hospice social worker telling me I should have stopped working when Alex was diagnosed, not the day he entered the hospital—a decision Alex and I made together. Why do I dwell on this? I lalalalala away the voice of my mother: "Pride, just plain pride, Lee Lawrence Lindsey. If you know what's good for you, you will lose it."

The cats inch their way over to the chair's matching footstool and look up. When I lean over to pet Yin, Yang butts his head against my hand.

I look up and then at Yang. Will I be prepared for tomorrow? "I can't afford to allow my feelings for Frank and his illness to get in the way of my studies." I return to my habitual way of dealing with the thoughts that lead to intense feelings, a slogan I learned in my twelve-step recovery program: "Don't make mountains out of molehills." Frank is not going to die from this. The doc caught it before the lab did. What would I be doing right now if I hadn't heard Frank's news? Working on the dratted paper. Not going to happen. Another day lost.

Within the week of my decision to allow someone into my life to counteract the selfishness and self-centeredness I'd gotten into since living alone, I met Frank. While wearing my college sweatshirt at Lake Ella, my favorite place to run and walk, he stopped me with "Western Carolina University. That's in Cullowhee, isn't it?" We discovered many things in common, not the least of which, he could pronounce the town where I went to school. We also hold private pilots' licenses, work at maintaining our health, and are connected through our North Carolina towns, separated by the Blue Ridge Mountains.

Timing was right. I was in the market for a life outside of academia, in the market for a playmate, in the market for someone who understood my need to work long hours. Easy-going Frank was glad to accommodate.

He was a distraction from my studies, until the afternoon the upstairs neighbor clued me in. What could I do but choose to love him, although I still have my doubts? As early as our first date, I began to have doubts. His "I wish I could have known Alex" seemed false.

Sometimes he calls at the last minute and says, "I'm in a crappy mood. Think I should stay home and not spread my miserable cheer." Something I appreciate, but still…then when I boot up my paper and begin work, he calls back. "My mood is much improved. Am I still welcome to come over?"

Did loving him begin building when Frank had his biopsy? Would I love him if I weren't facing the possibility of losing him? Just when I've allowed myself to love him—cancer. Is this reaction because my two closest experiences with cancer ended in death? First, my cousin, through which Alex supported me, and then his, through which he also supported me.

I know prostate cancer is not a death sentence. An elderly fellow artist, who used to set up his easel next to mine some Saturdays, has lived with prostate cancer for what? Over twenty years now.

What kind of meaning will Frank place on his diagnosis? He's the man who jokes about his sexual appetite. "I plan to die in bed, at the hands of a jealous husband," a statement that always wraps me in a pencil-yellow cloud of caution.

Yet when Yin and Yang, who hide from everyone else, crawl on him, I too shed my wariness. I'm flattered when my male friends say I bring color to Frank's life.

He brings adventure to mine, like the time we flew over a nearby forest fire and watched the helicopters fill large buckets from a nearby lake and then dump them on a fire. And he's teaching me patience about doing something over and over in order to get it right.

How will he handle the impotence from surgery? How will I handle it? Sex is not something I want to give up, but Frank is my first since Alex died. Didn't miss having a partner during those dry years. I can handle it.

Besides, how do I know he'll have surgery? Medicine has surely advanced in the twenty years since my elderly friend was diagnosed. Alex's illness taught me how vital positive attitude and expectations are for recovery. Alex's doctor had been adamant about a positive mindset. Can I help Frank stay positive?

I return to the safety of my office, tucked away in the back bedroom, strewn with papers, books, and note cards—looks like my study room in North Carolina at semester's end. When I finish a project, I reorganize. Living alone, I can no longer blame someone else for the lack of organization. I still hear the amusement in Alex's voice while I ran around the house complaining that I couldn't live in such a mess. "Look around, honey. Whose mess do you see?"

I pick up the small pillow one of the cats dragged from my bed and hug it to me. *Adia* by Sara McLachlan drifts in from the open window. I'd give anything to hold Alex and have him hold me right now. God, I miss him so much. He surely ripped my heart out and took it with him.

I can't get the memory of the day Alex was diagnosed out of my mind. I knew those first six weeks after his diagnosis were bad, but I didn't realize how bad until I relived them. Got to pull myself together if I'm to be of any help to Frank. I pull out one of the many books on crisis and the fight or flight response. What's going on? No fight. No flight. Paralysis. Mental paralysis. Numb.

An hour later, I scramble around to find something for dinner and settle on a quick pasta sauce of tomatoes, garlic, and basil. The sauce bubbles in the pot while my stomach roils to the same rhythm. The sauce's sachet escapes, fragrancing the apartment. It won't be as good tonight as it will be tomorrow, but that's what I have on hand. Thank the gods, Frank's not a picky eater.

While the sauce simmers, I set the glass-topped dining table with black placemats, matching napkins, and silverware. I pause and lean forward on the table. How will I survive this? How will my education survive this? Frank's cancer is not about me. It's about Frank. "Stop being melodramatic," I declare.

The cats skitter away. "Sorry, kitties. Didn't mean to yell." My clients' melodrama must be contagious.

Frank will be fine. Need to separate Frank's cancer from Alex's. *Breathe, Lee. Breathe. Breathe.* Can't imagine what I would do without the stress reduction class I took years ago when I first started back to school.

I survived Alex's death in the middle of my thesis. I'll survive this. Cut the drama. This is not about survival; it's about completing the program. My survival would be about my life.

Beauty makes the world better, I think as I open the drawer of my narrow, high chest and pick up the tapered candles for the sterling candelabra. The candles remind me of another lifetime. An existence before death changed everything. As hard as I try, I can't get Alex out of my mind. I return to the kitchen, take out two square white dinner plates and two wineglasses.

At ten of seven, I put on the water for pasta and set the oven for the rolls. I place the butter and Parmesan on the table.

Frank sounded lost earlier. He must have found working difficult after his diagnosis. "Stop obsessing. It changes nothing," the voice of my twelve-step sponsor rings in my head. "What you focus on is what you get."

Cooking was how my grandmother dealt with life's blows. I grab a large, wooden bowl from on top of the refrigerator, and then gather salad ingredients. I combine them in the bowl. I sprinkle the salad with Parmesan and oregano. I'll dress the salad after Frank arrives. I pull down the clear glass bowls from the cabinet.

At seven, I turn the boiling water to low. I'll turn it back up when he arrives.

I choose the wine, a Beringer zinfandel. After removing the seal, I uncork the wine to give it time to breathe—if I focus on what I'm doing, I won't resurrect the past or invent the future.

I look at the clock. Late again. Why, when we set a definite time, is Frank always late? Months ago, I'd stopped cooking meals that required more than fifteen minutes to finish after he arrives. We eat an abundance of pasta and sandwiches these days. Get over it, Lee. Tonight's a special case.

At seven forty-five, my concern mounts. Just before I call to see if he's okay, the doorbell rings. I rush to the door. Frank pulls me outside. We hold each other, standing in the doorway, for what seems like minutes. I'm not used to displaying affection in public. Not since Alex.

He lets go and looks over my shoulder. "Sorry I'm late. Been on the phone. My daughter called as I was closing the park. Such is the life of a park ranger." He gives me another longer-than-usual hug while I breathe in the fresh-air scent of his clothes. I sneeze.

When I let go, his disarranged, gray-streaked, sandy hair, his ragged form-fitting sweatshirt and pants showing off his slim physique, and running shoes with at least five hundred miles of wear, all tell me he's distracted.

Holding my hand, he follows me inside. "Smells good in here." He removes his shoes and leaves them in the marble entryway.

"Thanks." I push a stray hair from my face. "How are you doing?"

"Okay, I guess." His volume tapers off. I strain to hear. Yang wanders over and, with barely extended claws, gives his leg a tug.

"What did your daughter have to say?" Did he tell her? She's twenty-three. She should be able to handle it.

"Not much." With the unsteady gait of a much older man, Frank moves towards the dining room.

"I'll pour some wine." I turn towards the kitchen. "We can eat when the pasta and rolls are ready."

I hand him a glass and he moves into the dining room. From his place at the table, Frank talks to me through the kitchen doorway. "How was your day?"

"Painted the first coat on the cabinets and then came home."

"Great. Work on it this weekend?"

"That's my plan. I can't make myself work on the review paper, especially on the weekend. I either have to change my attitude about my topic or I need to change topics." The timer goes off.

Frank's face relaxes. "Thanks. I need the distraction."

I stumble against the cabinet. "Almost forgot, while I was at the coast, I had the feeling I was being watched. I chalked it up to paranoia, but when I got home, Joy called."

"The Girlfriend?"

"Same one. Wanted to complain about Vinnie stalking her."

"Wasn't she stalking him?"

"Yeah. That's what's so funny about it. She leaves notes in his mailbox all the time. Crazy letters, asking him to stop contacting her."

I've seen this often on psych units where I've worked. The patient yells into the pay phone, "I will never ever speak to you again. Never call me again. Never." Then she redials and repeats her words to the same person five minutes later. "Anyway, she slammed down the phone when I told her I couldn't talk."

I cradle the pasta on plates, take the rolls out of the oven, and as I carry them to the table, I bump into the doorframe. Hate it when my balance is off like this. As I sit, the sight of Frank's fastidious unfolding of his napkin fascinates me. It reminds me of my prissy mother.

"Doc says this is in an early stage." He picks up his fork and begins to twirl the spaghetti with the help of a soupspoon. "He wouldn't have caught it if he hadn't felt the nodule."

"Thank the gods for the mix-up about your appointment in November. Don't think the doctor would have detected anything then." I pick up my fork. "Not with routine lab work."

"Been thinking the same thing." Tension scurries across his face and then disappears.

I tell him I looked up prostate cancer in a book by Louise Hay. "Hay's belief is that this form of cancer is caused by sexual guilt." I laugh to lighten the mood, and point my fork upwards. "Do you feel guilty about sex?"

Frank lowers his head imperceptibly as he looks down at his napkin. "Yeah. Sometimes." His voice sounds sheepish.

Really? Not the reaction I expected. I place the fork on my plate and pick up my wineglass. "You might want to get over it." I smile and sip the wine.

"Yeah." He shrugs and looks down at his plate.

I place the glass on the table. "Well, whatever the cause, we can get through this together."

Frank's face registers shock. "Thanks. Blythe just wished me luck. But no offer to help. You're willing to see me through this?"

My brain tilts. What the— "I'm confused. Why would you expect help from your former wife?"

Frank's fork drops from the table. "She's the mother of my child, for God's sake." He grabs for the fork and nearly knocks over his wine.

Is that a touch of hostility in his voice? They've been divorced for years. "Sounds like you're still attached. Even after twenty some years?"

"Maybe."

I wait. He doesn't elaborate. "How's your paper going?" We spend the remainder of the meal discussing my ever-so-boring review paper. Frank's interest in the content of my schoolwork is new. Tonight new.

He refolds his napkin. "Sit in the den?"

He moves from the table to the den, and I bring in coffee, placing Frank's on the table beside my chair and mine across the room on the floor under a nearby table. Less likely to tip over there. I sink into a rough-woven floor pillow.

Frank walks over and pulls me up to face him. "I love you." He draws me tight against him. He kisses the hollow of my neck and releases me.

"When I first heard something might be wrong . . . ." I move my coffee to the table next to his, "I realized how much I love you and don't want to lose you." I settle into his lap. "What can I do to help?"

He shrugs. Then looks at me hard. "Will you go with me to the doctor on Monday?"

Is that fear in his voice?

His foot paws the floor. "Two sets of ears are better than one."

"True." Particularly since his set wears hearing aids. The irony of my need to be understood is not lost on me. "What time? I have an afternoon session."

"Nine," he says. "We should be out by eleven, at the latest."

I can postpone working on my papers. "Sure."

"Would you research treatments for prostate cancer for me? I want to be informed when I see the doc." He curls and uncurls his toes on the footstool. "You're better at computers and have more time."

My arm muscle tenses. I may be better at research, but he has more free time than I do. What does he do that's so time consuming? Besides, I'd think he'd want to do his own research. I would.

But then, why did I offer to help if I'm going to resent helping? I stand and kiss the top of his head, hoping to change my attitude. I don't smile because I'm happy…"More coffee?"

I bring two cups back to the table beside the chair. I set the coffees down and then plunk onto my pillow with a thud.

Frank studies my face. "You drunk?" Is his tone curious or accusatory?

"No." I reach for my coffee. "Why'd you ask?"

"You stumbled as you walked into the kitchen and your landing on that pillow wasn't exactly graceful."

Probably curiosity. "Oh, you noticed. My sinuses are affecting my inner ear causing balance problems."

Frank pulls me up and into his arms. He puts his hands on the small of my back and presses against me. He kisses the side of my neck. His voice is low and husky, "How about we take a walk to the bedroom? I'll keep you steady."

He walks me into the bedroom with his hands on my shoulders. I lie on the bed, suddenly dizzy. Should probably have taken an antihistamine. No need to mention this. The room spins as he caresses me.

Afterwards, for the first time in years, I want a cigarette. Oh, I don't smoke.

As we lie side-by-side, Frank strokes me. "Almost glad I have this cancer," he says. "Brought us closer together."

Because I've been practicing an attitude of gratitude for years, I don't question his statement. No matter what life throws at me, I can usually find something for which to be grateful. Makes my life more serene.

I snuggle closer. "Me too."

I amaze myself when I go from annoyance to loving feelings this fast. It reminds me of the meditation tape I used after Alex died, in which the speaker took me through a series of feelings: from deep grief to joy in five minutes. I felt each one.

Frank's fingertips kiss my hair. I turn my head toward him and catch his frown. "There will be impotency after the surgery. Maybe lifelong. How're you going to feel about that?"

The sheets turn scratchy. "You know, we make a big assumption here. We don't know if surgery is the only option—I haven't done the research yet, remember? But assuming surgery is the best choice, I'd rather have you cancer-free. Sex is important to me, but I can live without it." I lean over and kiss him. "How will you deal with it?"

Frank enfolds me in his arms. "I can live without sex. I've been thinking about it. It just isn't that important."

Startled, I sit up and lean on my elbow. Is this his response to my question about sexual guilt? Our English-Scotch-Irish ancestors taught us both to be stoic. Still, I'm not indifferent to my emotions right now. Is he?

I reach over and touch his shoulder. "We'll deal with that when we come to it. I'd prefer a healthy you to sex."

"Yeah. Well…thanks." He sits up and puts his feet on the floor. "Time to ease on outta here."

Once out of bed, he dresses and then goes to the living room where he methodically puts on each shoe and takes time to make sure his laces are just so. "Have an early day tomorrow."

As the front door closes behind him, Frank leaves me with concern for his health and trifling misgivings about…about what?

Chapter 5

We plan on an easier drive to the beach by going down Friday morning. Frank has taken a day off. As soon as we arrive, Frank opens the Kilz, pours some into a roller pan for me and another one for him. He hands me a roller. We each take a room and paint. I end up with more paint on me than on the wall. I've never experienced how quickly painting an empty room could go. We have the walls done by early afternoon.

I'm in the master bedroom. "Hey, Babe, ready for some lunch?"

We take our sandwiches to the deck and sit, leaning against the rail. He takes a bite. "After we eat, I'll bring in the extra ladder I brought, and we can start cutting into the ceiling and the corners."

He catches me with my mouth full. I finish chewing. "Sounds good. Do you think we'll finish today?"

"We should if we keep at it." He tosses the remains in the trash and gets up. "Come on. Time to get back at it." He gives me a hand. We work in silence until it turns dark-thirty and my stomach growls. "Finish in here," he says. "And start cleaning up. I'll be done shortly."

I go outside and wash brushes and rollers. Before I can finish, Frank brings me his stuff. "Think we should stop at the little green restaurant on the way home. You okay with that?"

"Sure." I continue the cleanup while Frank takes care of the ladders and paint cans. I take the rollers and brushes into the house. "I'm glad you bought the extra rollers. With this humidity, I doubt these will dry by tomorrow." Something I'd not thought about.

We pack up our things and drive to the small, Panacea seafood restaurant. By this time, I'm exhausted, and the smell of fried fish and hushpuppies triggers my hunger.

Frank reaches across the booth's Formica tabletop and runs his hand down my cheek. "Don't know what I'd have done if you hadn't bought the house. It gives me something to think about besides the cancer."

The waitress brings menus. "What would you like to drink?" Her kelly green top accentuates her frizzy red curls and emerald eyes.

"Beer for me. Coffee, Lee?"

"Please. Maybe coffee will give me some energy. Right now, I have none."

"You worked long and hard today. Didn't eat much lunch, either."

Glancing down to spread the napkin on my lap, I notice splashes of white paint on old running pants. I look at Frank, who has paint on his clothes and sweat stains under his arms. "Would you look at us? We look like a couple of vagrants in these old dirt and paint-spattered clothes."

"We fit right in here." He grabs a grease-stained menu. "Gonna have scallops. Ya know they're the real thing in this place."

"Crab cakes for me." I place the menu on the table. "As hungry as I am, I'm almost too tired to eat." Hmm. Something my mother used to say. My stomach growls.

I lean on the table. "If you'd like, you can have first dibs on the shower."

A little coffee sloshes into the saucer as the waitress sets the cup down in front of me. "Sorry, Shug. Ready to order?" I place a paper napkin under the cup.

While Frank orders for us, two fishermen in their white oyster boots—known as Panacea Nikes—at the next table light up. They turn to stare. I'm sure it's because we look so unkempt.

When I mention their stares to Frank, he says, "Know you hate to look grubby, but think you may be imagining the reason for their looks. You are a good-looking woman, after all."

The restaurant walls and furniture are encrusted with years of nicotine and cooking grease. The smoke in the air causes me to see the room as if through the waterfall of cataract eyes. At least that's how my artist friends would describe it. The idea of cataracts sends a chill of fear down my spine. Can't stand the thought of eye surgery. Thank the gods, the food makes up for the dingy atmosphere.

Frank and I make small talk through dinner, mostly about the house and timing of carpeting and countertops, all the components it takes to complete the majority of work. "Think we can get most of the painting done tomorrow, maybe all of it." Because he works next weekend, we make plans to work the following Monday and possibly Tuesday. "We should be able to complete the painting Monday."

Our next trip to the coast is a repeat of Friday, except Frank is quieter than usual on the drive back to my apartment. Once we've settled in with coffee, he stands. "Listen, I'd like to check on living wills and medical directives."

After the fiasco where a Florida woman was kept alive in a vegetative state despite her wishes, I should probably do the same. We move into the office where we share a chair. We're looking at medical directives on the screen when Frank asks, "You know I love you, don't you?" He'd asked this the other day, in the same tone.

I smile and lean towards him. I peck him on the cheek. "Love you, too." He looks at the floor. When he speaks, his tone is flat.

"I can't marry you."

I turn toward the window. The moon has disappeared. "What? I told you the day I met you I wasn't interested in marriage. And, since that time, I've never mentioned marriage." A flash of lightning crosses the sky. A patio door slams overhead. A loud crash of thunder follows. Then large drops of rain plunk on the window.

When I turn back to Frank, a marble-like mask pulls down over his face. "I'm still married."

A jerk takes over my diaphragm when I exhale, and then relief spreads as I register Frank's words. So that's the cause of my reticence. I'm not crazy. My gut was correct when I kept sensing something wasn't right in this relationship. My doubts began as early as two months after we started dating. At the time, I had no reason to doubt him. But. The big but.

The air conditioner kicks off, leaving the room in total silence except for the rain and the rhythmic drumbeat of my heart, louder and faster than usual. The piles of papers and books on the floor around the desk look as if someone picked up everything and tossed it in the air to see where it would land. The wooden desk scents the room with wafts of lavender oil spilled days ago. The bookcase above it is crammed with CDs, flash drives, books, a stapler, a hole-punch, and a small round palm-held antique oil lamp my brother brought back from Egypt. The office suddenly becomes a five-by-five-foot box. Without

Roberta Burton

windows. Frank's leg and shoulders against mine become invasive. Too close. Too close. Too close.

My gaze moves to the watercolor of a man's white shirt hanging on a bedpost, tennis shoes underneath. Alex's shirt sparkles with emerald green, alizarin crimson, ultramarine blue, and yellow ochre. The colors continue in the background. The increased intensity of color pops out the white shirt and shoes. My cells remember the night before I painted this watercolor.

"Why are you still married?" My every muscle on high alert.

His jaw twitches. "For our daughter's sake."

"My god, she's twenty-three." My voice grates even to me.

"We're paying her health insurance since she's still in school."

This is crazy. "You lied to me. Why did you lie?" Tears float to the surface and stream down in tiny rivulets wetting my face. Then my shirt. I get up and move to the den in order to put distance between us. Amid my confusion, I try to name my feelings. Betrayal comes to mind and then anger. Damn it. Cuts and bruises to my psyche hide behind anger's skirt.

Frank follows me and sits in my chair. He beckons. Instead of going to him, I retreat to my floor pillow. The material's rough against my bare legs where my pants creep up my calves. The still lingering remnants of the tomato and basil soup I'd heated up for dinner edge their way into my throat. "Why? Why would you lie to me?"

His face remains as unreadable as an uncarved gravestone. "I felt single. Not married," his voice an automaton.

Blood rushes to my face. "I don't give a damn how you felt. I had a right to know. You are married. I'd never have dated you had I known." In the background, my mother says, "You're nothing but a fishwife." Don't care. Yell anyway.

"I want you out of my sight. I'd like you to leave. Now. I want time to think this through. I'll call you."

Frank's lazy eye travels back and forth in its socket. Had it ever jumped before? "Guess it's time for me to ease on out of here."

Ease out. You're not as smart as I thought you were if you don't know that you just might need to run for your life if you stay any longer. As many times as you've told me that you expected to die at the hand of a jealous husband, did it never occur to you that you just might die at the feet of your enraged lover because of your lies?

52

I hold the door open. I slit my eyes and grit my teeth. "Just go."
He walks out. I slam the door.

As I process what happened, I remember when I expressed my doubts to an acquaintance that something about Frank didn't feel right. She recommended a spiritual intuitive, much like Edgar Cayce. Turns out, I'd attended several of his workshops on increasing intuition. His energy was that of loving kindness, so when he described a warm presence, which slowly increased until it filled the room, I knew it was Alex.

The message contained Alex's words as if he talked directly to me. I believed him when he said it was time to have adventures, the kind we would've had together, had he lived. Then Alex let me know, "I'll always watch over you, like a forest ranger in a fire tower." I believed. Since Frank is a park ranger, I was certain Alex was talking about Frank, giving me his blessing. Had I been wrong? In this process of learning to trust myself, I seem to take three steps forward and two back.

The following morning, before the Saturday meeting, I join a woman I sponsor in recovery at the converted rails-to-trails trailhead. The 5K run is perfect to work off some anger. My muscles move in orchestrated rhythm as I work up a dripping sweat. She complains about her current boyfriend. Seems he found out she was seeing someone else on the side, a seedy-past someone. When I ask why, "I want more excitement." Doubt she'll stay in recovery for any length of time unless she's willing to give up the drama. After our run, we towel off before going to our meeting. On my drive to the meeting, I wonder about her attitude and question if Frank might have the same thoughts.

Frank's best Naval Reserve buddy is at the meeting. While we're getting coffee, I ask her why she didn't tell me he was still married. Her eyes widen. She picks up a cup. "What? I thought he was divorced years ago, at least fifteen, closer to twenty. When the daughter was still a toddler." Disbelief resides in her tone. "Sometime after he moved out of their house," she fills her cup, "he installed a phone line under mine. He wanted to use my address so that his daughter could continue at her school and then go to Leon High when she got older." She stirs in sugar and then cream. "Maybe his marriage is a convenience, too."

I spend the rest of the day running errands and working on the boring review paper. With the school stuff handled, maybe I can take care of my emotional issue. I pull down my journal from the top shelf of my bookcase and move into the den. I embrace my coffee-filled black and white porcelain mug as I perch on the wide arm of my chair, the one I often sat on as a child. Got yelled at for that, too.

I must get some clarity about what I should do. I slide off the arm and into the chair where I'd sat in Dad's lap when I was little. I take a sip of coffee, uncap my pen, and, using one chair arm as a desk, I begin to marry pen to paper:

> February 13, 1999
>
> Problem: Frank lied to me.
>
> Think about it: He's a jerk, a liar. Can't trust him. Feel guilty if I leave him with his cancer. Kick a sick man when he's down. Societal upbringing insists I make nice like a good woman should—do my duty and care for him.
>
> What else has he lied about? He's put me in a no-win situation: If I stay with a married man, I go against my moral principles. If I leave, I've not kept my word—lost my integrity.
>
> Feel about it: Angry, hurt, betrayed, stupid, humiliated, and ambivalent. Mostly ambivalent.
>
> How I wish to resolve this problem: Need a damn good reason why he's still married, why he lied.
>
> Remember the nice things he does: he cooks me dinner, supports my schooling one hundred percent. Being with him is fun and humorous, I've missed that since Alex.
>
> Five actions I can take to resolve this problem:
> 1. Leave the relationship
> 2. Keep asking why
> 3. Let it go
> 4. Make myself crazy with resentment
> 5. Write about it

What can I do about it right now? Let it go. For now.

As I look over my writing, my hand slides to my forehead as if to burn the last five words on my brain. Truth is, hanging onto this anger, even if it is justified, will turn it into resentment. I might as well drink poison and wait for Frank to die. Why should I make myself sick just to prove I'm right? I cap my pen, get up, and place the journal on the desk. While stretching out my kinks, I make my decision: no decision. I refuse to waste time thinking about him right now.

But think about him I do. Funny, when I decide not to think about him, I ruminate over his willingness to fix anything his friends ask of him, from washers and dryers to cars and motorcycles. Even though he hangs onto a dollar as if it's a branch extending over the edge of a cliff, he often makes things for me like the time he fashioned a porta-Jane from a bleach bottle so I could pee while on long flights in his Piper Cherokee. Then I'm back to that night not so long ago when I came home late from class. After ten.

I open the car door and drop the keys into the pocket of my jacket. I grab my burgundy briefcase, punch the automatic lock button, and promptly slam the door.

Shit. My right thumb and first two fingers. Locked. In. The. Door. What had I done? Carefully, very carefully, I bend over with caution to reach into the right pocket that falls mid-thigh. I turn clockwise to retrieve the keys with my left hand. Got them. Now, unlock the door. A few seconds—they seem like minutes. Two tries later, I stab the key in the lock and turn the wrong direction. Other way. Open. I remove my hand and relock the door.

I look at my fingers and watch red splashes of blood spurt and hit the ground. No pain. Only nausea. I'm going to vomit right here on the sidewalk. I know from my history, when the injury's severe but I can't feel it, I become nauseated. I knock on the door of Mrs.

McPherson, a nurse. I say through the closed door, "I smashed my fingers in my car door. Would you look at them?"

She keeps her door locked. "Go call that man you're seeing and get him to take you to the emergency room."

And she calls herself a friend? Yeah, when *she* wants something.

I rush to my apartment and leave behind a trail of blood. I speed to the sink and turn on the water, then snatch paper towels and wrap my hand. I call *that man*.

He picks up on the first ring. "Be right there."

I'm in shock and must work off the rush of adrenalin that pulses through my veins, I pace and pace and pace while I wait.

When Frank arrives, he gently takes my hand and turns it over. "Let me see."

"Do you think I need to go to the emergency room and get stitches?" My tongue moistens my arid upper lip. "They don't look so bad now that I've washed the blood off."

"Look again, Lee. Those cuts are deep. Come on, I'll drive you."

"No...No...No emergency room." I hate it when I sound like a whiney five-year-old. I grab another paper towel and begin to pace again. "Stitches will keep me from typing for at least a week, maybe longer." Tears begin to build. I cough to stop them.

"Let me run to the twenty-four hour store and see if we can close the wounds with butterflies."

"Please." I touch his face with my uninjured hand. "Thank you."

While Frank is gone, I pace. Have to pace. Shocky. Can't seem to walk off the adrenalin. Unable to think clearly.

When he returns, he cleans the wound with peroxide and applies the bandages, then cups my hand in his, and watches. "Looks like they're doing the job. Don't see any blood oozing."

"Thank you for being here and for suggesting the butterflies." The idea of having Novocain shots in my fingers sends unpleasant thoughts scurrying down a dark path. I touch his neck. "If you hadn't thought of the butterflies, I wouldn't be able to type. Or hold a pen. We'd have spent hours in the emergency room, and you have to be at work early in the morning."

He pulls me to him and holds me. "Would've been glad to sit with you. But glad you don't need stitches." Frank leads me into the den.

"Sit and rest. Heat you some coffee." He turns on the desk light next to my pillow and bends down. "Add some brandy, too." He puts his fingers under my chin and turns my face towards the light. "You're so pale, you're almost white. Looks like shock."

I sit on the large, white linen floor pillow, looking at the painting I'd done of a calla lily, the one hanging over the entertainment center. Not bad. The white lily is filled with yellow ochre, cerulean, cobalt, violets, and greens with hints of scarlet set against a background of greens mixed with the same colors in the lily. The colors blur like oil on a puddle.

I jump when Frank leans down and kisses my forehead as he hands me the coffee laced with brandy.

"Some brandy?"

"Half. Thought that would help ease the pain and bring back your color." He moves to my chair.

Yin and Yang appear and snuggle, one on each side of me. They comfort me.

"Strange, there is no pain." I flex my fingers. "Just sensation. Not really numbness. Pressure. That's it."

We drink in silence. Frank watches me. "Your color's returning."

"I feel a rosy glow." Not quite a buzz. "Thank you for all you did tonight."

Frank looks at me, his eyes soft like a fuzzy blanket. "You're welcome." He shifts slightly away from me. He looks as if he wishes to say something else, but he doesn't. Yin wanders over to him and Yang snuggles closer to me.

My fingers move to my lips as I smile. I have so much love for Frank at this moment that my heart might fly apart. I reach for the spiked coffee.

Yang jumps on me and places his paw on my cheek. I reach over to pet him, but my thoughts return to Frank and the decision I must make.

I dwell on Frank's good qualities, not the fact that he lied to me. His lying doesn't negate his kindnesses, and I gave him my word. I choose to keep my word.

I'll see Frank through his surgery. The least I can do is care for him during his recovery. I claim I'm in love with him, don't I? I must let go of my fear: if he lied about his marital state, what else has he lied about? *Drop that thought.*

I said I'd be there for him. I can do anything for a couple of months. What's more important, maintaining my integrity or not compromising my morals? After all, he hasn't lived with his wife for at least fifteen years. They seem to be married in name only.

I call Frank. "I've made my decision." Was my tone neutral? "Would you like to keep the standing plans we had for tonight?"

Frank takes in a sharp breath. "I'd love to." His release sounds like relief. "Does this mean we can work on the house tomorrow?"

"We'll talk about that when you get here." I almost forgot, "Seven for dinner?"

"Tell you what, I'll bring dinner. Okay?"

Before Frank arrives, I costume the table with dark green placemats and napkins, which pick up the pale green of the Wedgewood china luncheon plates.

I'm showered and dressed when Frank rings the bell promptly at seven. He comes bearing microwaved chicken, one wing and one small drumstick each, two small microwaved potatoes, a mug of microwaved, frozen, mixed vegetables. No seasoning. He also includes his customary packaged, mixed salad greens. "Hey, Hon, thought we could use your oil and vinegar for the salad."

The normality of the moment feels like being in my family where dissension was smoothed over and tucked away into the past without discussion.

I add butter to the table and remind myself to act as if. If I'm going to do this, I'll have to change my attitude. "Thank you for dinner." I hug him.

I pour the merlot while Frank plops food on the plates. He sips the red wine. "Perfect, Babe. Just the right amount of water and ice."

Chardonnay would be much better with chicken, but Frank drinks only diluted generic red. Well, this is not generic, but he's not paying for it.

As we sit down to eat, Frank's demeanor is one of caution. Does he expect me to lose it again? Surprise! I was not out of control last night. However, I still have reservations about allowing him full access to my heart. I'll act as if I'm already allowing him entry, and see if I can change my attitude. The best I can do tonight is to consider this a gift to him for all he's done for me. He's said before that working on the beach house will help him focus on something besides his illness. And, for me, some help would be nice.

We make small talk throughout dinner, but not until we're settled in the den with our coffee, do I bring up what's on my mind.

"I wish to tell you where I stand right now."

Frank has the paralyzed look of someone waiting for sentencing.

"After thinking about it, and reminding myself of all you do, and have done for me, and because I said I would be here to help you deal with the cancer, I'm willing to keep my word."

Frank moves his head up and down so slowly that I hardly perceive the movement. "W...w...what about working on the beach house?"

I know he's more interested in having a distraction than the fact that I've distanced myself. He also knows he'll have to earn my trust.

"Think about it. I'd be a fool to refuse you. Even though I can pay someone for the repairs and cosmetic facelift, you'll find a way to do it the most cheaply, and you're reliable when it comes to fixing things. I'll also know when you'll do the work. So, yes, you can work on the house."

"Thanks. I'll go crazy if I don't keep my mind occupied while waiting."

"I know. Right now, I'm still angry, but I'll get over it. I always do." He should know that by now. "Usually sooner, rather than later." Acting as if, I walk over to Frank and kiss the top of his head, then pull away.

"Down to business. I'm thinking we can work on the house tomorrow."

"Great. We can hang the cabinets and then measure for the top. We can stop by the cabinet shop and order the top after my doctor's appointment."

"Sounds good."

Frank pulls me into his lap and kisses me. "I love you."

The warmth of his voice causes me to lean into him as I return his kiss. "Me, too."

He signals me off his lap. I follow him into the living room where he sits on the sofa to pull out his shoes from underneath. He tugs on the old sneakers. "Time do you wanna go tomorrow?"

"Around eleven sound all right with you?"

"Sure. Have the van loaded with my tools and measuring equipment. Lunch?"

I move into the dining room. "I forgot to pick up something. What about stopping at the deli in Panacea and doing take-out?"

As I clear the dinner table, he stands and puts his arm around me and gives me a sideways hug. "Going to ease on out so you can get your work done. Thanks, Hon," his voice soft as butter on a warm day. "I take it you're still able to go with me on Monday."

"That's my plan." I smile at him. How many times is he going to ask this? "I do have a client at four, but that shouldn't be a problem."

"Good deal." He turns to go, then swings around. "Almost forgot, will you still go with me to the doc's on Monday?"

Didn't we settle that seconds ago? Fear? Stress? "Planning on it. Why don't you bring your clothes over tomorrow and spend the night? That way we won't have to rush in the morning."

He gives me another hug before he walks out the door.

Although Frank's visit appears uneventful on the surface, something is missing from our conversation. That something fills the room.

Later that night, my usual dead-to-the-world sleep is crowded with dreams of Frank begging me to marry him, my house in Jacksonville filled with my furniture and my second husband Todd with his new wife Karen, who in real life is married to Richard, my first husband. I awaken confused and battered by the forces pulling on me. The feelings evoked in the dream are similar to my feelings around Frank and school, each pulling in a different direction. The power resides in outside forces, not within. I tuck the information away in my for-further-review folder stashed in the briefcase. Time to allow the power to reside within.

The next morning, prior to Frank's arrival, I pull out my journal, and process the dream:

> February 15, 1999
>
> The more I write, the deeper I dig myself into a tumultuous pit. I can do nothing about the pull of graduate school. It's demanding. I can, however, keep my focus on the next task. The review paper. What about the furniture in the Jacksonville house? I have no pull towards the furniture. Could the house and furniture represent my excitement about the beach house? Something else? What does the mix of husband with wife mean? The conflict between school and taking care of Frank?

Is there more hidden information about Frank's marriage? Am I ready to balance care-taking with school yet again? What was I feeling in this dream? Confused. Guilty. How is that a familiar feeling for me? Well, that goes back to the time Mother set me up with mixed messages by bragging about running from her mother to avoid a spanking. Mother hid under the bed and made it sound as if that were okay. The next time she called, I ran and hid, too. I got spanked. Is Frank simply a new face in this pool of mixed messages?

Is the guilt about my lack of desire to follow my cultural inheritance? Women take care of the men in their lives. I'd just read that ten percent of men stay with women who have drug and alcohol problems; ninety percent of women stay with alcoholic and drug-addicted men. I'd also read that anger could be turned inward as guilt. How does that apply to me?

Like I'm going to figure that out anytime soon. I close the journal and shove it into a drawer.

Now, as we drive to the coast, I think about how I've always assumed I won't get what I want. I'll add this to my list of shortcomings.

The road to Alligator Point is filled with Tallahassee drivers on their way to the beach and country folk on their way to or from church. We're in Frank's antique blue Volkswagen van. The heavy traffic slows us to fifteen miles an hour in some places, twenty in others. Even though the van, with its peeling blue paint, looks old and decrepit, it runs well. In it, Frank hauls his tools and whatever else we might need. How has he managed to keep it running for over thirty years? He's always working on it. It seems to serve him well, thanks to his mechanic, who is also my mechanic. "It costs him twice as much to fix his mistakes as it would to have me correct the problem in the first place." Frank can jerry-rig anything, but apparently, in the long run, he's a much better builder than mechanic.

When we pull into the drive, Frank reaches over and squeezes my hand. "Thank you for allowing me to work on the house."

"You're thanking me? Well, just call me Tom Sawyer." I'm glad I'm doing my part in making this time a little easier for him.

Chapter 6

Monday arrives and we sleep later than usual. Frank brings me coffee in bed, a luxurious start to my day.

As I pull my black turtleneck over my head, Frank suggests breakfast at a fast food restaurant near the doctor's office.

I slip into a pair of black slacks. A gray and black print corduroy jacket tops my sweater. I add stockings and heels for the professional look so my questions will be acknowledged and answered with candor. Frank wears gray slacks, a crisp white shirt, and his navy wash and wear sport coat. I give him a light slap on the arm. "You know, you clean up nice." I wish he would dress up a little more often instead of wearing his usual stained shirts and jeans. They make him look like some bum I picked up off the street.

We pull into the fast-food parking lot, go inside, and order our food. Frank picks up a paper left on a table and reads it. I remember back to the day when Alex was diagnosed at Emory with the breadth of his illness, Squamous Cell, Stage IV. That day in the clinic, we clung to each other, energetically, if not physically. Even the air prickled my skin. Now, as Frank and I leave the restaurant, his clammy hand squeezes mine.

The wait at the urologist's office is brief. A nurse shows us into the examining room. "Dr. Peters will be with you shortly." When she closes the door, Frank's jaw tightens. His thumb and forefinger rub together in that rhythmic manner he has when agitated. So that's why he kept asking me if I would come with him. I walk over and give him a lingering hug, hoping to send him peaceful energy.

In the small room, Frank won't sit in the straight-back chair. Instead, he paces like a caged animal as we wait for the doctor. The urologist finally flurries in the door. He perches on a white stool and patiently goes over each option while Frank sits and listens. Frank's facial muscles let go and his breathing slows. My research seems to have paid off. Being informed ahead of time appears to help him understand what's being said.

Dr. Peters pushes his glasses up on the bridge of his nose. "I'd recommend surgery." Frank glances at me, his thumb and forefinger still. I nod. Good thing I researched this option. The protocol is in line with the research.

Surgery is set for the second week in March. I stand with Frank at the medical records window while he names me his healthcare surrogate. He doesn't tell the person behind the glass he's married to someone else.

We continue to work on the house when we can. Once the painting is complete, I go to the carpet store Frank recommended. As I reach into my purse to pay for my carpet and linoleum, I jostle the person behind me. I turn around, "I'm sor—" and read the FSU nametag: George Hunt. I look up and stare into a familiar face. Is this really my childhood best friend whom I haven't seen since we spent summer afternoons in his empty dog cage talking? And talking. Always talking, mostly about how to get along with our parents and our friends. Was that the beginning of my therapist bent?

"Oh, my god, George? Is that really you?" He studies my face. I can tell he's puzzled. "It's Lee. Lee Lawrence. Well, Lee Lindsey now."

Recognition flits across his face. "Lee!" He grabs me in a bear hug.

He looks just like his father with his gray hair and expanded waistline. Maybe fifty pounds heavier. "What have you been doing all these years?" I haven't heard from him since his freshman year at Johns Hopkins. I take a breath. The person ahead of me is finishing up.

"Got a doctorate in sociology. Ran the counseling center and taught psychology at Iowa. Now teaching here at the community college and doing research at FSU." He pushes me far enough away to see me. "How are you? You look great. What are you up to these days?"

"I'm a late bloomer." I shrug my shoulders. His laugh is the same as it was when we were children and dropped road shells on passersby from the treehouse on the corner of my parents' property. "Short version: Married three times. Widowed too young, and now one step away from doctoral candidate in marriage and family therapy at Florida State."

His eyes widen, and then I move up to pay my bill. I wait for George near the door. When he arrives, "How about coffee?" Two strips of sample hardwood flooring stick out of his jacket pocket. "There's a little place just down the road." He holds open the door.

"Sure." I watch him climb into his truck as I fasten my seat belt. I should have known he'd drive a truck. Wonder what he thinks of this tomboy gone awry.

I pass him on the way to The Green Frog Café. I can't believe I haven't run into him before now. At the parking lot, he pulls in next to me. He gets out of the truck and eyes my car. "I see you still have a penchant for risk-taking."

Hah. He remembers my sneaking off to ride on the back of a boy's Cushman scooter. I laugh. "Guess we've outgrown licking Jell-O and Kool-Aid from our hands."

Once inside, he orders our coffees and I find a table. We settle in. George pulls a napkin from the container. "What are you getting your doctorate in?" He dumps two packets of sugar in his coffee and pours in cream.

"Marriage and family therapy."

He grins the same grin he had when we were twelve. "Got mine in sociology when it was connected to the marriage and family program."

I must have let out a small gasp at how our paths have paralleled over the years because he grins as my face reddens.

Living in Crawfordville." He stirs his coffee, "Bought a house on the Ochlockonee River."

I'm not surprised because the year my family moved from Bradenton, his parents built a house on the Manatee River.

As we begin to share our lives, it's as if we'd seen each other throughout the years. We spend our time catching up on our families and old friends since the last time I'd seen him, immediately after my father died, but we didn't get a chance to talk. His mother is still alive and well on the river; mine has been dead four years. He's single, never been married. I tell him about Frank. We exchange phone numbers and agree to keep in touch. He leaves to teach a class and I to meet a client. My heart sings with delight at running into him.

Three weeks before surgery, Frank and I share breakfast and talk about what we want to accomplish at the house today. He puts down his fork. "We gotta talk about my living will." He rises from the table and moves into the living room.

When we're seated, "If I'm a vegetable, no heroics. If I'm unable to do the things I do now, just keep me alive until my daughter gets here. Okay?"

Without waiting for an answer, Frank walks over to the French doors. He looks out, hands in his pockets, and then turns back to me. "I will donate my organs only on these conditions: no felons, no alcoholics, no drug addicts, nor foreigners."

I lean back in my seat. I know better than to say this, "What about blacks, gays, people who pick their noses?" Had to say it anyway.

Frank's body tenses and his eye twitches. He is so busted for his intolerance.

"Would you stay until I'm released from the hospital? With pain medication and effects of anesthesia, I might not be able to make good decisions. You may have to talk with staff."

The fact that he ignores my smart mouth tells me this discussion is either stressful for him, or else I've pissed him off. Most likely the latter, but it could be the former.

"Going under anesthesia can sometimes cause memory problems." He reaches down to scratch Yang behind the ears. Ah. He's been doing his own research.

I want to know. "Were you really serious about who you'd stipulate to receive your organs?"

Barely noticeable, his eye twitches. "In case I'm incapacitated for any length of time, I'd like you to take care of my bills. I'll give you the checkbook. You know where my papers will be. If you'll write the checks, I'll sign them." He reaches into the pocket of his jeans, pulls out his phone, and looks at it. "We should be going if we're going to get much work done on your house."

Damn. If he doesn't want to deal with something, he finds a way to ignore it, like changing the subject. Could be the stress. I can't go back on my commitment to see him through this. I'll give him six months before I make a decision about staying. After all, crises can change personalities.

I pack a cooler with sandwiches along with a container of water mixed with vitamin C for me. I intend to stay healthy during this busy time. "Want anything besides sandwiches?"

Frank appears at the kitchen door. "Don't forget the tomatoes and apples I put in the ice box. Oh, and the Coke I brought last night. Have some extra Coke?" He snatches his half-gallon insulated mug, fills it with ice, and adds half Coke and half water.

When we arrive at the beach and walk inside, I can hardly believe what we've accomplished in such a short time: repainted all walls and doors, ceiling repainted, and cabinets repaired and painted. The soft glow of the new, pale-yellow paint, as the sun washes across the walls, welcomes us inside. This time I get what *I* want.

We work easily together. Frank re-installs the bottom cabinets while I clean the refrigerator, which Frank has moved into the dining area to give us both space to work.

"Hey, Hon, did I tell you I picked out the carpet Friday?" I'm not sure when I would have had the chance. "White Berber and white linoleum for the kitchen and bathrooms. The installer will be here Tuesday. We'll soon be ready for furniture."

"Great! Should be finished today with everything except the countertops. Come hold this cabinet in place while I attach it?" Frank gets out his electric screwdriver and prepares to fasten the first upper cabinet in place. I hold it up. "May have to touch up these cabinets after I finish. Do it later though, not today."

"Oh, and while I was ordering the floor coverings, I ran into my childhood friend from Bradenton."

Frank attaches a screw.

"I hadn't seen him since he and his mother came by the house to pay their respects when my dad died." We'd barely said two words that day.

Frank continues to concentrate on the cabinet.

"We didn't get a chance to catch up with our lives then. We did a little the other day." I feel like I've been talking to a brick wall.

While Frank drives in the screws, I study Frank. He's graying around the temples. The color brings out the cool grayed cobalt of his eyes.

He looks up and gives a half smile. "Great!"

The first cabinet hung, he steps back and admires his work. Minutes later, he stops. "Not bad. Mind handing me one of those sandwiches? Gettin' pretty hungry."

I snag one from the cooler. I hand it to him along with a paper towel.

He uses one of the upper cabinets for a table. "Thanks." He takes a bite and goes on with his mouth full. "After I eat, I'll be ready to hang the rest of the cabinets. Aren't you hungry yet?"

"Not really. I'll grab something later." After I place a tomato on his makeshift table, I go back to my cleaning.

"Is that tomato handy?"

I laugh. "It's by your elbow." Frank shakes his head as he picks it up.

By the time I finish cleaning, Frank is ready for help again. We work until the sun slides below the horizon. We're about to leave when Frank remembers to measure for the countertop. "Want to give the cabinet man dimensions tomorrow."

I'd already picked out butcher-block laminate because it won't show scratches. The measuring process takes more time than I'd expected because of Frank's measure twice, cut once philosophy, but I prefer his way. Beats paying for two tops.

Because we've worked later than anticipated, we stop at the seafood restaurant on the road home. At least this time we look almost presentable. Frank takes a slug of beer and then reaches for my knee. "Thank you for letting me work on the house. It has made my wait bearable."

"You're welcome. Remember, I am benefitting from this as much as you are."

Because Frank works next weekend, we make plans to install the countertops the following Monday. The installer will lay the carpet early Wednesday morning. We are nearing completion.

When we arrive at my place, Frank walks me to the door, encircles me in his arms, and kisses me. A long, lingering kiss. "I hate to leave you, but I've got to work tomorrow. If I come in, I won't want to leave."

During the week, Frank and I catch a couple of hours here and there to gather things for the house. By the following Monday, Frank's day off, we're ready to complete the repairs. We pick up the countertops and head for the beach.

When we enter the house, I'm struck by the feeling of welcome the house gives me. The pale yellow, the color of sunshine, gives a warm glow to my new home. Although I'd shown Frank the floor covering samples, when he sees the installed product, he whistles between his teeth. "Babe, this looks beautiful. You did a good job picking these out."

I help him carry the counters up the flight of stairs and install them. Since this is the last of the repair work, once Frank gets the tops on the cabinets, I'll clean up so that the house will be ready for the furnishings.

Time has moved at the speed of water rushing for drains during a heavy rainstorm. We mostly furnish my dream with extra furniture from my apartment, a few things from Goodwill and other used furniture stores. I hang some of my beach paintings from my Jacksonville days.

The day before surgery, we move in dishes, silverware, and other kitchen items. I make the bed in the master bedroom and stock the towels and toiletry items in the baths.

As I vacuum the living room, I glance toward the harbor. "Frank, come here. That must be Joy's car parked across the street."

"Could be. Ignore her."

By the time we take the final walk-through, the car is gone.

The house is ready, a perfect place for Frank's recovery. I stand at the open door. The salt air and sounds of the gulf create a healing environment.

I close and lock the door.

Frank is quiet on the way home. He must be scared about tomorrow. At my apartment, I heat up coffee in the microwave and make Frank his customary Coke float. We move into the den, and Frank settles into my chair, silent. This is one of those times when my therapist persona pays off. I know that if I question him, I will increase his tension. Thank the gods I can sit for hours without having to talk. If he wants to talk, he will.

He stares at the ceiling a minute, sucks at the inside of his cheek. "Do you have the tape you made for me to play during surgery?"

"I do. I even made sure that you would awaken pain free."

"But what if—" His voice tight.

"The surgeon will get it all." I say with certainty in my voice.

Frank's shoulders drop and he slumps back in the chair.

The next day, surgery arrives, carrying its own brand of anxiety. My mind returns over and over to the loss of Alex and memories of his hospital stays. Are Frank's thoughts on the potential loss of his manhood? His life? Is he one of those people who believes that the outcome will mirror an ancestor? His grandfather died of prostate cancer.

If asked before his diagnosis, I would have said he's focused on his sexual prowess. Is he as willing to give it up as he claims? I keep remembering his "I want to die in bed at the hands of a jealous husband."

The next morning, before the sun powders the black sky with its golden glow, I drive Frank to the hospital. A staff person shows us to his room to await the surgical prep. My backpack contains a textbook and a piece of fluff-fiction for me, and a *Flying Magazine* for Frank. This will be a long day.

Frank changes into the hospital's back-flapping gown. Before either of us can pull out our reading material, an aide comes in, checks his vitals, accompanied by non-stop chatting. An orderly shaves him. The anesthesiologist arrives to explain what he'll be doing and to have Frank sign the treatment permit. When the line of personnel slows, I say, "You sure are popular this morning."

"I thought this was going to be boring. I was wrong. Not even time to open my magazine." He gets up and goes into the bathroom, his backside showing with each step.

Before he comes out, a nurse arrives with the shot to relax him. When the orderly wheels him out at nine-thirty, I open the book on domestic violence in teenage boys in preparation for my review paper. How many more studies are needed to show that abused boys become abusers?

In between checking my watch every few minutes, I sit in the patient recliner next to the air conditioning vent to read. I tuck first one hand and then the other underneath me to warm them. A squeak outside the door catches my attention; it's only nine forty-five. I go back to my book. A pigeon interrupts my reading when it lands on the sill. I check my watch. Not yet ten. Just as I begin to get into the book, a meal cart rumbles down the hall. Trays clang. Lunch already? I check my watch, ten o'clock. I practice a tapping exercise called emotional freedom technique or EFT that Errol taught me. Once I compete the simple exercise, I'm able to concentrate.

After a couple of hours, hours that seem like days, Frank returns. He's awake and looks like he's had a simple or minor procedure. The nurse expresses concern about his low pulse rate, fifty-two. "I'm a runner," irritation in his tone, "That's normal." This is why he wants me here for his entire stay because the drugs keep him from making good decisions. Outside, a chameleon clings to the window, watching and puffing out his red throat.

To me, Frank's stay is uneventful. He's given a morphine pump, used, at most, three or four times the first day, and one or two the next. To Frank, the third day was eventful. When his bowel movements attempt a return, he curls into a ball, grimacing. "I've never had stomach pains like this."

Try having a baby, Babe. Morphine, plus the results of the incision, cause constipation. He didn't have that much morphine.

"This pain is intolerable. Can't stand it. Get the doc to give me something. Fast." He squirms in the bed.

This is why the gods, in infinite wisdom, made women capable of birthing babies instead of men. "Honey, I know you're miserable, but what you're feeling are normal gas pains following surgery. You'll feel like you're going to die, but you won't." I take a deep breath. "I asked the nurse to get you something when I walked down the hall looking for coffee. She's trying to contact the surgeon now."

"Well, tell her to hurry up. I'm in pain."

His irritability reminds me of my dad's last hospital stay, when he'd had gallbladder surgery. The surgery went well and he was expected to recover easily. Three days later, when I called Mother to ask how he was doing, she said he was swearing at all the staff, calling them names she'd never heard leave his lips.

I chalk up Frank's peevishness to the pain and the remnants of anesthesia. I offer to stay but he shakes his head. He looks so pitiful, curled up in a fetal position. I keep my lips tight. Bite my tongue. This is not the time to remind him that nothing comes to stay. It comes to pass.

After these weeks of juggling my review paper, Frank's illness, and the house, I feel like I'm just treading water. Lake Ella is my life raft. The minute I step on the sidewalk, fresh air breathes new life into me, clears the dust motes clogging my brain. As the turtles lie on the bank, sunning themselves, some poke their heads up out of their shells and turn their fat necks and heads toward the sun, reminding me of all I'm missing. I run slowly, in the calming rhythm of a well-turned wheel. My stiffened muscles relax and work to capacity with ease.

After I've done my three miles, I drive home to feed Yin and Yang. They greet me as I walk in the door. "Miss me?" They sprint to the kitchen and stand in front of their bowls. "Hungry, huh?" After I clean their box, I shower and return to the hospital.

When I arrive in Frank's hospital room, he is groaning. Within an hour, my reading is interrupted by a long, loud noise and lingering odor. His grimace replaced by a half-smile. "Sorry, Babe. But damn, that felt good."

On the fourth day, my phone rings as I walk around the lake. "Hi, Hon. It's just me, Frank Islip. The doc was just here. The cancer was contained in the prostate. They got it all."

Relief spreads through my muscles. I stop and look out over the lake. A rainbow radiates from the fountain. "That's wonderful. I'm so glad. What great news! I'm just finishing up here. I'll be up in about an hour."

"Take your time. I'm being released. It'll take the staff that long to do the paperwork."

Why does he always tell me not to hurry? It does calm my need for instant action. Do I put too much pressure on myself? Something to tuck away in the for-later-review file stored in the burgundy briefcase.

My arrival at the hospital coincides with Frank's instructions on the care and cleaning of the catheter, which will remain for the next week.

Frank will recuperate at my apartment until the catheter is removed, a true test of our compatibility. He's an easy patient, not demanding, quite happy to read or surf the web. He shows no sign of the earlier irritability.

While he's at my place, I make my weekly research meeting. Simon reminds me to finish my review paper, and then tells me the new department head is looking for a research assistant for his new study. I should apply. I do, and I walk out of his office as his research assistant. I know I got the job because of my pilot's license. The new head is learning to fly a Citabria, an acrobatic plane.

As soon as Frank has his one-week check-up, we retreat to the beach house. On the way back from the doctor's office, we stop by Frank's to pick up some clothes, a cane, and his .38 Special. He goes nowhere without it. Being an alcohol, tobacco, and firearms agent taught him to carry it at all times, he claims. I wonder if it is because he's only five-foot-six and slightly built.

As we leave, Frank is careful to avoid the other rangers, who are in and out of the office, immediately behind Frank's house. "Don't want to look too healthy." From there, we pick up my things and the cats. I'd ask Errol to care for them, but he'd just snoop into everything. Besides, they'll provide entertainment in an area where there is no cable and only snail dial-up to the Internet.

Within two days of settling in, Frank, ever my Mr. Fix-it, changes all the outlets in the kitchen and bathrooms with ground fault interrupters, "To bring them up to code." The man can't sit still. He's been a teacher, parole officer, an ATF agent, private detective, as well as a contractor, real estate broker, entrepreneur, and now park ranger. Oh, and he had some sort of secret job in the military reserves. What is his reason for being secretive? Which came first, secretiveness or secret jobs? Why so many different occupations, and why do I view that fact as inconsequential? I file these questions away in my *think-about-later* file.

One afternoon as we return to the beach house from the Crawfordville hardware store, Frank listens to some call-in show bashing President Clinton for his escapade with a White House intern.

I've had enough. "Will these people ever let this go or will they continue for another ten years?"

"They should've impeached the son of a bitch."

"Why? Because he did what many other presidents have done?"

"He lied, dammit." Frank slams his fist on the steering wheel. "He lied."

"And he's the first president to lie? He's a product of the fifties and early sixties. We all lied to ourselves about having sex. If it wasn't," I make air quotes, "all the way, it wasn't sex."

"He still lied. He lied under oath."

"You might have done the same thing if you'd been in his position."

"Never!"

No, you just lie about the little things, like being married. Bet you've lied about where your dick's been, too. "Don't tell me you've never lied about your sexual experiences."

Frank's eyes point straight ahead and his knuckles turn white on the steering wheel. Uh, oh.

"Look, let's just drop this." I shift in the seat. "We're not going to agree. There's no sense in ruining our day arguing over something that has no bearing on our relationship." Except that you lied to me. Do you still lie to me?

While Frank works on the house, I write to get some clarity.

> March 14, 1999
>
> Problem: My inability to confront Frank. No, my refusal to confront Frank about his lying. What do I think? There's a possibility that his surgery has left him with a form of post-traumatic stress.
>
> How do I feel? Uneasy. Afraid. Afraid of what? Of making a mistake.
>
> Five actions I can take to resolve this: (1) Leave the relationship, (2) Confront my fear: If you say you love me, you will physically harm me, (3) Make myself crazy with resentment, (4) Talk to George, (5) Get sick.
>
> What can I do about it right now? Let it rest. For now. Talk to George the next time I have alone time. I need to trust my instincts about confronting him. They are saying no. Absolutely no.

The fear comes from my mother. It was her, "This hurts me more than it does you," while she thrashed me with a switch that was a whip with a leaf or two on the end. Even as a small child, I knew she hit me out of anger, not as a means of stopping a behavior. Of all the people who spanked me as a child, she was the most vicious. She'd then tell me she loved me. I knew better.

Two weeks post-surgery, Frank spends most days at the beach house, strengthening the pilings to hurricane-proof the house. He drills holes through steel, bolts the steel to the wooden pilings, using all his upper body muscles, including the abdominal ones that were cut during surgery.

However, he always uses a cane in public, "In case someone from the Park Service sees me." He stretches his two-week recovery time into six. Not something I would do, but I am enjoying our time together. Once a week, we're in Tallahassee for errands and doctors' appointments.

When not outdoors helping Frank, I spend my time on the computer, working on the review paper. Once I pass the defense, I'll start on the prospectus. I'm also working for the new department head researching studies for a project he's doing. Both are a slow process as the dial-up Internet rate is thirteen bits per second. Click. Wait. And wait some more. If I still smoked, I'd light a cigarette about now.

I meet with the department head every two weeks—tomorrow is my day. I print out the articles, his and mine. This morning Frank takes off to run errands while I opt to stay at the house and work on the research section of my prospectus.

After spending three hours of click and wait on the Internet, I pick up my frustration and take it for a walk along the beach towards Bald Point. The afternoon is warm with a gulf breeze that whisks my brain clean of impatience and fills it with a sense of well-being. All is as it should be.

The tide is low enough that sand stretches from the water to the rocks. I notice a seagull struggling to move. Does it have a broken wing? I switch to problem-solving mode. The bird needs a vet. My car is in Tallahassee. Frank is on his errand. During the day, midweek, the houses are empty. It's not in my nature to let the bird suffer. I'm not an instant decision maker when it comes to life or death. I continue my walk. I ponder my dilemma: Let the bird suffer until it dies, or smash it in the head with a large rock? Instant death is kinder than a long, suffering death.

The sun plays hide and seek with rain clouds, as if deciding whether to stay or disappear for a stretch. While saltwater air, cries of gulls and anhingas, and the smell of new sea life announce spring, the

Roberta Burton

impending choice stalks my thoughts. I must concentrate on the beauty of the day and the decision will come to me. I will have no regrets.

After what seems like hours, I return to the spot where I found the gull. Still not on its legs, it lies closer to the gulf-front house and now its beady black eyes give me an I-will-be-fine-without-your-help stare. I send it healing energy and, filled with awe, I walk across the road to my house.

I walk into the house renewed in spirit and energy. I'm ready to get back to work. Frank walks in a few minutes later with more construction stuff. I tell him about my experience.

Frank starts toward the door. "Should we go check on the gull?"

I feel good about my decision, but if we can help the bird, I'm all for it.

We take off down the beach, only a few houses down. I point to the house where I last saw the gull. It is gone. Frank puts his arm around me and points to the sparkling windows overlooking the gulf. "Suppose it could have flown into a window and knocked itself out."

Whatever the cause, I'm content with my choice.

With his arm still around me, "How about some lunch?" We return to the house, and he checks his purchases while I prepare lunch. We take our drinks and plates out onto the deck and listen to the waves swish to shore, a gull's cry, interrupted by an occasional car going by on the main road. A rare day when we both take time to enjoy this peaceful place.

"Gonna work on the breakaway rooms underneath the house." Frank gets up and goes down the outside stairs.

I clear the table and take care of the lunch remnants. I call my department chair and set up our meeting time for tomorrow. Then I go back into my office and get back on the computer.

Later, when I mention going to campus, Frank offers to drive me into town. He can run some errands and go by his house while I'm at the university. A real gift. Finding a parking place is such a hassle, there are times I'd sell my soul for one.

The next day, when the meeting is over, I wait for Frank outside the building entranceway, scanning the street. "George?" I break out in a grin as he heads towards me. "What are you doing here?" I hug him and in return get one that encases me in his muscular arms.

76

"Meeting one of my old professors for lunch. He's retiring at the end of the semester." He looks at my now empty briefcase, "What are you doing here on a beautiful spring day? Looks like official business."

"Brought the department head printouts of all the research I did for him these past two weeks. I'm his research assistant."

"How'd you land that?"

"Think it had to do with the fact that I hold a pilot's license and so does he."

George takes a step back and raises his eyebrows. "Thought you were never going to fly. Not after getting stuck under the bridge in the little sailboat."

I laugh as I remember my dad promising me that if I'd learn to tack a sailboat, he'd give me flight lessons. "Yeah, well, he never told me planes have instruments to help me tack. Funny, he wasn't overly happy about my taking lessons."

"How did your boyfriend's surgery go?"

"Excellent. Now that my only class is my once-a-week research group, I'm staying at the beach house. He's been doing heavy-duty labor since the week after surgery. Actually, it just feels like I took the semester off since I'm not going in every day. I am researching for my review paper and for the department head."

"Nice. I'd like to see your house sometime."

I pull out a piece of paper and write down the number. "Didn't have a phone at the beach the last time I saw you." I hand him the paper. "There's no signal on my cell at the house."

Frank drives up. "Here he is now. Come meet him."

I introduce them, and then George leaves to meet his retiring professor.

"Call me," I yell after him. He waves a *yes*.

I kiss Frank's cheek as I settle in the van. "Hi, Honey."

"Seems like a nice chap." Frank starts the van. "You need to keep in touch with him now that you two have renewed your friendship."

We drive away. "How was your meeting?" We chat about my project for the department head as we leave the university and set out for the beach.

That night, Frank chooses to spend the evening on the computer rather than spending time with me. I lean a shoulder against the doorframe and watch him study the screen, absorbed.

He took me to, and picked me up from, campus. Then he came home and did things to make this house more livable for me, and then he finished digging a ditch, the one I quit on.

Remember? What makes me think I'm the center of the universe? Talk about being self-absorbed. He certainly has the right to do as he pleases at night. Or anytime, really.

I stare for a moment more at his head silhouetted against the monitor. I can read. I've already spent much of the afternoon researching on the Internet. Now it's his turn. Why am I kicking the-time-for-reading gift horse in the mouth?

Days pass. Weeks pass. Frank makes room for, and installs, a used washer and dryer underneath the house so I can rent out the house—his idea. He updates both bathrooms. While here, we've completely furnished the house from the Salvation Army and Goodwill, the new chic for beach house furnishings.

George calls a couple of times and comes by. Frank welcomes him and seems to enjoy George's company. He's comfortable with Errol, too. I like that he's not jealous of my male friends.

Before we're ready to leave, Frank finds a real estate agent who just happens to have a client needing a place to stay for six months while her house is being built nearby. The tenant calls the day before we are to leave for Tallahassee. We agree that I will pay the utilities and she will reimburse me. Perfect timing for finishing my review paper and then writing up my prospectus; everything I need is in Tallahassee.

After an overnight cold snap, the temperature continues to drop as we pack to go back to Tallahassee. I change from shorts to jeans and add my FSU sweatshirt. I call to Frank, who is in the next room, "I'll pack the kitchen. Would you check the bathrooms? Will that work for you?"

"I'm packing my own things."

I look up from the cardboard box on the counter. Did I miss something? I walk into the master bedroom. Frank bunches up a shirt and stuffs it into his duffle bag. "Does that mean you won't check out the bathrooms? I'll take care of the cat box."

"No. You blind? Can't you see I'm packing my things to leave?"

I add on "stupid bitch"—a term Todd used in the same tone—as Frank turns and glares. I don't understand. I've not seen this side of him before. What does his nastiness mean? Is he having some sort of traumatic reaction to his surgery? Why now? Look, buster, stop acting like such a prick. You do not want to be in the fallout if this keeps up and I have a way to escape.

I glance out the bedroom window. The waves idle in to shore, without agenda.

"Leaving tomorrow, for five days, to see my daughter." His speech tight. Clipped.

My solar plexus coils. My lungs squeeze, and I can hardly breathe. I've been here before.

When husband number two, Todd, had his second open-heart surgery, that same sudden hostility swept in without any more warning than a summer thunderstorm when I mentioned my surprise at the number of sponges used during his surgery. I didn't understand Todd's tone then, and I don't understand Frank's now. Remnants of their surgeries?

Since my divorce from Todd, I've read studies about how major surgeries can induce post-traumatic stress. Is that what's wrong with Frank? He's never been like this before. I want to ask when he talked with his daughter. I won't.

It isn't that he's going, but how he puts it, that irks me. The implication in his voice, pulsating jaw muscle, and the intimidating cop stance say, "Don't even think about objecting." As if I would.

I say nothing. I'd like to know how I feel and how to respond before I simply blow up. Finally, after a few seconds, "When are we leaving?"

Frank narrows his eyes. "You're not!"

I take a step back, seeing the look on his face, the look my mother claimed I often gave her when I was fifteen. She would say, "If looks could kill, I'd be dead." So that's what she meant. What have I done to infuriate him? Did mother have the same question about me?

"What's all the hostility about?"

Frank's eyes slit and his jaw tightens. His hands clench into fists. Would he actually hit me? His thundercloud face looks as if he could.

His jaw spasms. "Why are you asking so many questions? You're not my therapist."

Thank the gods for that. "This is unexpected and the hostility is…never mind." I move away to finish cleaning and packing. "When did you decide this?"

"When I talked to her this morning, not that it's any of your business." Frank storms out. He grabs a cooler. He slams it into the van. He comes back inside. He grabs the duffle bag. He snatches more things. I rush to have more ready. He throws them in the van. Slams the door. My personal items are not included. They remain at the front door where I placed them.

"Hurry up. I want to leave."

Mean, hostile, old man, it may not be my business, but he didn't talk with anyone this morning unless she was hiding in the closet. I don't get it, but it's not worth getting into an argument. He's going to do what he's going to do.

As I pass by the open door, I notice the familiar old Volvo parked across the street. Joy? What's she doing here? Glad I changed the locks.

"I said hurry up." My stomach clenches as his voice becomes cold, controlled.

I square my shoulders, "I'll be there as soon as I finish the bathrooms."

I rush to the bedroom, strip the bed, and bundle the sheets into one of the pillowcases. I march into the master bath.

"Hurry up. I don't have all day."

My hands shake as I clean the porcelain fixtures, grab the towels, and mop the floor. I repeat the efforts in the guest bath. I add towel and washcloths from the bathrooms and kitchen to the laundry pillowcase. Finished. At last.

I look out the window at the water across the road. I'm going to miss this place even though all I want right now is to get to my apartment safely.

Is Frank trying to start a fight so it'll be easier to leave? Alex and I did that a couple of times until we caught ourselves doing it. One of us would say, "I'm going to miss you while you're gone." That stopped the argument.

The house is complete. I make two last trips to the van. Why, if Frank is in such a hurry, do I have to make two trips to the van? I look in and see that he did bring the laundry and the litter box. My god, where are Yin and Yang?

"Where are the cats?"

"You tell me. It's your job to keep track of your animals."

"You're the one who was stomping around and going in and out the door. Did you leave the door open?"

"No."

"Will you help me look for them?"

"Hurry up." Frank thunders through the house.

If they're in here, they'll never come out. "Check under the bed in the guest room and under any furniture. Please."

He goes outside and calls, "Here kitty, kitty, kitty." His voice is calm and welcoming.

We search and search. Frank opens the van door. "I'm leaving. If you don't get in this van now, you'll have to find your own way back."

Now all my things are in the van, even my purse and cell. I have no choice. With a churning stomach, I get in the van.

During the ride back to Tallahassee, Frank's excessive passing and yelling at other drivers, his constant checking of his cell phone for the time, and his grinding teeth seem significant, but what is the significance? What's this about? Any attempts at conversation are met with silence. I give up. I don't feel like talking anyway. If he hears tears in my voice, another round of hostility is sure to follow.

When we arrive at my apartment, Frank unlocks the door and dumps my things in the living room. "I need to ease on outta here."

Good riddance.

I walk into the apartment, my heart jolted from its moorings.

Chapter 7

Fifteen minutes later, as I root among my dumped belongings on the living room floor, looking for my purse, the phone rings. Oh, calling already to apologize? I pull the cell from my pocket. "What?" I demand.

"Hey, what did I do?" It's George. "Just called to see if you're in the mood for some company."

"Oh, George. I'm so sorry, thought you were Frank." I search through the pile for my purse. "How'd you know I was back?"

"Intuition." He laughs. "I talked to Frank this morning. He said you were heading to Tally. Check which phone you're holding."

"Oh." Thank the gods, I hadn't put it in my purse this morning. But the cell shouldn't be in the stuff Frank dumped. "What's up?" I drop off the package of cat food in the kitchen, amble to the den, and sit in my chair. I take a deep breath.

"Can we start over? I'd love some company, but I need to drive back to the beach and search for the cats." Tears prick my eyes. Have to find my purse and keys. I drum my fingers on a nearby table.

"You sound discombobulated. Can't tell if you're angry or crying." He's still the listener he always was. "Want to tell me about it?"

"Both. Angry at Frank, and crying about Yin and Yang." I explain how Frank became hostile and then left me with no alternative but to leave without the cats. "I couldn't get back into the house, and I had no other transportation back to town."

Sweat swooshes from my underarms as my temperature rises. "I was trying to find my purse in the pile of stuff on the floor, so I could drive back to the coast when you called." I untangle my legs and prop my feet up on the footstool.

"Wait—you left without them?"

"Yeah, Frank was in too much of a hurry to get back to Tallahassee to bother about the cats. Fortunately, I must have put the cell in my pocket. My purse was in the car—god knows where. Had to come back to town with him."

"I'm in town. You're upset. Would you like me to drive with you back to the beach?"

"Would you?" I go limp as a Raggedy Ann doll. "Oh, George, that would be great. I didn't realize how much I dreaded driving back there."

"I'm about fifteen minutes away."

When we hang up, I close my eyes and lean back. I take three long, slow, deep breaths. I sit and breathe until something rubs against my foot and meows. My heart quickens, and I jump up, startled. I reach down to pick up Yin, but she squirms out of my arms and insists I follow her to the living room.

A tiny meow comes from the laundry bag. I reach in to disentangle Yang from the racy red bra wrapped around his legs. The same bra I'd chosen for the first time I slept with Frank.

"Poor baby." I pull him from his web of red lace. I pick him up. His heart races. I hold him against mine until it slows.

I call George and let him know the cats are here.

"Good. See you in a few."

I take care of Yin and Yang and then sort through the mess on the floor. Most of it goes into the laundry. Can't deal with it now.

As soon as I finish, I write:

> April 10, 1999
>
> I don't understand why Frank was so aggressive when he informed me he was leaving town. He was hostile and cruel about the cats. I feel confused and uneasy about the cats. I want to know if he knew the cats were in the pillowcase. The old standbys of leaving, getting sick, becoming resentful, or expecting him to change will not solve the problem. At least George will soon be here.
>
> Problem: The way Frank informed me he was leaving town, his sudden aggressive manner, forcing me to leave without the cats—mostly the cats. What I

think: He's hostile and cruel. How could he just leave with the cats missing?

What I feel: Confused and uneasy about the fight, confused about cats.

How I want this problem resolved: By preceding his information with how do you feel about? Or what do you think about? I want to know if he knew the cats were in the pillowcase.

Five actions toward resolution: (1) Leave the relationship, (2) Ask him to soften his demanding response and expect him to be compassionate, (3) Make myself crazy with resentment, (4) Talk to George, (5) Get sick.

What I can do about it right now: Let it rest for now. Talk to George—glad I told him about Frank's marriage and my decision.

George arrives carrying a quart of Ben and Jerry's Rocky Road. I spoon the ice cream into two bowls and give one to him. Once he settles in and we catch up on the last six weeks, he leans in. "I take it you have decided to stay with Frank."

"At this moment, I'm not so inclined." I squirm in my chair. "I entered into this relationship knowing I needed to look at myself. Frank gives me the perfect opportunity to change those old behavioral patterns and beliefs that cause me to attract someone who, it turns out, is just like him." I take a bite of ice cream. "But maybe not. I never saw this behavior before the cancer diagnosis. I want to make sure this is not a temporary condition." Ahhh, comfort food. "So my decision is to stay. For now."

George spoons ice cream into his mouth. "I take it he's recovered from the surgery."

"Yeah, physically." Chocolate, marshmallow, and nuts dance on my tongue. "He was back to speed in less than two weeks."

"Two weeks? Why so long at the beach?"

Coffee would go great with this ice cream, but I don't have any made. Food supply is low, too. "He has too many hours of sick leave. He wanted to use as much of it as he could before he retires."

"You stayed at the beach while he took extra sick time? Didn't that interfere with your life?"

A knot forms in my neck as I identify the source of my general irritation with Frank. "No wonder I was so nitpicky about how Frank spent his time at night." I wanted to spend time with him. His recovery time was a chance to become closer. Because of my previous experiences with others' surgeries, I let it go. "Except for the click and wait forever, I could do my work at the house. The office set-up there is more convenient than the one here. Besides, he worked on improving the house during the day."

George takes another bite. A look of pure pleasure spreads like honey across his face. He is serious again. "What exactly happened that put you in such a state when I called? Besides losing the cats?"

"While we were packing up this morning, Frank informed me he was flying to Fort Myers to see his daughter for five days. It was how he put it that bothers me." I give him the blow by blow.

"Not like you to overreact. Tell me more."

"Not much more to tell. I just asked if he'd empty the bathrooms and check to see that they were clean. His reaction was completely unexpected. When I asked about it, he turned hostile." I stare at the melting ice cream in my bowl. "There was a moment there when I thought he might hit me." I get up and move to the kitchen. "Making coffee. Want some?"

"Coffee? Always."

I start the coffee then grab a spoon of peanut butter before I return to the den. "I journaled about it before you got here. I came up with letting it go and talking about it. I wanted the problem resolved by his softening the statement to something like, 'I'm thinking of going to see my daughter tomorrow.' That gives me the opportunity to have some input such as 'That sounds like a good idea.'"

The look on George's face tells me I am so busted. He leans back in his chair, his hands clasp the back of his head. "It seems to me that you want him to change."

"Well, damn. I should know better by now." With a whack on the side of my head, "I've certainly worked on that one for years." I lean back. "He may never change, but he definitely won't as long as I'm pressuring him." Even if silently. Hadn't seen that in my journaling. "Thanks, George."

He gets up and goes into the bathroom. I pour our coffee and bring it into the den, along with sugar and cream for his.

When he returns, "Did you say you thought he might hit you?"

I nod. Guess I didn't squeeze that one by.

He stirs his coffee so long it seems like a meditation. "What would you tell one of your clients if she mentioned that possibility?"

I take a sip of coffee. Too hot. "I'd tell her this is not something to slough off." What's with my eye tic? "While waiting for you earlier, I realized how often I see important things as insignificant and unimportant. I've never addressed possible violence in my journal, either."

George's eyebrows lift. "And you're studying domestic violence?"

I nod. "In fact, I've never focused on anything that I view as inconsequential." My face grows hot. "Duh! If they're inconsequential, they're not worth the time to attend to them. That's what I did with the hostility." My knuckles have turned white on my cup. Damn it. I should know better. I even did it again—made something important inconsequential—by failing to write about it. "You're right. The real issue is Frank's hostility."

George leans forward in the chair as if to punctuate his next utterance. "You going to be safe?"

"Sure. Because he's gone, and we don't live together." Is this what my dad would call flippant? I don't know.

He takes a slug of coffee. "Have you developed a plan?"

"A plan?" Damn, his clinical experience is too much like mine. He knows exactly what to ask. "Hadn't thought about it." I sip my coffee. "Previously, he's never given any indication that he could be violent. I can always have an escape route. Done that one before. I'll be on guard." That is, if I ever see him again.

I remember my conversation with Errol. That superiority thing bothers me. Why not ask George what he thinks. He'll tell me the truth. "I almost forgot. I have a question for you."

"Ask away."

"Do I come across as acting superior?" Yang walks up and nudges me for a little attention. I lean over and pull him into my lap. Ahh, the rumble of a purr.

"Not unless you've changed completely since we were kids." He reaches out and knuckle-rubs the top of Yang's head. "You've always been open to others' opinions."

"So, are you saying that I don't normally come across as superior?"

"That's what I'm saying." He grasps his coffee mug. "You're a doctoral student, so you're supposed to act superior. But if you do, you have the knowledge to back it up." He takes a slug and puts the cup on the table. "Where'd you get that idea, anyway?"

"Errol, from an anthropological drawing I did years ago in one of my classes."

He looks me in the eye. "Things are not always as they appear."

I should know that.

The conversation turns to George's volunteer work, providing dogs for people to pet in nursing homes. He not only uses his dog Suzie Q, but he coordinates for a nearby nursing home.

After George leaves, my mind turns to the possibility of abuse from Frank. I go over similar behavior patterns after surgery and hospital stays. According to Mother, my dad said things she'd never heard from his mouth before. My second husband, Todd, was hostile after his open-heart surgery. I remember reading a memoir about the behavior of the author's husband after open-heart surgery. Her book had a profound effect because I read it within a month of my dad's death. I don't want to take the chance of making a mistake with Frank.

Two weeks after the beach house experience, the phone rings. "Hi, Hon." My muscles go into high alert. "It's just me. Frank Islip here."

As if I would forget that voice, probably haunt me on my deathbed.

"There's a seminar at the community college on financial planning day after tomorrow. Want to go?"

"That's a hot come-on." Not that I want one.

Silence.

My voice rises. "You can't even ask about Yin and Yang? Don't you even care what happened to them?"

Silence.

"You there?"

"I, uh, forgot about that?" His voice rises at the end as if questioning whether I believe him. Damn, no acknowledgement of the way he'd dumped my things on the floor either. "I'm sorry about that. Don't know what got into me." His voice honeyed.

A fit of nastiness, that's what. Could that have been a sign of post-traumatic stress? I would expect any male would be traumatized by Frank's surgery, particularly one who seemed to live and breathe sex before surgery. "When did you get back?"

"Haven't yet. About twenty miles from Tallahassee. Have to work tomorrow." No phone calls, and he doesn't seem anxious to see me. Not that I really care. What's going on with him?

"Need to drop my stuff off at the house, and if it's all right with you, thought I'd come over. Missed you."

Silence.

"You there?"

I take a deep breath. "Missed you, too." Don't do it. "Have you eaten?" Damn.

"Thought I'd catch a bite at home, and then come over."

You've been gone two weeks and you have food to eat at home? Do NOT do it. I ball my fist and stuff it in my mouth to gag the voice. Then release it. "If you don't mind leftover black beans and rice, you're welcome to have dinner here."

"Thanks. Can you wait a couple hours to eat? Need to drop off my stuff and get cleaned up. I'll bring the information on the seminar."

"Sure."

"See you then." He hesitates. "Love you."

Later, when Frank arrives, I open the door and am smothered in a bear hug as soon as he steps inside. He closes the door with his foot and nuzzles my neck. "I've missed you, Babe." His lips meet mine in a long, lingering kiss.

"Hello, fur balls." He greets the cats as if he expected to see them. Does he even remember that last day at the beach house? Is this his way of avoiding confrontation? One of these days, I'm liable to bite off the tip of my tongue.

While we eat, Frank tells me about the seminar. It sounds helpful, so I agree to go. I yawn while we relax over coffee. "Been a busy day today and I have an early appointment in the morning so I'm going to chase you out of here in a few minutes."

He stiffens but says nothing. He then reaches across the table and clasps my hand. "You know I've really missed you."

Not going to work this time, buddy boy. "Missed you, too, but I've got to get some sleep before my meeting."

The next day, he calls and chats for twenty minutes about nothing in particular. If I were playing hard to get, I'd have won that round. The following evening, we attend the seminar.

Will Fox, Simon's archrival, is seated in front of us. At the break, he turns around and asks about my dissertation topic. When I tell him Simon has me doing a qualitative study describing what it's like for troubled adolescent boys to live in a violent family, he laughingly says, "Tell Simon he's not qualified to head your committee." Something in his voice lets me know he already knew I'd painted myself in a qualitative corner with my review paper.

When I see Simon at our weekly research meeting, I jokingly tell him, "Will Fox told me to tell you you're not qualified to head my committee," and laugh. I barely register Simon's raised eyebrows and forget about the incident. I'm too busy to give it much thought. I spend little time with Frank as I focus on research of juvenile boys who are violent. When I learn exactly how I'm to judge other research, I discover more flaws than good research. Errol reminds me to focus on the goal.

The weeks fly by as I struggle to get my prospectus ready for defense. In my research meetings, Simon first has me move a section of chapter one to chapter two. The next week, he has me move the same section back to chapter one, and the following week again to chapter two.

During these back and forth research weeks, George and I take a Journey workshop—another parallel in our lives—with new instructors. These instructors are trying to get the client, who is emotionally shut down, into feeling. Nothing is working. Mindful of my conversation with George, I sit without comment until one instructor looks at me, "Lee, can you get her into feeling?"

I go up to the front of the room and start shaking my arms and torso, bouncing on my heels. "Now, do this with me," as I take her hands. We continue until I see a flush to her face. We stop, and then I take both of her hands, and look her in the eye. "Close your eyes. Go inside your body and tell me what's happening there."

Her words tumble over each other. Her voice rises, "My leg is shaking. I can't get my leg to stop shaking."

"Don't try to stop it. Describe the sensation," I squeeze her hands.

"It starts in my foot and travels up my leg into my hip."

I ignore the movement behind me as people get up for snacks or drinks or bathroom breaks, a sign that I've hit a universal issue. "What color is it?"

Her eyes clinch tight. "It's…red."

"Does it have a sound?"

"Scream." Her leg begins to shake uncontrollably.

"If it were a bumper sticker, what would it say?"

"Run like hell." Tears stream down her face. My heart goes out to her. I don't want her to shut down her tears, so I place my hand on her back behind her heart. "Let it out. Let it all out." When I'm dismissed, I return to my seat.

At break, George walks over. "Good work, Lee. Where did you learn that?"

"Thanks. I took professional training in Hakomi. I think I learned it there."

"How do you know when to use it?"

Examples work best. "Have you ever gone through something so terrible that you cried?"

He nods.

"I found that most people pat you like they would burp a baby or pet a dog. Patting shuts down the emotion, so whenever someone cries in front of me, if I do anything, I put my hand behind his or her heart. It causes one to feel supported in the pain."

"That's such a simple technique—"

"Not technique, George. Gesture. Gesture of support."

His eyes open wide, "I get it. If I think technique, I won't use it with family and friends. Thanks."

"You're welcome." I shift my weight to one foot. "Did I come across as a superior bitch?"

"No, you came across as kind, but your skill was superior."

Getting her into feeling was a good piece of work if I do say so myself. It was an intuitive thing. "Thanks."

After the long weekend, research day arrives too soon. I haven't heard from Frank in over a week, but today I'm more concerned about an imminent conversation with Simon about what seems like busywork as I drive into the center of town on the one-way street to what used to be a nineteen sixties motel, turned … what? FSU uses it for their children and families programs. Traffic's not bad. I speed up to five miles above the speed limit so I can make the lights. With most state workers on their jobs, I easily move over to the far right lane to avoid the bottleneck from construction on the combination condominiums and shops. Sleepy Tallahassee is becoming cosmopolitan.

I'm the first to arrive for research group. Simon comes from a back room, "Why are you here?"

I look around this room with its concrete-block walls, painted industrial green. "It's Tuesday. We have a meeting. Where is everybody?"

"I called earlier to tell you the meeting was cancelled."

I squirm on a non-padded folding metal chair. My thin pants provide no barrier to the cold metal. Something's not right. "I didn't get the message."

Simon's body remains steady. His face retains its neutral expression. "You must have already left by the time I called."

Remind me why you are surprised to see me. We'll be alone, easier to confront without an audience. I slide the prospectus from my burgundy briefcase, set it on the table, and take a deep breath. It's time to confront him about his lack of productive feedback. "What's the purpose of moving this section back and forth between chapters?"

He leans back in his chair. "I know you have abandonment issues and I'm not abandoning you."

That is not the question I asked, you simpleton.

He taps the prospectus with the point of his pen, and then drops the pen with a clatter. "I can't chair your committee."

The air deserts me like a deflating balloon.

Simon wears his therapist demeanor, the kind, fatherly professor who cares deeply for his students and clients. A meanness creeps through the mask.

My mind flips. What the…what do my abandonment issues have to do with moving words back and forth between chapters? He's firing me as his student. Now what? Will I be able to complete the program?

Because he knows about my issues: they come up in supervision, in writing the theory of therapy paper, and in a number of other little ways, I'd think he'd be more compassionate.

Although he sits with feet apart and arms open, his jaw twitches and his back is unnaturally straight in the chair. He keeps his arms uncrossed. More twitches escape along his neck. Beads of sweat form on his forehead. "You will write a better dissertation with another chair."

My hands begin to shake. The room temperature drops ten degrees. Without the distraction of my dissertation, the uncomfortable room gains focus, anything to avoid feeling the terror coursing through me. What a drab place to counsel marriage license applicants, a new Florida law requirement. If I were counseled in this room, I'd break off my engagement, run for the highest bridge, and jump.

My thoughts return to Simon. Right. Now he wants to dump me after he narrowed my focus so much that I'm no longer studying what I chose.

Simon's red hair is turning gray around the ears, and he's put on weight, ugly weight. With his graying beard, he transforms into second husband, alcoholic Todd. Unlike Todd, who would have blurted out a similar edict, blamed me for it, and then left without a word, Simon struggles without success to hold his composure.

Not Todd. The suddenness of Simon's pronouncement catapults me into an incident with Todd when he tells me I will not be going to New York with my daughter, nor will I see her graduate. I know even now that my beautiful sixty-year-old home, with its southern charm, ten minutes from downtown Jacksonville, is not worth staying in the marriage.

I tell him there is no way he can stop me as I watch his fists clench. Uh oh. Although he's never hit me sober, I know to soften my attitude or he might.

"After all," I say, "she only graduates from high school once and she wants me there. She's had a rough year." A move from the town she's called home since kindergarten. She's missed being with her friends and doing the fun stuff, like going to the prom, the senior trip.

We are in my home office. My desk overlooks two walls of paned-glass windows and a glass door to the terrace. Todd stands over me. "You're not going. I forbid it."

Spring has arrived. Dogwoods bloom by the old servant's quarters over the garage, now an apartment for Todd's son. The fig tree has greened out by the fence. A breeze dances with new growth on the magnolia. Sun streams in the windows, creating a shimmering shadow on Todd's baldhead. Just as the sun raises the office temperature, Todd's words raise mine.

"Excuse me. I am not some child you can control." The azalea by the house needs trimming.

"There you go starting another fight," his eyes cold. "I'm getting tired of your always wanting to fight." I listen to his footsteps as he storms out through the family room, banging the breakfast room doors, as he continues to his car. He drives away. He would have left rubber on the driveway if he hadn't bought that Audi diesel he wanted so badly. No rubber today.

I see Todd all over again when Simon places his arms across his chest. "I recommend Megan Raes to chair your dissertation." I still see Todd. What had I done to cause the same reactions in these two men? I mentally drum my fingers on the notebook in my lap as Simon drones on, "You've painted yourself into a qualitative corner, and Megan is a qualitative researcher. She can help you write an excellent dissertation. Here is her number." He thrusts a sticky-note at me. He is alcoholic Todd, with a different face and issue. Not entirely different face, he does look, as well as act, like Todd. And, according to Errol, he's an alcoholic.

I knot my hands under the table. "I still feel abandoned. I am *not* happy about this." Damned right, I feel abandoned. Even worse, he's wasted four weeks of my time with meaningless busywork. Time I could have made progress on my prospectus. He acts like he's doing me a great big favor when he can't admit that he's not qualified to chair my committee. Oh, this isn't about me. It's about his damaged drunken ego.

"I'm sorry you feel that way. Give her a call."

"Well, damn, Doctor," I stand. "How therapeutic of you."

Simon's face turns red. "Remember, you can always sell your paintings if you don't get your doctorate."

Touché. "We're not here to discuss my watercolors. I can't believe you would thwart my progress for a month, and then with no warning, you dump me on another professor. You leave me no choice, do you?" I stalk out the door.

When I leave the building, I step into a sauna. Within the twenty minutes I was inside, the sun ascended twenty degrees. Both temperature and humidity rose with it. The air is so saturated it's palpable. One flight of stairs feels like three. The sun hitting the whitewashed concrete nearly blinds me.

Simon is lucky I've spent a number of years learning to control my tongue. Otherwise, I would shred him with my words and leave his jiggly-bits on the floor.

Chapter 8

I'm still shaking from my confrontation with Simon when the cats greet me as I walk inside. As if they know, they disappear into the office as I make my apologies. "Sorry, babies. I need to write stuff before I take time with you." I go straight to my journal, tucked away among the textbooks. Must stop this monkey-mind before I make myself crazy.

June 8, 1999

Was Simple Simon looking for an excuse? For what? To keep me from graduating? Stop. That's paranoid thinking. What does clarity on my prospectus have to do with abandonment issues? How did this turn into a vitriolic conversation? Oh, comment about abandonment triggered my irrational reaction.

Feels way too familiar. Todd could get me to react early in the morning so he could justify his drinking. Left me feeling doomed the rest of the day. I'm afraid I won't graduate.

Go deeper. Childhood? Less than five. Mother's set-up: she bragged about running away from her mother and hiding under the bed because she'd done something wrong. She'd gotten a spanking for running, not her bad deed. I would never have thought about running until she told me her story. I ran. I received a switching, had to pick out my switch from a bush that had whips for branches. Felt like a set-up even then. Just like this does.

Who set this up? Simon? Will Fox? Why do I feel guilty? Crazy? I can't understand this man. It's the addiction. It's his sense of entitlement to treat me any way he wants and then to blame me for his treatment, so I end up feeling guilty. He gets to feel righteous indignation because his student behaved badly and stormed out of the building.

What is my part in this? If I create everything I experience, how did I cause Simon's reaction? When I told him what his nemesis said about not being qualified to chair my dissertation. I thought Fox was kidding. Until today. Moreover, I thought Simon took it that way. Lack of awareness is my part.

I put down my pen. The journaling has calmed my thoughts. Now I'm ready to call Megan. What will I do if I'm stuck here forever running the Florida State maze? She must be some new professor who needs dissertation students.

Before I reach for the phone, it rings. "Hey, Babe. It's just me. Frank Islip here."

I'm not ready to talk with him about the Simon thing. "Hi. What's up?"

"Dr. Peter's office called. I have an appointment for my six-month check-up. Can you make it?"

"Hold on." I check my calendar. "When?"

"One o'clock next Wednesday."

I pencil it in. "Sure."

"Thought I'd come by and see you this evening." There's a question in his voice.

I need to get my doctoral program on track. "I can't tonight. I have to work on my prospectus for a meeting tomorrow." I hope I'm not spitting in the wind and that I'll at least have a meeting set up with Megan tomorrow. "Can I take a rain check?"

"Call you later. Okay?"

After hanging up, I stop a moment and scratch Yang as he rubs against my leg. Yin has disappeared.

I take a deep breath and pick up the phone. I schedule a meeting with Megan. Tomorrow afternoon at the Green Frog Café. As soon as we get off the phone, I email her the requested first two chapters. She sounds nice enough, but what does that have to do with her ability to chair my dissertation? Besides, she's in the home economics department of the college. My mother's degree is in home economics. I will not follow in Mother's footsteps. How can I possibly get a degree from this college? "Pride goeth before a fall," an oft-repeated phrase of Mother's. Where did that come from?

The next morning, I wait for George at the Frog. Once the panic subsides, I realize my degree will come from my college, not home economics. I watch the regulars walking around the lake in their blues, greens, reds, yellows, and all colors in between. Some saunter while others race-walk or run. A man I used to see often plods along on a walker, accompanied by a younger woman. Must be his daughter. Is this why I haven't seen him in a while? A stroke? My gaze moves on and passes a clump of trees. The woman who tore up the beach house stands as still as one of the tree trunks and looks this way.

When I turn back to the table, George straggles in. He looks like he's just gotten out of bed. He gets a coffee, and then joins me at the table. "What's up?"

I'd planned to process what happened with Simon yesterday. Instead, I take a sip of coffee. "Had the strangest dream last night."

He stirs his coffee. "Want to tell me about it?"

My shoulders tense as I remember the confrontation. "Let me tell you what happened yesterday." I quickly relate my confrontation with Simon. "In the middle of this confrontation, I flash back to Todd and feel the same feelings I have with Simon."

"You might want to consider the possibility that you have some residual PTSD from your marriage."

I nod as I consider his idea. "I think the dream's connected to my encounter with Simon. Hope I can gain some clarity by talking about it."

A casual acquaintance stops by to look at the painting of the climbing-tree across the lake hanging on the wall next to the table. After saying her hellos, she moves on toward the counter.

George rests an elbow on the table. "The dream?"

"I'm in Simon's boat." I lean in. "Maybe a rowboat with a trolling motor attached." I scoot forward towards the table to make room for the person squeezing in behind me.

"Anyway, we're out on one of the waterways, when suddenly we're surrounded by snakes. So many they're churning the water. The motor stops. Simon hands me an oar. 'Beat them away.' Before I put the oar in the water, I take a closer look. These are brown water snakes, at least six inches in diameter. Maybe five feet long."

George shivers.

"I'm not afraid of the snakes and don't put the oar in the water. Simon yells to fight off the snakes. I put the oar in the water, and pull it back in the boat. I don't want to disturb the snakes any more than they're already disturbed. Simon yells. This time I hear panic in his voice. I wake up."

"Damn."

"I know snakes mean transition in Native American medicine, plus my Chinese birth sign is snake. Guess that's why I wasn't afraid." Ahh. I was the one with the power in the dream.

George cocks his head. "I want to hear about your new major professor."

I give him a rundown of our phone call. "We're meeting here later this afternoon."

"Do you have time for lunch?"

"If we don't take too long. I'm starving."

"I was thinking about the little restaurant across the street in the shopping center, the one on the side."

"The fish place or the other one?"

"Other one. Good food."

Because crossing is dangerous on foot, George drives. Nothing on the menu appeals but hummingbird cake. That'll last me all afternoon. I pay, get my cake and a cup of coffee, and find us a quiet booth where we have some privacy. The icing reminds me of the afternoon I wondered what it would be like to hit a bridge abutment.

"Damn, is the cake that bad?"

"No. I haven't tasted it yet. I was thinking…."

He leans forward, elbows on the table, when his name is called. "Hold that thought." He hurries to pick up his food.

The cake reminds me of another day when I had a large piece of hummingbird cake. The taste, the smell of this cake takes me right back to that day.

What would it feel like to run into that bridge abutment? Confusion and disorientation swirl around me as I return home from Todd's and my deposition.

Safely inside my Jacksonville apartment, I go straight to the freezer. I pull out Alex's leftover birthday cake. The one made with real butter and butter icing that he insisted I keep. Three-fourths of it is left. It is so rich I can eat only a small slice at a time. I cut a tiny slice, put the cake back in the freezer, and sit down to eat it. Still frozen. Not the best way to enjoy such a tasty morsel.

With each bite, I return to the room where the deposition takes place. I listen to Todd testify that my name is on our jointly owned house for the protection of his assets. HIS assets. "Lawsuits against architects are so prevalent these days, and liability insurance is so high, that I dropped my insurance. It has eliminated further pursuit of frivolous suits. With Lee's name on everything, I can save at least half of my assets."

I traipse back to the freezer. I pull out the cake. I cut another slice. This time I leave the cake on the counter. I can't believe that I'm resorting to freezer eating. With that thought, I put on a pot of coffee. Can't have cake without coffee.

I'm back in the deposition. This reluctant eavesdropper hears Todd whine he is in such poor health that he needs all but my measly two thousand a year contributions to the company retirement fund. That is to be the sum of my compensation for running your office for all these years. Being Secretary-Treasurer of the business was not a figurehead position. I did all the paperwork required. You had me doing your menial labor on the renderings, making lines of different sizes to fill in spaces, something that you didn't want to pay our draftsman to do. You know I put in as many hours, sometimes more, than you. We didn't even start the retirement fund until five years ago.

He tells the judge, "I don't know how much longer I can work. I've had three open heart surgeries."

You neglect to say that you continue to smoke and eat foods not on your restricted diet. Can't the judge see that you are so overweight it is obvious you aren't taking care of yourself? I'm surprised you don't report that I told you when you had a stroke, I was going to put you in a nursing home as you were causing your own demise.

Back to the kitchen. I pour coffee. This time I cut a man-sized slice, one with all the roses on top. Rich, gooey icing. My favorite. I dig in.

Todd touches his lips. "You know, she is nothing but a gold-digger. She only married me for my money."

Hard to do when one marries a bankrupt alcoholic who is recovering from open heart surgery. You know the one. The one who begged me to marry him because he needed me to survive. Was that survival linked to my good credit? How can you blatantly lie like that?

You forget that I ran your practice for the month you were in treatment for your alcoholism. You forget that I negotiated payment on a bad debt from your most powerful client. You forget that when you got back, you told him to forget it. Yeah, I'm a gold-digger all right. Who are you? It is your own vindictiveness that you see in your ex-wife and this soon to be ex-wife.

The cake has grown on the plate. I can't finish it. I stop eating. I cry. My tears release the knot in my stomach. My neck relaxes. My shoulders drop. The hole in my stomach is not from hunger. The belief that I was a good wife died in that room along with the belief I was an even better helpmate. Has my entire marriage been based on fantasy? Whose?

George returns to the table. "What were you thinking?"

"About the deposition during my divorce from Todd."

"What brought that about?"

"The smell of the cake." I unfold my napkin and place it in my lap. "I flashed back to that time." I take a bite.

"Must have been vicious."

"It was." I sip my coffee.

George looks at me hard. Has he ever seen me angry?

"The more I ruminated on the deposition, the more cake I wanted." I take a small bite.

I can almost see George's mind working. No marriage equals no divorce. "I watched Todd go into helpless mode. He told the judge he just didn't know how much longer he could work. After all, he'd had three open-heart surgeries. He neglected to tell her that he continued to smoke and eat all the foods that weren't on his restricted diet." I wash the cake down with more coffee.

"How could the judge not see he was so overweight that it was obvious he wasn't taking care of himself?" Or had she blamed me for his weight?

"I was surprised he didn't tell her about the time I told him that when he had a stroke, I was going to put him in a nursing home because he was causing his own demise."

George's eyes widen. "You told him that?"

"Yeah. Afterwards, I felt free of the burden he would have placed on me."

"How did that free you?"

"By telling him in advance the consequences of his continued behavior, I was no longer responsible for taking care of him at home. As nasty as he was following his surgery, I can't begin to imagine how much worse a stroke would have been." I lick some icing off the fork. "He did have a stroke, by the way." I lean back against the booth. The sickening sweet smell of the cake on the plate turns my stomach.

A mayonnaise-covered tomato slides from George's sandwich to his plate. "I had no idea you'd been through all that. Your mother bragged about how well you'd married."

"I know. According to Todd, she called him to find out what I'd done to break up our marriage. God only knows what Todd told her."

Yeah, if I'm a gold-digger, who was he? Couldn't he see that his rants about his former wife's vindictiveness were really about his own venom?

George leans over his plate as juice from his hamburger runs down his fingers. "I didn't know you'd divorced him. I thought he died."

"He died after I moved here." I push away my plate. "Funny thing, as I remember how I couldn't finish the other cake, I've stopped eating this piece. I remember tears rolling down my face, tears over the death of the fantasy. Seems like my entire marriage was based on fantasy." Whose?

As we talk, I continue to work myself up over Todd's testimony. "Not only did I deserve to be paid for the work I did for the business, but I should also have received combat pay for the trauma of living with his active alcoholism and abuse for the first six years of our marriage, and an ill-humored crazy man for another six." We had one good year in the middle.

George pulls another napkin from the container on the table. "What was wrong with him?"

"He later told me, after the divorce, that a twelve-step person told him I was having an affair with Alex. If I was in love with Alex before I left Todd, I didn't know it. I even had misgivings about moving into an apartment complex near Alex's. He was my friend. I was focused on school, not on finding a husband. In fact, another husband was the last thing I wanted."

I finish my coffee. "George, are you sure you want to hear this?"

He gives a go-ahead. "This is the part of your life I missed, and it's part of who you are now. I'm having a hard time understanding your mother."

"Maybe this will help explain it. Amidst the squalor of our marriage, Todd gave me a diamond bracelet. It took me two years to understand why I was so angry when he gave it to me. The bracelet said everything was perfect in our marriage." My stomach tightens. "At the same time, behind the garage apartment, the original nineteen twenty-seven windows were arranged in sloppy piles and made the house look like the Clampetts from 'The Beverly Hillbillies' lived there." I take a deep breath. "Mother focused on the diamond bracelet." Did she even notice those windows? "I couldn't have cared less about a piece of jewelry."

"Doesn't sound like a gold-digger to me."

"I know. Todd used to accuse me of being a reverse snob because I preferred to drive my old Volkswagen over his new Pontiac Bonneville."

George takes our plates and his drink can to the awaiting trash bin. When he returns, he thanks me for sharing that part of my life with him. "Even though it's hard to hear."

I gather my things. "Thanks for listening." I reach up and touch his shoulder. "Aren't you tired of my saga?"

He shakes his head. "Tell you what. I have a class until six on Tuesday nights," he pulls out his keys, "why don't we catch a bite to eat and then head to the American Legion for their swing night?"

"I'd love it." We'd learned to dance going to the teen club on Friday nights when we were in seventh grade. We hadn't yet learned to dance with other people. Our parents alternated dropping us off and picking us up. "Like being thirteen again." I grin.

As I get in my car to pick up the papers for Megan, I'm disoriented from turning the belief that I'd been a good wife to Todd upside down and sideways.

How could my own mother believe a man who was more adolescent than adult? I immediately return to the night Todd and I entertained our next-door neighbors. They'd been smoking pot before coming over. Unbeknownst to me, while I was dishing up the spaghetti, they gave Todd his first experience with the drug on top of his pre-dinner drinks.

The conversation turns to the skull, a recent find on the part of our complex still under construction. Todd explains why he'd said nothing about the skull. "Once the city finds out, construction will be stopped for the anthropologists to dig on the site for more Indian—" His face drops into his plate of spaghetti.

Our neighbor seated next to him grabs the few hairs on top of his head, raises it, and pulls out his mostly full plate. "Have the munchies bad." She then replaces his plate with her empty one, drops his head, and begins to eat.

I am horrified.

While I walk to my car, I laugh aloud at the image of Todd with his face planted in his spaghetti. What horrified me then, elicits a belly laugh today.

As I drive home to get my notepad, I shift my thoughts to the meeting ahead. My laughter has rid me of my fear of not graduating, and I'm looking forward to meeting Megan. When I reach the Frog, I sit by the window where I can see the entrance. I'm startled when I see a lanky woman walk through the door. I'd not seen her here before, but every Tuesday afternoon at three o'clock my first semester, I saw this woman at the campus post office, looking disheveled. Her long, stringy blonde hair appeared to be allergic to shampoo, her clothes, a Jackson Pollack canvas of food. With her red nose, swollen face, and blank look, I'd pegged her as an alcoholic meeting her parole officer.

The woman walks toward me. Although she's cleaned up, she could still pass for Twiggy on the skids. Chalk dust replaces food. Puzzlement covers her face as she approaches.

"Lee?"

No. This cannot be my worst nightmare arriving. I sink into mental quicksand, certain I'll never graduate. I smile and beckon Megan over. She sets her black leather briefcase on the chair across from me. "Back in a minute. Coffee."

She returns and settles in. "What do you want to know by doing this study?"

I pause a moment to get my thoughts in order. "What meanings the participants make out of having been exposed to family violence as children."

"Sounds exciting. I recommend this book on the five qualitative designs." She points to the information on the first sheet of my chapters. "Check over the different studies and you'll find one that suits yours. The author also provides good outlines for each study type."

My shoulders drop from around my ears. "I'll order it today." Maybe Megan will be a good chair. "I should have it by the end of the week."

Megan turns the chapters around to face me as she points to the crossed-out section in chapter one. "I'd take out this whole section and eliminate the entire chapter two."

"Thank you. Thank you." I laugh and shake my head. "Thank you! I saw no reason to keep it, but Simon kept moving it from chapter one to chapter two and back again." This is a woman who knows what she's doing. "To be honest, I saw no reason to write it. He must have been married to his ideas." I stop a moment and consider what I'm about to say.

"I was sure Simon was passing me off to a new doctoral faculty member who needed dissertations to chair. Instead, I finally have someone who knows what I'm doing."

Megan gives me a smile of encouragement. "Thanks. Your writing is good, and I think your study is exciting." She really did read chapter one. "When Simon asked me to take you on, I thought I'd have to write your dissertation for you."

After we conclude our business, I take a risk. "You know, I'd see you Tuesdays during my first semester...at the post office." Megan nods as if she, too, recalls the weekly encounter. "I was certain you were an alcoholic meeting your parole officer. In North Carolina, those pillars of the community met at the post office so their neighbors wouldn't spot their cars near the parole office."

Her eyes widen. "Alcoholic?" She laughs. "Well, yes. That was a bad year."

I discover her husband died six months before the fall semester when I first saw her. By summer, she'd adopted a baby from Honduras, the young Jackson Pollock. Telling her about my experience with Alex seems to bond us together in widowhood.

She looks at her watch. "Time has flown. I need to pick up my daughter from school. Shall we meet again in two weeks? The parking is easy and I can find something healthy to eat."

I take a couple of turns around the lake as I piece together my conversation with Megan. She seems excited with my topic. For the first time in months, I have hope.

The book Megan recommended arrives. She's right. It is good. I choose phenomenology because the study is about the meaning participants make. Funny how I'd known that was the research for me when I took a history of the science of psychology as an undergraduate.

Finally, someone who doesn't insinuate I'm a poor researcher because I like qualitative research. Now I have my topic. It's still in the field of domestic violence but completely different from Simon's intentions.

When I turn my phone on, I see where Frank called while Megan and I met. "Hey, Babe. It's just me, Frank Islip. Sorry I missed you. I'll call you later tonight, so we can make plans for tomorrow."

So much has happened in the past twenty-four-hours, I'd forgotten Frank's doctor's appointment.

The next day, Frank picks me up at noon and takes me to a fast food restaurant near the urology office. Although we're a few minutes early, we have no wait. Once in the examining room, Frank sits on the doc's stool, his foot moving up and down as if in time to a fast-paced song. I know to keep my mouth shut. Frank moves to the examining table when Dr. Peters breezes in. He motions me over and gets out a diagram to show us where to inject and has Frank practice on a rubber penis. He then injects a fifty-cubic-centimeter dose of Trimix to jump start Frank's erection, and then gives Frank a prescription. "Don't use this more than every other day."

Frank has the prescription filled at the one pharmacy in town that carries the drug. He then stops at another drugstore to buy syringes, cotton balls, and alcohol. All this time, I'm realizing just how much I've missed our lovemaking. I'd just blocked my feelings about not having sex.

Now I run all kinds of scenarios where Frank's erection disappears before we get to use it. I know better than to rush him, but damn. I want him. Now.

Once in the apartment, I leave a string of clothes from the door to the bed. Frank undresses. We make good use of the shot. But. There is a difference with an injection. The penis doesn't lose its erection right away.

When I reach over to snuggle to his back, he moves. "Can't get comfortable. Damn this hurts." His back muscles tighten. "Haven't felt this much pain since I was eighteen."

He gets up and goes into the shower. "Didn't help." He puts on a loose pair of sweats. He paces. Twenty minutes pass. He calls the doctor and puts the phone on speaker. The answering machine recommends the emergency room. We climb into his old blue Dodge van and drive towards the hospital. Frank calls again. Same response.

We pull off on a closed road and Frank tries once more. The line is busy. Frank punches the repeat button as soon as the busy signal beeps.

My heart beats faster and I have to sit on my hands to keep Frank from seeing them shake. Even as I imagine gangrene setting in, I must hold it together. For his sake.

When he reaches the answering service and explains his predicament, Dr. Peters calls back immediately. Frank puts the phone on speaker. "If your erection lasts four hours, then go the emergency room and get a shot to counteract the effects of the Trimix." Frank's shoulders slump.

I let out a breath. I'd been so caught up in Frank's panic that I'd forgotten all the stories my upstairs neighbor regaled me with about this predicament and the four-hour limit.

In the ten-minute drive back to my place, Frank's penis returns to normal. I go into the kitchen to start dinner. Frank gathers his things, "Think I'll ease on out of here and head home."

Instead of dinner, I pull out my journal:

> September 10, 1999
>
> Frank just left after the shot experience. I have a feeling he blames me for his blue balls. Maybe he's embarrassed that I witnessed his panic. Whatever it is, something's changed in our relationship.
>
> What can I do about it? Wait and see. My perception could be wrong. If I feel the same tomorrow, wait and see some more. Given enough time, it might change on its own. Then I can decide what to do about it. Thank you, my friend, who gave me that piece of advice years ago. My attempts at solving these problems always end in the situation I don't want. Yet, when the timing is right, the problem solves itself.

As ghosts and goblins make their yearly rounds, it is time for me to choose my committee, submit my proposal, and then meet with the chosen few. I set an intention that I will make this happen before the trees lose their leaves. I've heard rumors of nightmare committee members from all disciplines, so I ask Megan for recommendations. When I look at her list, I relax. That was my list.

George and I fall into a pattern of dinner and dancing on Tuesday evenings. I look forward to spending time with my old friend. We discover that our paths have crossed and intersected a number of times during those years we didn't connect. He left Florida State before I arrived, he taught at the same school as one of my close friends who has since died, and he even visited a family who lived a block from me in Jacksonville.

Frank and I see each other once or twice a week while I'm busy with my prospectus. We usually go flying or hiking the Munson Hills Trail. He finds things to fix around my apartment. We enjoy our time together. At least I think *he* does. I just want peace. There've been no more crazy episodes. I begin to relax into the relationship. Our sex life is random as Frank attempts to find the right dose for him.

The rental agent calls to remind me that the six-month tenancy on the beach house expires in three weeks. Hurricane season has been kind to my house. I can't wait to spend some time there even as Frank grumbles about the perils of hurricanes on this section of the gulf. As we drive through Panacea on our way to the seafood festival in Apalachicola, he says, "Remember the devastation of the last hurricane that blew through here?"

I bob my head. When I first saw the house with Joy, a bluebird-colored cottage across the road from me was crumbling into the water, its foundation undercut by storm surges. By the time I bought my place, the cottage had disappeared and the property had been donated as beach access to us residents across the road.

"It's just a matter of time before another one hits." He pulls into a real estate agent's office in Panacea. "Want you to meet my old Navy buddy. He's just set up shop here in town." He opens the truck door. "Come on."

By now, I know when Frank has an ulterior motive. I'm not ready to sell my dream of living on the water, but I meet the man, and we chat a few minutes. Frank and I are soon on our way. Our chatter runs along the lines of the seafood festival we are about to enjoy. Frank plans to take me by the museum where he worked. He spends much of the ride explaining how John Gorrie discovered air conditioning. After spending two hours in the sun and eating my fill of seafood, the cool museum is a godsend.

On the ride back to Tallahassee, Frank brings up the beach house again. "Have you thought about selling it? You could take a big profit."

I don't want to sell my dream. I lick my lips and try to slow my breath. "Nooo …"

Frank frowns. "Insurance rates are going out of sight, what with all the hurricane damage from last season."

"I know." I roll my neck from side to side to remove the sudden kinks. I don't want to talk about this now.

"You're not using it, you know." His neutral tone tells me his concern for my finances is genuine.

I don't want to spoil our outing with a refusal. "I'll think about it." Driving back and forth to the beach while I have to be in close contact with FSU is inconvenient, but this isn't forever.

The stars are out, and the moon lights the way to my apartment. I check my mailbox while Frank opens the door. As I walk in, Frank hands me a piece of paper. "Found this taped to the door."

I take the notice from the owners of the complex. "What the—" the paper shakes in my hand. My rent will go up thirty percent if I sign a year's lease; if not, it will increase sixty-five percent. Frank recommends a Tallahassee real estate agent—another friend of his— and gives me her number. "I use her for all my transactions."

First thing Monday morning, I call her. We make an appointment for the next day. She picks me up and shows me several condos, including one I'd looked at when I first came to Tallahassee. I love the area, but the interior is too dark. Next, she shows me a townhouse in a small community that, when you drive in, you feel like you're in the woods. The leaves are turning bright red, burnt orange, and golden. The colors stand out against the gray buildings. The interior of the condo is a mess, but the price is right, and it has a large, fenced back yard. It is the best location in this hidden community. The buildings have been kept up and the property is well maintained. She then shows me another one across town. I like it, but no yard.

I have Frank look at the one I like with the yard. He thinks I can get it in shape for about five thousand, including shoring up the foundation. I call the agent and make an offer. The owner can't afford to lose money on it, so I pay the asking price. Now I'll have a mortgage. We shoot for closing before the rent increase and barely make it.

I hire movers, and Errol is to set up my television and computer. He's drunk when he arrives and leaves within thirty minutes. Frank works late but brings food when he comes to check on my progress. As we sit down to eat on the barely cleared off table, Frank picks up his napkin and spreads it across his lap. "Have you gotten your mail today?"

I'd forgotten it. "Would you mind running me over there to pick it up?"

He finishes the fork full of salad he'd stabbed from the bowl, "Be glad to. Know you're tired."

After we've eaten, I put the dishes in the dishwasher. Frank pulls on a flannel shirt. I grab my navy cardigan. We drive the short distance to the old place. I gather the mail and we return to the condo. I set the mail on the dining table without looking at it.

"You might want to check your mail." Frank's voice has an edge to it.

I start to sort the pile, mostly junk, something from the insurance company. I open it. The company not only informs me of the higher rates, but also that it will no longer insure beach houses as second homes. My legs shake. I sit at the table. I watch my dream drift off into the clouds. "Did you get the notice today, too?" Frank and I are insured by the same company. Tears prick my eyes.

His eyes tell me yes. "Hon," he touches my shoulder. "You might want to think about selling the house. It's too far to commute back to Tallahassee every day, and now that you own a townhouse in town, it's a second home. Your insurance…" his voice trails off. "Just think about it."

"I'll do that." Tears try to surface. I don't need two places. "Let me get settled here first. Then I'll meet with your friend, but I can't promise anything right now."

Please, Universe, no more major changes until I meet all my doctoral requirements.

Chapter 9

I have the condo organized within the week and am ready to turn my attention back on my prospectus when the air conditioner goes out. It is a Saturday, and the temperature is ninety-seven degrees. No chance of getting a repairperson today. I call Frank and leave a message. I spend the weekend questioning my purchase. Do I need a new air conditioner? The repairperson traces the culprit to a clogged line in the dirt under the house. What else can keep me from my prospectus?

I hear nothing from Frank until Monday evening. "Been in the woods. No signal," is his excuse. I stuff my agitation and move on.

Three days before I'm to defend my proposal, my outside committee member asks for an outline of the entire dissertation. Thanks to Megan's recommended book, I fill in the outline form with my information and drop it off the following day. I will give copies to my other committee members at my defense.

The day before the defense, I'm practicing my presentation in front of the cats when the phone rings. "Hey, Babe. It's just me. Frank Islip here."

"What's up?"

"Just got a call from my cousin in Pensacola." His tone upbeat, "I need to run over there and see my sick aunt."

I can't imagine anyone letting his schizophrenic cousin know, for fear of sending him over the edge. He was diagnosed years ago. Ever since, the family tiptoes around him. "I'm so sorry." I grip the phone. "How serious is it?"

"Won't know 'til I get there." He coughs. "Leaving in a few minutes."

"Be safe and give her my best wishes for a speedy recovery." I walk over to the French doors and rest my eyes on the profusion of berries on the crepe myrtles. "Let me know how she's doing?"

"Will do. Call you when I get back. Good luck on your defense. Love you."

"You, too." I tuck the call away in my *things-that-don't-add-up* folder, the one I should have started months ago. Don't have time to think about it now.

I try to ignore the stomach growls as I go over the presentation one more time.

Morning arrives too quickly. I dress carefully in one of my professional suits and heels. I learned early in my college career that when I look the part, I perform better. I'm in the conference room fifteen minutes before eight.

When I walk into the room, Megan waits for me. She gives me some last-minute cheerleading. We establish how I'm to present. We've already decided that I can do four participants, four female and four male. The other committee members arrive, three from my college, including Megan, and my outside member. I make my presentation. The outside member asks, "Where are your stats? You can't do a dissertation without stats."

I sidestep the statistics question by reiterating the research question: What meanings do adults who witnessed family violence as children make of their experience. "I will have to see the data before I can decide if it is amenable to running statistics."

"You can't write a dissertation without statistics."

I smile and nod my head. "Oh."

We move on to the number of subjects I will have. The other members ask for six, but agree to five. "I could do five, but I want equal male and female." They know how long an hour session takes to transcribe and my inquiry will take longer, much longer. They finally agree to four. I want to finish and they want me to finish. My outside committee member mumbles under his breath but agrees.

In what seems like longer than two hours, I move from doctoral student to doctoral candidate. It's time to put out some feelers for an internship.

I spend the next three days updating my résumé and curriculum vitae—a résumé of my studies. I work four hours a day researching my curriculum and experience. In just four years, I've added two pages of experience including supervised visitation for abused children, acting as guinea pig for a new treatment for compassion fatigue, not to mention the Lee-Errol-team's co-therapy. I've also had several journal articles published: Joe's is currently in press, all co-authored with Errol.

I attend a meeting of the local marriage and family association where I run into a marriage and family therapist working at the campus-counseling center. I mention I'm looking for an internship. She insists I apply at the counseling center. I do.

The telephone rings. It's Simon. "The University Clinic called asking for a recommendation. I wrote you a glowing one because your therapy skills are excellent and you would be a welcome addition to any setting you choose." He tells me he's emailing a copy of his letter to me and snail-mailing the original to the clinic administrator.

I thank him and hang up. This must be his way of making up for dumping me as his student. I check email. I edit my resume and curriculum vitae and email them to the director of the clinic with a note that a paper copy will be in the mail today.

I see that I have a message from Joe, my supervising practicum professor, asking me to call him. I do. "I'm writing your recommendation for the campus clinic. You'll be a good addition anywhere you go." I thank him. "I'll email you a copy." He hangs up.

Two recommendations are required and now I have two glowing ones.… Perhaps too glowing, particularly Simon's. They'll raise questions: the department wants to get rid of me, I'm so good I'll show up the director, or I won't be teachable. None are true. Simon must be trying to make up for firing me. Since I cannot make anyone else give me what I want when I want it, I've learned that all I can do now is wait.

I need a break. I change into my Lake Ella clothes and drive to the lake to clear my head. As I begin my walk, I feel the pressure to get the internship immediately, as if it should have been done yesterday. Intuitively, I know that when I find one, it will be perfect for me, and it will be exactly what those particular clients will need. It's a spiritual thing, a matter of trusting the Universe.

I love this lake I know so well. It teaches much about life in general and about relationships in particular. I learn something new about the inhabitants of the lake every time I come here. Today is no different. As I near the pavilion, a raft of ducks grieve for one that has been hit, maybe run over. As I come around for the last lap of my three miles, they still stand respectfully. Something in their demeanor shows their sadness. They have me rethinking what I thought I knew about these creatures. They bicker and they mourn and they babysit each other's babies. Maybe they're more like humans than we give them credit.

By the end of three miles, I let go of any expectations and know that the perfect internship will be mine when the time is right. I've been guided throughout this doctoral program, from writing papers to doing therapy, from Simon's firing me to acquiring Megan as my major professor. All I have is this day with which to be concerned. What happens tomorrow will happen tomorrow.

Two weeks after the sick aunt phone call, "It's just me. Frank Islip here. Sorry I missed you. Having to go to North Carolina from Pensacola." He coughs. "The cabin-roof's leaking. Will try to call from the cabin. You know how the reception is. Love you."

Another piece of information to file in the *things-that-don't-add-up* folder. Don't have time to think about it now.

My next hurdle is acceptance of the proposed research by the human subjects committee, making certain I'm not harming the participants. Red and yellow leaves float to the ground as I drive along Levy Avenue to turn in the proper forms at the research center.

When I return home, Frank has left another message. "At the hardware store in town, so thought I'd try to call you. Work is progressing slowly, but steadily. Hope to be home by the weekend. Love you."

I call back and leave a message. "Sorry I missed your call. Miss you. Love you." Maybe he'll get it. I don't hear from him until Friday afternoon.

"It's just me. Frank Islip here. Just got back in town. Thought I'd come see you. I've missed you."

My shoulders tighten. Thank god, I'm to meet one of my twelve-step buddies for dinner and a meeting. "Missed you, too. Wish you'd called sooner." With, I hope, disappointment in my voice. "I have plans for this evening." My shoulders drop.

"What about tomorrow evening? Can't see you during the day. I have to work tomorrow."

"What do you have in mind?"

He doesn't answer. I'm not going to invite him over for dinner this time. "You there?"

"Want to go flying when I get off work?" He sounds confused. "Think the weather will be good."

"Sure. What time?"

"I'll give you a call in the morning and let you know."

"Look forward to it."

When he hangs up, I'm unable to rid myself of the feeling that something's off. Why am I not enthused to see him? I shrug off the question to file away, and I pour a cup of coffee.

Frank calls around noon the next day and suggests meeting at his place at four-thirty. "I can leave early. One of the rangers agreed to take down the flag and leave it on my porch. I'll lock the gate when I get back."

The trip over is spent with lively banter. He gives me the latest North Carolina gossip, and I brief him on my new topic. Before we leave the ground, we stop by the mechanic's shop. Frank hands him a check, "Sorry, Bud, didn't expect to be gone so long."

Bud shoves his ball cap back and winks. "You'd better be careful about staying away. Some guy's gonna come along and steal your girl here."

Frank puts his arm around my waist, looks at me, and laughs.

I laugh, hands on my hips, "Okay, boys, fight over me. Make my day."

As we walk back to the plane, Frank places his hand on my butt. "You know he's interested in you, don't you?" He climbs into the old Piper Cherokee.

I follow. "I know he likes to flirt, but I've never taken it seriously. To be honest, I'm not interested."

He starts the engine and we taxi out to do the run-up. Once in the air, we fly over a new housing development that had just begun the last time we flew over. "My god, they have the landscaping in already."

"I'm surprised, too." As we climb higher, the air cools quickly. Frank turns on the heat.

I lean over and kiss him on the cheek. "Thank you. I was getting cold. Didn't think about the sun going down and the higher altitude when I decided to leave my jacket home."

He returns the favor by looking over and squeezing my knee. Maybe we should take time off from each other for long periods more often. I like what is happening.

On the ride back, his hand on my knee, "Hey, Babe. Mind if I spend the night tonight? I've missed you and want to spend more time with you."

I put my arm around his shoulder. "Sure." This is the man I fell in love with.

"When we get to my place, I'll unload my gear and then head on over. Do I need to bring anything for dinner?"

"I don't think so. Have some leftover chicken and yellow rice in the freezer. It won't take long to heat it up in the microwave."

"By the way, must be back at work at seven to raise the flag."

The next morning, he brings me coffee in bed, and then kisses me goodbye. "I'll call you later. Love you." He leaves. I smile as I go back to sleep.

Early Monday morning, the phone rings. It's the woman who wants to supervise my internship. "Lee, I'm so sorry, but I'm not going to be able to supervise you. My boss said he couldn't have an unpaid intern in the clinic and he couldn't pay you. I'm very sorry. I so wanted the opportunity to supervise a marriage and family intern." We chat a few minutes, and then I thank her for calling. Granted, I'm disappointed, but I know something better is waiting out there.

I don't have the go-ahead from the human subjects committee; however, I turn my entire focus to the dissertation. I work on strengthening the justification for my study by elaborating on the paucity of work on my topic.

So far, this is the calmest and easiest time in my relationship with Frank since his surgery. He calls and comes over a couple of times a week. During his visits, he shores up the condo's foundation by pouring concrete pads around the pilings. I hand him the tools he needs when he asks. We spend most of his days off working on the house. Once the cats have adjusted to the move, Frank installs a cat door for them to come and go at their pleasure. We take out his canoe on warm evenings or go flying when the weather suits. He's been the kind Frank with whom I fell in love.

Focusing on school, I choose to forget my impending decision about staying with him or not. Don't want to add to the stress by disrupting the relationship, and my theory is being borne out. That one-time flare-up was connected to his surgery.

He spends Thanksgiving with his family but leaves from— and returns to—my place. George goes to Bradenton to be with his mother. I spend the holiday with Errol and his wife, as I've done every year I've been here. Ever the gossip, Errol mentions that Simon had planned to visit his son in Nova Scotia for the holidays, but was told not to bother.

Since George was in school with Simon, I mention Errol's gossip to him.

"You don't know?" George asks. "His son was a big high school football star who had a scholarship to one of the big-name colleges when a freak accident caused by some kind of negligence ruined his football career."

"Oh. That explains why his son doesn't want him to visit. I thought it had to do with his alcoholism."

"I don't think so. The gossip is that Simon settled for a paltry sum."

"What do you mean?"

"The settlement could have been a lot larger because the wife blamed her husband for the accident when it happened. There had been talk of criminal negligence."

My hand flies to my mouth. "How awful for the kid. Didn't he have a say in the settlement?"

"He was seventeen."

I'm not sure what to make of this. I wonder why Simon let it go without pursuing it. Maybe he, too, had learned that pursuing a lawsuit would cause more problems, rather than resolving them.

Christmas is a repeat of Thanksgiving. As part of Errol's family, I'm invited for the opening of gifts. Mine is the most memorable one I've ever received: a plunger. Two days before Christmas, the toilet backed up. I had no hope of getting a plumber. Errol, always my Plan B, came within the hour with his plunger and fixed the problem. I now have my very own, and we all have a Christmas story to tell.

Frank and I drive to the North Carolina mountains the weekend before New Year's. The white Christmas gift of snow remains on the ground when we arrive. We spend our time hiking and playing in the snow. The gas heater keeps his cabin cozy when we've had enough of the cold. It is a few days of drinking hot chocolate and eating chili to warm our insides after we play in the cold outside. We find an old sled in the storage room and slide down the hill from the cabin to the private drive, just hilly enough to have fun, but not so steep as to be dangerous. In the evening, we drive around and look at the lights.

Snow. Colored lights. Stars above. It is a magical time. By New Year's Eve, we've had enough fresh air at the high altitude that we are in bed asleep long before the clock strikes twelve. This is the first time I haven't rung in the New Year since I was sixteen. I am content.

Before the holiday decorations come down, Frank and I drive to Panacea to meet with his friend. I sign a contract allowing him to sell the beach house.

When I talk with George about the sale and my intention of giving Frank some of the profit, he asks. "Do you think his insistence is due to making money?"

"Not really. As much as I want to keep it, I'd be unable to insure it. And how practical is it to live at the beach when I can barely get an internet connection? I have to be able to do my research."

Within two weeks, an offer comes from a couple in Georgia. I agree to sell the house complete with furnishings. The agent insists I remove the paintings and let him sell them separately. I refuse. They are part of the furnishings and are not excepted in the contract. I won't do that to the purchasers. After the closing, the agent expresses surprise at how easy the closing had been. "Never had one go that smoothly."

Perhaps trying to cheat buyers causes problems at closings. I almost doubled what I paid for the house. I offer Frank part of my profit, but he refuses to accept payment for his work.

I don't take the time to grieve the loss of my dream house. I push on.

By the first week of spring classes, I have permission to begin my study. Serendipity shows up in the form of a new book published the week before. While searching for another book, I discover this one online. It is the missing piece to my theory.

Immediately after approval, participants line up to be in the study. One comes from a dinner discussion one night. "Can I participate?" Two come from a conversation while buying vitamins. "I'd love to do it, and my husband would probably do it, too." The final one comes from a chance meeting at the market: a mother volunteers her son. I'm in awe of the ease with which everything falls into place.

I wish my internship would go as smoothly. One social work professor, who promised he would supervise me if I needed it, backed out. His excuse was that the marriage and family department head "needs to change before I can work with her."

His statement goes against all my beliefs about therapy. I can't change anyone. I can only change my attitude about the situation. I came to Florida State because the program taught a theory of self-responsibility.

I turn to my alternative medicine professor. He will supervise me, but he would like for me to do more clinical experience in my field of interest: alternative healing using meditation, massage, and herbs instead of drugs. He knows of a new unit connected to a hospital in Genteel, Georgia. I'm waiting to hear from him.

Chapter 10

I pull into the space marked "Visitor." I'm to meet George at his office. We plan to brainstorm a collaborative project, connecting his sociology and my marriage and family studies, a possibility for a long-term project. I reach across the console to grab my briefcase, which contains my journal encompassing my progress through the Twelve-Steps, case-notes of alcoholic clients and their family members with names blacked out, and notations from my domestic violence study. When I step from the car and turn toward the building, I glance at my phone as I turn it off—a courtesy to George. Oh, a missed call. I never hear the phone when I have the windows down and radio playing.

When I walk into George's office, I point to a blossoming pink camellia in a window box. "I like. Did you plant this?"

His smile says he did.

I put the phone in my purse. "Green thumb. Unlike me, who kills them with what passes for kindness."

"Thanks." He studies me. "You look distracted. What's going on?"

My god. An empty office chair. A first for an academic. That's George, always organized. "I just noticed a voicemail when I turned off the cell ringer." I plop into the overstuffed chair, kick off my ballet flats, and tuck my legs under. "I've been hoping for a return call from one of my professors about ideas for an internship."

He glances at the clock and then back at me. "What happened to the clinic on campus?"

"It didn't pan out. The woman who wanted to supervise me told me the director said he didn't have money to pay me and I couldn't work for nothing." I still think the recommendations were too good, too good to be hired. "I talked to one of my other professors about either supervising me privately or helping me find a place."

"Check your voicemail."

The call was from the professor. "Call the director of the new alternative medicine center in Genteel, Georgia. The number is…" I write it down and place the phone back in my purse.

"I may have found an internship." Now I'm fully present.

George appears to mull something over. He straightens. "I have been trying to decide how much to tell you. I don't want to get your hopes up and then have them dashed."

"Tell me now. We will worry about my hopes later."

He hesitates. "Okay. I have written a grant for a longitudinal study of the physical, psychological, and social effects of addiction on families." He looks down at his hands. "You have the skills I'm missing to make this a comprehensive study. I want to make certain that your background won't interfere with your objectivity." His eyes twinkle as he grins. "So I want to hear all your dirty little secrets."

Relief drops my shoulders and loosens my neck. I return his grin. "All of them?" I don't give him a chance to respond. "Yes. I will do it." I know I need to do this anyway and who better than my childhood friend who has never betrayed my trust.

"Okay if I record this?" George smiles as he reaches over to turn on the recorder. "Good. What new insights did your journals bring you?"

"Childhood stuff about my dad." Some I'd written for classes in grad school. "Well, not until Dad told me he'd been in the program that uses the Serenity Prayer did I realize he must have had a problem in his younger days."

"What makes you say that?"

I pause to gather my thoughts. "I did an early memory exercise in my clinical psych program. I must have been seven. I'd remembered early morning phone calls that agitated Mother. We walked over the bridge to Nana's. Mother walked. I ran as she held my hand. I knew they were both upset, even though they were trying to hide it. They looked like this." My mouth marches into a straight line and then pinches itself. "In hushed tones. Snippets of words, 'he's'…'can't find him'…'didn't show up'…." My stomach tightens as I remember.

"Sometime in the afternoon, a phone call came. I could feel their relief. The tone of the day shifted. Words spoken, 'been sick'…'food poisoning'…'allergic to shrimp.' As I tell you this, I think, likely story, because much was made of the allergy over the years, in a way that felt like a cover-up. My child-bullshit detector."

"What did you take away from the exercise?"

"Adults lie. As an adult, I'm pretty sure he must have gotten drunk and was hung over."

"What else did you take away from your writings about your father?"

I shift in the chair. "He loved me. He was proud of me. He was a good father ninety-nine percent of the time, and he had flaws. Not enough to prevent me from loving him, though. Not until I was older did I appreciate that he protected me as best he could."

I stand and walk to the window and watch a bright red cardinal float like a feather for a landing on a camellia branch.

"Both he and Mother gave me my love for the written word. I'm a voracious reader, a gift from both parents." My paternal grandparents were the ones who provided *McGuffey Readers* for me when I visited. They encouraged self-study. "Dad continued to study all his life. He worked at increasing his vocabulary, and he learned Spanish when we moved to Tampa." Funny, how I always thought of Mother as the intellectual. That's how she presented herself to the family.

George clears his throat. "We've gone off track."

Good catch, George. How did I do that? "I think there's something I'm not ready to see."

"We've been at this for a while. Why don't you leave the materials you brought so I can look them over—maybe keep you from reliving this."

I take a deep breath. "What exactly are you looking for?"

"You know I want to do this project with you. I have to be sure that I can trust your research and thought processes." He scrutinizes my face. "Don't look so concerned. I want to know if you have worked through most of your childhood issues around addiction."

I almost laugh. "My most pressing issues came later."

"Don't worry, we'll get to them. From what I've seen so far, you seem to be aware of them, at least most of them."

My shoulders let go. Hadn't realized how tense I'd been. We make plans to meet again next week. Same time. Same place. He hugs me before I go out the door.

I drive straight home and call the center. The director answers immediately. "I'd love to have you as an intern, but we just opened and don't have any clients right now. Let me give you the number of the supervisor for the psychiatric unit at Genteel General. She's expecting your call."

Things are looking up. When I reach the supervisor, we make an appointment for the next morning at eleven.

Later, when Frank calls to see how my meeting with George went, I tell him about driving to Genteel in the morning. He offers to bring his van. "Noticed your tires are getting a little thin, and with the mileage on your car, it's about time to change them. I'm off tomorrow. I'll take your car in and make sure everything is good for a road trip."

My first thought is *No, I don't need help*. It's only thirty miles to Genteel, but I'll let him do this. "Thank you. Were you planning on spending the night tonight?"

"That's the reason I called."

"Dinner?"

"Let me take you out. Need to celebrate."

"I don't have the internship yet."

"Know you'll get it."

"Thanks for the vote of confidence." I wish I could be so sure. "See you this evening. What time?"

"Seven-thirty okay?"

"See you then." I hang up.

I look back at our conversation and wonder why I have such a hard time accepting help. I'm certainly no expert on my car. Something to ponder. Not accepting help could affect my work with George. As I think of George, I hear his voice asking, "Why do you always let Frank be in charge?"

I hear the voices of the past. "Women have to let men be in charge." No, it's "Women have to let men think they are in charge. Otherwise, we are labeled as "ballbusters." Damn.

As we leave for dinner, Frank unlocks the van. "Also, want to get a deer whistle for your car so you don't hit a deer driving back and forth."

"How thoughtful of you." I'm always surprised when Frank does something so unexpected. "I'll take you up on it." I fasten the seat belt. "Let me know what I owe you, and I'll write you a check." I lean over and kiss him on the cheek. "Thank you."

"No problem," his voice smooth as satin. "Know you'll pay me back." We adhere to an understanding of reimbursement. "Just want you to be safe when you're driving back and forth."

As I lean into him, he turns and kisses me.

I lean back. "I appreciate you." It seems every time I think about ditching Frank, he does something to change my mind. The new tires and whistle are a perfect example.

On the drive to Genteel the next morning, my mind is on Frank's thoughtfulness. Thank goodness, he offered the van rather than the big diesel he usually drives. Wouldn't have enjoyed driving the truck. Perfect weather today for driving without air conditioning, a real plus since the van's unit isn't working. Finding the hospital is easy. The supervisor waits at the door as I walk into the lobby of the unit. The interview is short. She shows me around the unit and introduces me as the new intern. After the tour, I'm directed to the personnel office located in a separate building across town from the psych hospital. It won't take me long to learn my way around this little city. I'm taken aback by the courtesy shown me in Genteel. Even drivers are polite, unlike the aggressive people on the roads in Tallahassee. I complete the paperwork and have blood drawn, and then a tuberculosis test administered. I'm to return in three days to have it read. Then I'll be able to go to work.

Because of all the dead zones between Tallahassee and Genteel, I wait until I'm home to call Frank and tell him the good news. "Congratulations. That's great, Babe. Glad you got it. Now you are on the last two legs of your journey. It won't be long before you'll be Dr. Flunky."

And Dr. Dishwasher, Dr. Garbage Person, and whatever else we can dream up. A long-standing joke about my degree, one that keeps me humble.

"I'm at the hunting store now picking up the deer whistle. I'll bring the car by when I'm done here."

When he arrives, Frank answers his mobile as I open the door. "Hey, how're you doin'? I think I can manage next week. Let me call you back in a few minutes. Okay?"

Frank gives me a quick kiss and says, "That was the North Carolina neighbor. Said he thought I should check on the cabin after that unexpected snow storm in the news."

"When will you leave?"

"I'll go up Monday." He shuffles his feet and looks at the floor. "Mind if I spend Sunday night here?"

After all he's done to make me safe, why would he act like he's afraid I'm going to tell him no? "You know I'd love that. I'll have to leave here around ten to have my arm read, but you'll be on your way by then."

"Yeah. You're going to be busy all week getting ready to start your internship, aren't you?"

"Pretty much."

"I'll ease on out of here. Call you later."

"Thanks again for taking care of my car."

"Oh. Before I go, let me put the deer whistle on."

My internship occurs with perfect timing. One of my first patients teaches me that therapy is a puzzle to be solved. My new black Moleskine notebook, purchased to record my internship, is ideal for these reflections. I pull it out of the bag and enter my first patient:

> July 8 2001.......Discharge Note
>   Janet—retirement age—arrived on the unit the weekend before I began my internship. She was assigned to me with the diagnosis of severe depression with suicidal thoughts. This is her first psychiatric admission. She reported that she works at a Tallahassee hospital as a licensed practical nurse. She dressed in jeans and a tee shirt. She appeared unkempt. When I asked why she was admitted, she responded, "I feel so bad that I can't do my work properly."
>   When asked what precipitated her depression, she reported that her retired military husband of thirty years "won't let me retire. He says I have to work five more years to pay off our house."
>   Prior to her discharge, I held a family conference with the husband. I saw him individually before having

her join us. The room, located just off the information desk, was furnished like a small living room with a taupe sofa and two matching chairs. A wooden hardback chair sat in a corner.

The husband dressed like one of the gentry in a pair of well-tailored khaki slacks, an open-collared white dress shirt, and Italian loafers. The soft light of a lamp sparkled the gold watch. He wore no wedding ring. His hair was neatly trimmed and his nails appeared manicured. If I didn't know he was retired military, I would assume he was a successful businessman.

He was charming and kept repeating how much he wanted his wife to return to normal. He frequently checked his phone, the latest. When Janet joined us, she sat beneath a painting of the gulf at dawn. He became Mr. Solicitous. She brought up early retirement. He rationalized the necessity of her paycheck to pay off their home.

While he waited in the therapy room for her discharge, I took her into the unit to complete the necessary paperwork. She appeared happy to go home and looked forward to her month-long aftercare program, a daily commute to a military facility.

As the second week of my internship passes, Frank expands his North Carolina trip. After spending a few days at his cabin, he visits friends in Virginia and Tennessee. He calls when he's on the move, but in between, my phone remains silent. I wonder if he's using vacation time or sick leave. "If I don't use it up"—can't remember how many hours—"by the end of the year, I'll lose them." By the time he retires, he should have used up both.

I begin interviewing the participants in my study. Each story is different in context but the same in content. I have each interviewee pick out a name to be used in the study. By the time I interview the third person, I see how the chosen names fit the stories they tell.

At the psychiatric unit, I'm able to help patients who may have floundered on psychotropic drugs without addressing the problem.

One eighteen-year-old is on his third admission in as many months when I see him. Staff tells me his mother is a drama queen who has her own set of admissions, so I ask about his father. When he dismisses his father, I ask if his dad is as crazy as his mother. "No, he kind of holds things together. He doesn't let her rile him up."

"What happens when you go off the deep end?"

"Mom goes crazy," a smile of recognition crosses his face, "and Dad gets me here."

"You're an intelligent person. Which of your parents do you want to be like?"

He runs his fingers through his hair. "My dad."

"Good. Watch how your dad acts and copy what he does. You won't have to keep coming on the psych unit if you do that."

Fifteen minutes later, I get a call from the psychiatrist. "Come into my office, please." The patient and his mother are in the room. Doc says, "You cannot tell a kid he doesn't have to act like his mother if he doesn't want to."

Why not? "Well, I did." My heart speeds up. "He should know he has options." Is that a hint of a smile on his lips?

I use Frank's time away to conduct all the interviews and give them to a transcriptionist. Now I'm trying to understand a passage that clearly does not match the transcriptionist's wording on paper. Oh, a sentence is missing. Changes the entire meaning of the subject.

Annoyed at the interruption of a ringing phone, I mark my spot, and then pick up.

"Hi, Hon. It's just me, Frank Islip. I'm sitting in front of your old house in Charleston." On the way to Ohio to see yet another friend, he has driven out of his way to visit the West Virginia house where I spent the first nine years of my life.

"What? You're kidding, right? How does it look?"

"It's been kept up. Painted white with black shutters. There's a large apple tree in the front yard."

I nearly drop the phone. I take a deep breath as memories of being tied to the stake come flooding back—the trunk of that tree—being forced to gather my own switches for my spankings. But Frank doesn't know that. I put a smile on my face to take the tension from my voice. "That's what I remember." He's gone out of his way.

"I've taken several pictures for you."

"Oh, Honey, thank you." I turn over the pages I was reviewing. "I can't wait to see them. And you."

"You're welcome. Listen, I'd better go before someone thinks I'm casing the joint."

"Thanks again. I love you."

"Love you, too. See you."

As I hang up, appreciation of Frank's thoughtfulness softens my heart. Perhaps that softening is what allows me to journal about being tied to the stake.

> August 12, 2001
>
> I am five and tied to the crabapple tree in my front yard. I've been playing cowboys and Indians with the little boy down the street. He crudely, but effectively, tied me to the tree so I couldn't escape, and then his mother called him to lunch. The rope was so tight, my neck swelled.
>
> "Mommy! Mommy!" I can't breathe. I'm going to die here, tied to this tree. I don't want to be a cowboy burned at the stake.
>
> "Mommy! Mommy! Mommy! Help! Help me!" Why isn't she coming? Where is she? I don't want to die. Why did Havilland leave me here without untying me? The rope hurts. Why is it getting tighter around my neck? I can't move my head.
>
> MOMMY! HELP! Somebody help me! Maybe mean old Mrs. Kramer will hear me, or Perry. I want to go inside. I don't want to be here forever. I'll die here. I want my mommy. Where is my mommy? I have to scream louder.
>
> "MOOOOOMMYYY!" Why can't she hear me? The rope hurts. My wrist hurts. My legs hurt.
>
> "Shut up!" a voice yells out a window. "You're making too much noise."
>
> Mommy would be mad at you, Mrs. Kramer, for saying shut up. Mrs. Kramer doesn't like me because once I walked into her kitchen to bring her a bunch of wildflowers. I hadn't been invited.

"Please help me."

"Where's your mother?"

"I don't know. I want my mommy." Fresh tears cascade down my cheek.

After what seemed like hours later, Mother released me from my prison with a good scolding about getting myself into this predicament. And about disturbing Mrs. Kramer. Oh, wow. This is another example of my not knowing how to protect myself, and that I should have known. I believed her. Like always, I was the problem. But how could a five-year-old know these things?

In those days, no one owned an air conditioner. People kept their windows open. Where had Mother been? On the phone? Vacuuming? And now, as an adult, I wonder, could she have ignored me? I have a vague memory of her saying something about not exaggerating my predicaments like Chicken Little because then no one would pay attention when I was really in trouble. In a novel, the child would die because the mother ignored her cries. My mother would call my cries melodramatic.

No wonder I thought my mother wanted to kill me when she left me in a car that started sliding backwards down a mountain. Even at nine, I didn't have the cognitive ability to process this.

I stop writing as a new insight shows up. Both my brothers were in the car the day Mother parked on a hill to run into the cold storage locker to pick up meat for dinner. She put the car in neutral and pulled the emergency brake. The brake didn't hold and we began to roll backwards. A man jumped into the car and applied the brake. I decided that she wanted me dead. Not until I wrote it down did I realize she was being her flakey self—damn, she wasn't paying attention as I don't pay attention.

As I cap my ruby pen, a weight lifts from my brain as if I'd been carrying these incidents around forever, along with the rock under which they were buried. This leaves more room for the important stuff like writing the dissertation.

I fill my days off with cataloging and organizing information. I manage to walk or run most days. Health is my first priority. Without it, I have nothing. Walking is my touchstone to sanity. It clears away the fog. When I spend hours focusing on my project, I need to walk or run. Unlike some of my cohorts who gain weight during the writing process, I maintain mine. And, during my run, I begin to see how the dissertation wants to be written.

As my internship continues, four weeks after Janet's discharge, she returns to the unit. She is assigned to me. We sit on my office floor in navy back-jack chairs—cushions with backs—I brought from home in an attempt to put the patients and me on an equal level. A table lamp on my desk provides soft lighting.

She reports, "Aftercare was good. I learned how to relax and take care of myself." She smiles a wan smile. "When I got home, I took a long, soaking bath with candles and soft music to reduce any stress I might have about coming home."

Alex's two watercolors of his cancer hang on the wall across from me, a reminder that my patient knows what she needs. My job is to steer her towards her inner knowing.

"While in my bath, I kept thinking we needed to lock one of the bedroom windows because someone might come in and kill my husband."

I write on the notepad in my lap. "What happened to cause you to think someone might come in the window?" Something in her demeanor, perhaps her lack of emotion, causes me to think something else is going on.

After our session, I fill out my case notes then rush to begin my meditation group.

The following morning, I receive a call from Janet's mother in Phoenix. The first thing the mother tells me is that she's an alcoholic with twenty-eight years sobriety. Janet was already married when her mom got sober. And, yes, she still attends to her recovery regularly. She then adds a complete and more complex picture of Janet's marriage. Instead of the painted picture of a large, expensive home on the edge of a golf course, they live in a trailer, the same trailer with the same window through which Janet's then fifteen-year-old stepson escaped his father and has not returned to their home since. That was over twenty years ago. If they've lived in that trailer twenty years, it has to be mortgage free. Sneaky man.

When I hang up, I'm reminded how much of therapy is a finely crafted puzzle to be solved with the help of many. In our session later that day, I question whether Janet might also wish to leave through the same window. "Think about it."

Her heels bounce up and down. Her toes face the door as she shakes her head no.

"I'm not saying that's the case, but if it is, you might want to acknowledge it yourself. Admitting our feelings doesn't mean we have to act on them."

She again denies any thought of escape.

I must tell her. I take a long, slow breath. "I left two marriages because I dreamed I killed my husband." My throat tightens as I share my experience. "In the first dream, I had no remorse, but I was afraid of getting caught. He was the kind of husband who did what he wanted when he wanted without regard for my wishes or feelings." Like yours.

Her eyes become the size of quarters.

"My second husband was abusive when drunk. After he'd been sober six years, he pushed me out of his way with his stomach. That night, I dreamed I cut him up and stuffed him down the garbage disposal so I'd not get caught." I sort of laugh at how preposterous that seems now.

"I was controlled and bullied by both for a number of years before I had the dreams. I left soon after each one."

I take a deep breath and lean forward. "If you think it's possible that you might want to escape your marriage, by admitting it to yourself, you give yourself power over your choice to stay. You'll no longer be a victim. That choice also gives you the power to change your mind at any time, or not at all." I lean back, "You don't have to make a decision today."

When she's discharged, she still hasn't admitted she'd like to leave. She will stay, but now she knows she has a choice. Weeks later, she still hasn't returned. I assume she no longer feels powerless in her marriage.

By the time valentines appear in the stores, Frank returns from his trip and offers me the use of his house, close to the park where he works. Frank's place becomes my writing office. The usual distractions aren't present. No laundry to do, no dishes to wash or put away, no beds to make. Helping myself to Frank's food or doing my usual chores would be an invasion of his privacy. I don't even have the distraction of the cats. My job at Frank's is to write.

I work four ten-hour days in order to complete my internship in six months instead of nine, which gives me the extra day to work on my dissertation. When not at the hospital, I write at Frank's while he works, and at home on his days off. Since we see each other for lunch most days, I don't usually see him in the evenings unless he has the day off. This works well as I want to finish the dissertation. I'm too busy, and Frank's full support is a gift. What a relief to love a man who is confident enough to encourage me in my endeavor.

The dogwoods turn green, and oriental poppies dress the landscape. I complete my internship. I will miss my fellow therapists and other friends I've made on the unit. At the same time, I'm anxious to focus on the dissertation.

During the internship, Megan and I have kept in contact to discuss ways to go with the information the participants gave me. Once we looked at the names the participants chose for the study, we noticed they seemed to match the person's story. Megan suggested they were metaphors for the person. Sure enough, they were perfect metaphors for the way they saw themselves. The internship allowed me time to reflect on how I wanted to write the dissertation.

Now that my days are free, I arrive at Frank's each morning, write until noon when I prepare our lunches, and then write again for an hour afterwards. I often run in the nearby park, my favorite running spot, before I go home. There is a wood-chip path with bridges over a small creek. I easily lose myself in the calming energy of flowing water and overhanging branches. Since I run on Indian land, I imagine what it must have been like when the Indians inhabited this land. Some days, I feel such tender, loving energy from the land that I'd swear there are spirits here in the coolness of the forest. I've heard stories about people who seem to want resolution, seeing Indian spirits around the Trail of Tears.

Other times, I run at the lake, which is not so cool. There's so much asphalt and traffic on nearby roads that even the trees can't protect me from the heat. If I am still mentally exhausted from my morning writing, I watch *Oprah* and *Dr. Phil* to relax before picking up my writing.

One morning, I arrive at Frank's and become so engrossed in figuring out a puzzle in my results chapter that I'm startled when the door bangs open around eleven. Frank strolls in, dressed in street clothes, carrying his penile-shot bag with the refrigerated cold pack.

"Hi, Honey. Where've you been?" Although I'm curious about the bag and the fact that he's wearing slacks and a dress shirt, I don't want to create a conflict right now.

"Had a doctor's appointment this morning." He usually tells me when he has a check-up and then spends the night because he times his appointments so he won't have to work first thing in the morning, but I didn't see him last night.

I'm merely curious when I ask, "Why do you have your shot bag with you?" I catch a glimpse of his eyes narrowing before he turns away.

"I just told you I had my doctor's appointment this morning," in a tone that indicates I'm the world's most stupid person. His gaze shifts back in my direction, "I took it to show Doc."

My eyebrows rise. Right. And the moon is made of green cheese. How dumb does he think I am? "Why would you do that?" One of my first husband's favorite sayings flashes a neon sign: The best defense is a good offense.

"I just told you." His tone strident, as if to say, don't you dare ask.

So the doctor has never seen an empty syringe. Well, perhaps not one packed in ice carried by a patient. Beyond believable. I file it away in the *red flags* folder of my burgundy briefcase.

Frank stalks off, leaving a trail of acrid fear. He shoves the injection material in his freezer and rams the bag behind the bleach in his laundry closet.

The next day, when I'm in the middle of a rewrite, Frank walks in with a purple rose. "For you." He hands it to me, then bends and kisses me on the cheek.

"Thank you." I smell the rose and smile. "Where'd you find one that color?"

"Some woman was selling them alongside the road."

My stomach pings. No amount of roses will make me ignore yesterday's red flag. Do I want to continue loving this man? I'm not sure he's trustworthy. I vow to keep my eyes wide open.

Megan and I continue to meet on a regular schedule, every two weeks. I turn in what I've written, and Megan returns her comments. She always asks for more. "I want to see what happens next."

My gratitude pocket is filled to overflowing, unlike Simon's doctoral students who are like becalmed sailboats on the last leg to the finish line. "We were supposed to meet at the conference," relayed one of his students. "I flew to Boston from Atlanta, rented a car, and spent the night in the hotel so I could meet with him. I was at the appointed place at the appointed time, but he never showed."

While others chase the elusive Simon, I keep a rigid, rigorous routine until the beginning of July when I write the last word on the first draft. I'm at Frank's when I finish. I call his cell, twirling with joy. "The dissertation is done."

"Great, Babe! Call me later?"

I squeeze the laptop in my backpack, and the books, papers, and pens into my burgundy briefcase. I soar home, singing "You Are My Sunshine" off key. It is hot, in the high nineties. Even this heat can't melt my exhilaration.

Stepping out of the air-conditioned car, I enter a kiln. Ugh. Too hot to run. I'll walk instead. A postal worker sorts the mail as I enter my apartment. I'll pick mine up later. I drop the backpack beside the door onto a narrow box made from wood torn out of the old Sears store in Atlanta. Sitting on wrought iron legs, it serves as a narrow table.

I call Megan. "Whoopee! I did it! The draft is done!"

"Lee?"

"Sorry, I was too excited to think you might not recognize my voice." That's my ego working overtime. "The metaphors you suggested made the methods section so much more interesting than dull reporting. Thank you for that."

"When can I see it?"

"How about Monday? That will give me time to complete a first edit."

"Monday is good."

"Lunch at Bella Bella?" One of our habitual meeting places. "Lunch is on me."

"One-thirty okay? I have my qualitative research class until one. Can't wait to read it."

"Thanks. See you Monday." I click off and whoop again, sending the cats dashing for cover.

I call George and leave a message. Then I change into running clothes and drive to the lake. I park in my usual spot. I'm so full of myself that I hardly notice the heat as I start my walk. The thought of pasta with pine nuts, mushrooms, and sun-dried tomatoes causes my mouth to water. Monday at Bella Bella is not soon enough. I want to celebrate now.

I call Frank again. "Hey, I'm celebrating with pasta and sun-dried tomatoes. Would you like to join me at seven?"

"I guess so," his tone anything but enthusiastic. Must be the heat. "Want me to bring anything?"

"Just your sweet, charming self."

"Thanks. See you then."

When I think about the pasta dish for dinner, my stomach growls. I have everything ready to go by seven. Even the wine has been opened to breathe. Now where is Frank? Will I ever learn not to expect timeliness from him?

Before I become irritated with Frank, George calls. "Congratulations, my friend. Good work. You need to celebrate." His upbeat tone makes up for Frank's so what tone earlier. "How does lunch tomorrow sound?"

"Wonderful. Where do you want to meet?"

"I'll pick you up at noon. Wear something casual. I have a surprise for you."

"That sounds mysterious."

"I'll see you tomorrow."

While I wait for Frank, I turn off the sauce, and when the pasta is done, empty it into the colander. It may be cold, but it will not be overcooked.

At seven-thirty, Frank strolls in, "I got hung up on a phone call from my daughter. Couldn't just cut her off."

His excuses are getting as old as the way he starts phone conversations. Dirt is newer than his alibis. I will not get upset. Since past behavior is a good predictor of future behavior, if I ask him to be on time, and if he sees my irritability, he'll continue to be late. Another lesson in tolerance. Expectations, too.

I'm learning from this mirror and soulmate how to look for— and pay attention to—patterns. He is not an easy soulmate, but he teaches me about my character flaws. As an old mentor would say, "Makes for a good soulmate." I say nothing, and we have a pleasant meal. Hmm, glad I didn't confront. I'm learning.

We make it an early night because I have more work to do on the dissertation before it's ready to turn in to Megan.

As I pull up the file and begin my edits, I remind myself of all the times Frank has been there for me, but I'm still disappointed that he seems so disinterested in my big accomplishment. One in which he played a part.

Chapter 11

George arrives promptly at noon. He takes one look at me, "I think you will find those jeans to be too hot. Put on something cooler. And bring a bathing suit."

"Where are we going?"

"It's a surprise."

I change into a white one-piece sunsuit—sort of a long sundress with legs—and sandals. I pick up a shrug for my shoulders, my bathing suit, and coconut oil for tanning. I stuff everything into my carry-all.

As we drive toward Crawfordville, I think gulf. However, before we get into Crawfordville, he turns off onto another road toward Wakulla Springs.

"Wakulla Springs?" Todd and I often stopped there for dinner on our way to Tallahassee from Panama City, when he had apartments under construction, including one near me in Tallahassee.

"Maybe." He keeps his eyes on the road, but I see a grin form.

"How did you know?" I reach for my sunglasses. "As much as I love the place, I haven't been back in all the years I've lived here." Don't really know why.

I settle back and enjoy the ride as George hums along with the radio. I don't think I've heard him sing or hum before. I suddenly realize this is our first road trip together without parental supervision. Well, there was the night we rode to the beach with a friend in his new Edsel convertible, a Christmas present from his parents. He didn't keep the car a full year. I guess he couldn't take the jokes about the vagina-looking grille. I chuckle.

"What're you snickering about?"

"I was remembering our only other non-parental supervised road trip in Tom's new Edsel and all the jokes about it."

George laughs. "His dad traded it in before he'd had it six months. I think his mother had a problem with it."

"That's even funnier."

We're still laughing when we pull into the parking lot. George opens my door as I pull out my shrug. I leave the satchel in the truck. Once inside, George walks up to the person taking names, "George Hunt, reservations for two at one."

"Your table is ready, Dr. Hunt." We are shown a table with a view of the springs and are handed menus.

"Impressive, George. Do you ever get tired of being called doctor?"

"No, but it doesn't have the ring to it that it did the first year or two."

A waiter brings an ice bucket with a bottle of champagne. He opens it and pours the champagne down the side of the glasses so the bubbles rise. When he leaves, George picks up his glass. "To the almost doctor. Congratulations on finishing your dissertation." We clink glasses.

We spend the afternoon playing in the water and lounging on grass. Late in the afternoon, we change out of our suits and get ready to drive back into Tallahassee. I am so relaxed, I am almost giddy. My legs and torso have become rubbery. My brain focuses on the pleasure of a watery afternoon in the sunshine.

"George, thank you for such a perfect day. I can't think of a better way to celebrate."

"Thought you might enjoy it. You've been working too hard these past few months. It's time to enjoy the fruits of your labors today. Tomorrow, you'll be back at it."

He knows me too well. The return ride is quiet, a comfortable quiet. I don't want to spoil the pleasure by talking. I suspect George feels the same. Once home, he kisses me on the forehead. "Stay limp for the evening."

I reach up and give him a bear hug. "Thank you again for such a perfect day. I'm so glad to have you back in my life."

The next few days are spent going over the last section; having an outline ahead of time has organized the dissertation. I'm free to concentrate on the content and my writing. Since Frank is working this weekend, I have no interruptions. By Sunday evening, I email the last chapter to Megan, and I'm ready for some feedback.

Before I can call George, I hear from Frank. "Hey, Babe. Thought I'd come by, if it's okay?"

"Sure, what time?"

"Have to close the park. How about nine?"

I can grab something to eat and shower before he arrives. "That will work. I'm finishing up my changes for a meeting with my major professor tomorrow."

When we hang up, I call George and read him the conclusions. "Good job, Lee. Well thought-out, too. You'll have no trouble passing."

I trust George's opinion. I'll go to bed knowing that I did a good job.

Frank arrives a few minutes after nine. He hugs me as he walks in.

As he heads for the living room, I step into the kitchen. "Want some coffee? I just made a fresh pot."

I bring our coffees and sit on the sofa next to him.

He leans towards me. "Since you'll have turned in your dissertation, how would you like to go to New Mexico with me on Thursday? I want to look at that fly-in community I showed you. This is a good time of year to be out there."

I've been so focused on my writing that I haven't paid much attention to Frank. Can I go? I guess I could. "This might be a good time for me to go. Megan will be editing my dissertation, and I'll feel refreshed when I get back." My neck tightens. Too much computer work. "Why Thursday?"

"I have a colonoscopy scheduled for Wednesday morning and I won't feel like doing anything all day. Could I get you to take me and pick me up?"

"Sure."

We spend the evening making plans for the trip. It's the longest trip we've taken in the camper. Frank reaches over and pulls me to him. He kisses me, "I'll ease on out of here so you can be fresh for your meeting tomorrow. Glad you're going with me."

The next day at five to one, I turn off my phone and stroll into Bella Bella. Megan is waiting at a table by the window. I check the *Specials* list and see tomato basil soup, always a good choice. A menu awaits my perusal. As soon as I'm seated and greet Megan, a waitperson arrives to take my drink order. I order coffee. I know what I want. We both order the soup. Now we can talk, uninterrupted, until our food comes.

Megan pulls out my chapter. "This is quite good. I have a few little suggestions. Once you make any corrections, email me the entire dissertation, and we can go over it one more time before you turn it in to the committee." Coffee arrives. "There's not a big rush since several committee members are taking the summer off." She stirs in cream.

"I'm considering a trip to New Mexico." I drink my coffee. "Would this be a good time to go? I think I'll be gone about three weeks."

"Excellent idea. I can take my time editing and you need to forget about your dissertation for a while."

Our food arrives, and once we complete our business, we have time to chat. We catch up on departmental gossip. Nothing exciting. The newest department head, the one I worked with, is leaving. He took a full professorship at another school. "Other than that, the department seems to be getting along these days." She sips her coffee.

We walk out the door and head for the parking lot when Megan stops, "Give me a call when you get back, and we'll get together to go over your dissertation. I'd like to be able to schedule your defense in early September."

Can I be ready by then? I'll have most of the summer. "Thanks, I will."

When I arrive home, I dial George. "Thank you for the kind words last night. Megan likes what I've done."

"I knew you could do it." He pauses. "Did she give you an idea when you might defend?"

"We're shooting for early September." I take a long, slow breath. "Frank has decided that we should go to New Mexico. Would you be willing to feed the cats and clean their litter box while I'm gone? They're good for a week without care."

"I'll be glad to. How long will you be gone?"

As if they know what I'm asking George, Yin and Yang come bounding in through the cat door. "Anywhere from three weeks to a month." I'll miss him while I'm gone.

"Can you afford that much time off?"

"Megan seems to think so. Most of my committee will take off as soon as the semester is over. I'll be ready by September."

"When will you leave?"

"Thursday." I reach down and pick up Yang, who is the closest. "He has a procedure scheduled for Wednesday." The purring machine starts up. "Can't drive that day."

I check my mental list. "I need to get you the spare keys to my apartment. I can bring them by your office tomorrow or Wednesday morning, or I can leave them in the dryer."

Silence.

"You there, George?"

"I'm thinking. I could meet you at the lake either tomorrow afternoon or Wednesday morning." He sounds a little down. Is he going to miss me? "I don't have a class until one on Wednesday."

Yin walks over and puts her paws up as if she wants to join Yang on my lap.

I want to work around George's schedule. "What works best for you?" After all, he's doing me the favor.

"Let's say Wednesday at ten."

"Perfect. See you then." I hang up. "Hey, little one. You going to stay in my lap all day?" Yin saunters over. I pat the sofa. "Come on up, Sweet Girl."

Frank arrives with his laxative drink Tuesday evening after dinner. Because he is to have nothing by mouth after midnight, he waits until the latest possible moment to have his usual Coke float in a larger-than normal glass. We go to bed early in preparation for his eight o'clock appointment. When I drop him off, "We'll call you when he's ready to be picked up." A staff person adds, "Somewhere between ten-thirty and noon."

I meet George in plenty of time to walk after I hand him the spare keys. I give him the necessary information to care for the cats. "Remember, they can go three or four days without your attention, a week if necessary. Thank you so much for doing this for me. I owe you a dinner, maybe even two for this."

"Glad to. And dinner would be good. Your timing coincided with an appointment I have with a student in a few minutes at the bookstore." He gives me a hug. "Have a good trip."

When I pick up Frank, we return to the townhouse, and he spends the day on his computer. As I traipse up and down the stairs to prepare for the trip, I notice the light on the screen changes every time I go by him.

The changing screen raises my antennae. I wonder if he's on some porno site or if he's having a conversation with someone he doesn't want me to know about. I have to remind myself that what he does is none of my business. *Accept the things I cannot change.*

By late afternoon, he returns to his place. He had moved the camper to my townhouse once I had room for it, so while he's gone, I load my things into it then finish my miles by walking around the small community.

Frank slides the camper into the truck as I trudge up the drive. I wave and go into the townhouse. Frank comes in while I shower and change. He's already on his computer by the time I walk into the kitchen to prepare dinner. "Burritos okay? Need to use up leftovers."

He jumps. "Uh, okay."

As I'm completing dinner, "What do you want to drink?"

"Beer."

Sounds good to me, too. "Be ready in a few minutes." I place the burritos on plates, open the beers, and serve them.

I pick up the drippy burrito with both hands. "I'm so ready for this trip." Hot sauce and sour cream drip out the end. "I can put my schoolwork behind me and concentrate on having fun."

Frank smiles, one that creeps me. It feels like the smile of someone plotting revenge or with some other malevolent plan. We talk about the logistics of packing the camper for our trip tomorrow. "I put all my stuff in the camper before I came inside." He bites down on his burrito. It drips from the other end. "If you'll decide what needs to go from here, I'll load the camper in the morning."

Sour cream and salsa plop on my plate. "I packed my personal stuff and stocked the camper with all but the cold food and what I need tonight. You might want to check and see if I've missed anything."

He takes a swig of beer from his sweaty glass. "Want to put any of yours in tonight?"

I shake my head. "I stored my clothing earlier in my half of the camper cabinets." Didn't he notice? Didn't he hear me tell him I'd taken care of my things? "Just waiting for those last minute toiletry items that I'll use tonight and in the morning. I'll double-check the foodstuffs, but I filled our non-perishable cabinet with enough for several days." Such are the advantages of keeping the camper in my backyard.

I rise to start the dishes. Frank loads them on the bar behind the table and I take them to the sink. He goes to my desk and fires up his computer. "Like I said, this trip is going to be the trip from hell."

And when did you say that? To whom? As I start to load the dishwasher, I turn and look into flashing eyes.

"Your attitude's gonna ruin it for me."

I move away from the sink, grip the butcher block in the center of the kitchen, and look at him. "If you set that intention, I'm sure you'll get what you expect." Now, I don't know if I even want to go. I turn back to the task at hand.

"You're the one with the bad attitude." His accusation prods me from behind. My shoulders tense.

Silence. Keeping my mouth shut works.

The chair squeaks as he shifts weight. "See, you just turn your back on me when I talk to you. What do you mean I'm setting an intention? Just stating a fact." I hear the unspoken *Bitch*.

I whip around to face him. "Just what I said. If you expect that we'll have a bad trip, you'll get a bad trip. Personally, I'd like a good trip, so that's what I expect."

He throws up his hands in a gesture that makes soap opera queens look like Zen monks. "Stop your psychobabble with me."

"Why are we arguing?" Do I sound like I'm losing patience?

"You started it with your attitude."

Good work, Frank. I now, have an attitude. "Okay, I'm not sure what I conveyed to you, but I'm sorry. I was thinking about what I have to do to get ready to leave tomorrow."

"You look mad."

"I probably do now. I don't know whether I'm angry or frustrated at the turn of this exchange. I wasn't mad when you started the conversation."

He runs his thumb along the edge of the table. "Sure couldn't tell it by the way you looked."

"Okay, I'll concede that I may have looked irritated. You aren't the first person to misinterpret my concentration for anger."

"Your attitude is going to make this a bad trip."

"Whatever." I turn back to the sink.

Frank mumbles something I can't quite hear. I say nothing. I finish the dishes and go into the bedroom. I want to counteract Frank's bad-trip intention, so I concentrate on the good time we'll have. Not happening. I head for my journal to see if getting my anger out on paper will change my attitude.

Instead, when Yin and Yang follow me into the bedroom, I pick up Yang and whisper, "You'd never expect me to be mean, would you, little boy?" Holding him releases the tension in my neck and shoulders.

"What would happen if I refused to go and refused to let him take my camper?"

Yang wiggles out of my arms and jumps to the edge of the bed. "You think that would be mean?"

If I'm plotting revenge, that's a clue he's retaliating about something. How am I causing his revenge? Am I vengeful about his being married? "You trust me to figure it out, eh?" Yang looks at me as if I'm crazy.

Both Frank and I stress whenever we pack for a trip and have to coordinate our individual belongings into a couple-thing. Is he depressed? Where did that come from?

So much for focusing on the good trip we'll have. How can we have fun when Frank is always finding fault? He'll never act differently if I don't change my attitude.

The gloomy outlook for the extended trip invokes hours of slamming-door silence followed by minutes of vitriolic exchange.

Chapter 12

The next morning, Frank tells me he has to go back to his house to get an unmentioned something. He doesn't say what. Because he returns mid-afternoon, we arrive at his aunt and uncle's just in time for dinner. The three relatives talk, mostly about Frank's wife Blythe and their daughter. Frank's aunt has recently seen Blythe at a reunion and discovered, "Blythe is the same as ever: amusing, good humored, kind, and perfectly delightful."

The more they talk and reminisce, the more I feel like an outsider. Where I was once welcomed, I've become the shamed one. Even though I know it's my perception, I still feel like a *shunned* woman: as if I'm not there. I am not a part of the conversation.

When we go to bed, Frank holds me for part of the night, and says, "You're a good woman." He says nothing else. What does "good woman" mean, anyway? This is the first time I've had an inkling that he's with me out of duty, because I took care of him during his prostate surgery. He sleeps. Silent tears soak my pillow.

Mid-morning we leave his aunt's house. On I-10 heading west, we've driven less than fifty miles when the truck has a flat on an inside tire. Fortunately, we're at an exit. Frank changes the tire and we exit the interstate to find someone to repair the damaged one. While we wait for the tire, we have lunch at a nearby café. He doesn't complain about the disruption. Have to give him credit for retaining his humor. Maybe my intention for the trip will overcome his.

Once we get back on the interstate, Frank yawns. "Will you drive a while so I can take a short nap in back?"

"Sure." I'm much more comfortable driving because, unlike the passenger seat, the driver's seat doesn't pitch me toward the door.

Even though Edmunds.com didn't report the truck as having been in an accident, something heavy must have dropped on the passenger side of the cab, or else the truck rolled. The windshield on the driver's side has an eighth-inch space between the frame and the glass. When he bought the truck a year ago, my job was not to check out the truck, but to go online and verify any reported accidents. That's what happens when you buy a repossession from a family-owned, small town bank.

An hour later, Frank bangs on the back window. I pull over and then continue to drive after he climbs back into the cab. I've driven about fifteen miles in a construction zone when he commands, "Pull over at this exit."

I don't know why, but I have a foreboding. "There's a rest stop just ahead." I can see it from here.

"I said pull over now," he demands. "I'll drive."

I know better than to argue with him. Not when he uses that tone. We change places, and as Frank approaches the rest area in the middle lane, a truck in the right lane zooms ahead and hits a construction cone, sending it flying. WHAP. BAM. We've been hit. Frank pulls over just past the exit to the rest area. He gets out. "Camper corner behind you ripped open. Going to back up on the shoulder and enter the rest area."

Well, damn, Frank. If you'd let me continue to the rest area, we'd have missed the blown cone and we'd have entered going the right direction rather than backing in. I say nothing.

By the time Frank assesses the damage, talks to the attendant, and duct-tapes the corner, it's almost dark. The attendant offers to let us park in the back overnight, but Frank refuses. However, because I'm starved and he's hungry, we eat before going on to the next little town.

"First thing tomorrow, I'm going to find the construction company responsible for the damage and make them pay. That cone should not have been left where it was." He slaps the counter. "They will pay!"

By the time we find a truck stop in which to spend the night, tears rest barely below the surface, and my hands shake. I feel so insecure and inadequate. I'm not allowed to express an opinion or make a suggestion, and I'm nowhere near a town where I can catch a flight to Tallahassee. Frank's irritation causes my muscles to tense. I pick up his mood and no longer try to be pleasant. Time to go to bed before I say something to set him off again.

Frank spends the following morning looking for someone to blame. By one o'clock, he has an address and phone number. We stop for lunch. He decides to wait to report the damage to the camper, since the state now has a record. We only get another hundred miles down the road before we stop for the night.

Well, Frank, how's your intention about this being a lousy trip paying off for you? I am now convinced that we bring to us that which we believe. This is only our third day on the road, and I wonder what else can happen.

Days four and five are mostly pleasant. The string of earlier events seems to have calmed him down. I almost believe he likes crises. Not that they were major crises, but they were disruptions. He hasn't been friendly, but he hasn't complained about me, either.

Late in the afternoon, when we reach the Hueco Mountain Range near El Paso, the burning sun scorches the already burnt grass along the road. The blues and purples of the nearby mountains accentuate the dead color of the grass. We arrive at a pause in the road. Frank's jaw tics. "Let's find a truck stop to park the camper for the night," his voice a low grumble.

I don't respond. That tic lets me know whatever I say will be wrong. We stop at a motel along the main road. As soon as we settle in, we change into running clothes. We run a block to the business section of town and then run on the sidewalk. I'm so tired of sitting, I run with Frank part of the way, ignoring my hurting, bounced-around body. Not good with the truck-re-injured hip. The initial injury is from an old rollerblading accident. I make it a half-mile, and then bend from the waist, my hands resting on my knees. "You go ahead. I'll walk the rest of my three miles. Don't want to slow you down."

Frank has showered and popped a beer when I return. He starts talking about how he must run every day. The more he talks, the more the tension in my neck increases. What's the tension about? I strip and walk into the shower. I realize if I can't run, I don't want him to run, either. Not nice. Am I trying to control him on some subtle level? How do I do that?

I complain: He takes too long to run. Dinner is too late. I go to bed too soon after eating. I just get the camper cleaned up when he comes in tracking dirt all over the floor. My hip hurts. Damn, I'm whiney. Guess he has a point. Even if I say nothing, he gets the message.

As I come to this realization, Frank starts in on me about how I'm too good to stay at a truck stop. From there, he jumps to my controlling him.

I've had it. "Look, I'm with you only because I choose to be, not because I need to be." How can I catch a flight back to Florida? I'm not about to mention the realization that I'm angry about his being able to run while I can't. In his current mood, he'd slap me in the face with it.

He leaves and when he returns a half-hour later, he acts as if nothing took place before he left.

We get a late start the following morning. Frank takes the time to teach me an exercise to help ease my hip pain. His caring and concern erase the previous six days of the trip. He seems to be most considerate when I decide to bail. Then I remember. Todd did that, too. How do I let them know?

We stop for a late breakfast. While Frank seems amenable, I ask about his insistence that I stop the camper and let him drive the evening we were hit by a cone. "Did you sense something was about to happen?" I know he's intuitive like I am.

He nods his head as he takes a bite of his breakfast.

"I wondered about that after it was all over. I had the same feeling when you asked me to stop. Maybe we need to be more explicit in our communication. What do you think?"

"Yeah. Probably." He turns to the paper he'd picked up on another table.

By early afternoon, we arrive in New Mexico, not far from our destination. After a gentle climb around flattened curves, we find the state park indicated on the map. Scrub grass and rocks line the roadway to our campsite. A nearby hiking path meanders through this geode-filled park. We each pick up a rock to take home, a custom allowed and also encouraged. To be able to crack one open without destroying it fills me with anticipation. I won't crack mine today.

Later in the afternoon, we continue the drive to Akela Flats to look for the small fly-in community where Frank wants to live part-time when he retires. I fidget during the drive to the airstrip. There's something about not knowing where I'm going in the desert, even though we're on a paved road. Those Saturday afternoon cowboy movies with desert scenes I saw as a child affect me. All I see is blowing sand with a few cacti interspersed among the sagebrush. No lush green, no trees. For someone from a tropical climate I might as well be on the moon without companionship. There is no cleansing air from the gulf. Instead, the air is filled with stinging sand. I watch a sandstorm from the distance and imagine breathing in grit. I look to Frank for some reassurance. He stares at the road ahead.

We stop at the trading post that is Akela Flats where Frank calls the owners of the fly-in ranch and makes an appointment to meet them tomorrow morning at their house.

Oddly, my muscles relax when the pavement turns to a packed sand taxiway. A roadrunner passes by, and a couple of rabbits look for food a few feet from the runway. The mountains' purples and blues sit on a palette waiting to be highlighted by the late afternoon sun. The quiet beauty of this place strikes me with awe.

Could I learn to like this landscape? Guess we'll find out tomorrow what this ranch offers in the way of property.

The owner insists we stay with his wife and him in the attached apartment. After settling in, we spend the next day looking at two houses and three pieces of acreage. The properties are contingent upon the availability of water. The water on the owner's land is the best I've ever tasted. For the first time since I was a child, I want to drink water.

The owner's house is a large ranch-style with slate floors and warm-toned adobe walls. The entrance opens into the kitchen, one made for entertaining and entertainment. A large flat-screen television hangs on a wall where it can be viewed from the oak dining table.

While Frank and the owner talk about Frank's preferences, the wife shows me around her kitchen. I'm surprised to see she has the latest appliances, most of which are professional. Her pantry is a large walk-in closet filled with chili and enchilada sauces she's made from the chilies she's grown in pots on the walled terrace which is easily seen through the sliding glass doors in the kitchen. Along the terrace wall, cacti standing as tall as four feet fill large pots. In front of them, pots of bright red ripening chilies contrast with the dark green of the cacti. A large basket filled with fresh tomatoes, onions, cucumber, yellow squash, and potatoes sits on an island in the center. We're invited for lunch after we view two houses.

If I were planning to retire here, I'd prefer the house nearest the runway, even though it has a mobile home incorporated into the center. The warm, dark brown stucco and stone give the house a welcoming feeling. There's a large sheltered courtyard in the back. The four bedrooms and three baths would give me space to have both an office and a studio with convenient water. A magnificent stone fireplace separates the living and dining rooms and provides a focal point for both rooms. Even though the house appears to be a little too dark for me—the heavy drapes on the doors and windows remain closed—I'd seriously consider buying it if I were moving here.

The second house is smaller but much lighter inside. The layout doesn't flow as well, and the flimsy construction tells me it's also built around a trailer.

After a lunch of enchiladas, rice, and refried beans served with plenty of wine, Frank looks at property. While he's with the owner, I meet the residents of a beautiful home on the runway next to the landowners. The wife invites me to tea. While their house was being built, they spent a brief time in the house I like. They tell me the magnificent fireplace is home to a large family of rattlesnakes. The owner mentioned neither that small detail nor the fact that no exterminator has been able to remove the snakes. In a moment, welcoming becomes menacing.

Frank's only concern is land to park a motor home that can be disconnected for traveling. "Cheaper taxes." He chooses the cheapest piece of land contingent on the availability of water, a questionable strategy.

With Frank's business out of the way, we plan a trip into Mexico the following day. We have moved back into the camper, now parked in the driveway of the rattlesnake house. We awaken early. While having coffee, I begin breakfast, and Frank finds the radio to check the weather. Instead of weather, we hear a confused announcer. "It appears that an airplane struck one of the towers at the World Trade Center this morning, just moments ago. We don't have any other…Oh, my god! Another plane has just struck the second tower!" For the next hour, we hear more of the same, with some speculation that, "Now the CIA will get more funding," from President George W. Bush. The announcer soon reports that another plane has been hijacked somewhere over Pennsylvania and that the Pentagon, too, has been hit.

I move around in a dense bubble, one that allows me to take in only so much information at a time. Frank sits staring at his hands folded on the table. I pace. My entire body is on alert, my mind numb.

As we listen to the news about tightened security and the fact that all planes are immediately grounded, Frank twists his mouth, "There goes our trip into Mexico. Bet the border's locked down tight."

Since we don't want to sit around, and since we're pilots, curiosity sends us to the airport in Demming. There are few cars near the airport. Indeed, the airport parking lot is empty. As we enter the building, one man sits mesmerized in front of the television set in the lounge area. He doesn't acknowledge our presence. Where are the airport personnel? Have we entered into the middle of *a Twilight Zone* episode where everyone disappears?

Once back on the ranch, we stop at our hosts' house. They are glued to the television in the kitchen. We stay for lunch. Since the airport was so quiet, we plan to attempt to get into Mexico later in the afternoon. What will we find there? Will we be allowed to cross the border? Will we be able to return?

We drive to Demming, the area's Atlanta—all traffic going south or west goes through Demming. We take the highway to Columbus, New Mexico, and then to the border leading into Puerto Palomas, Mexico. The drive is hot and dusty. The good news is that we aren't experiencing a dust storm, a common afternoon occurrence according to roadside signs.

At last, we arrive. Frank parks the camper in the US parking lot. He recommends we take only fifty dollars, passports, and our drivers' licenses into Mexico. We're dressed simply: jeans, tees, and sneakers. When we start across the border, a machine gun attached to an arm waves us through. No one checks.

As we walk into the town of Palomas, nothing is open. No shops. No restaurants. No markets. A ghost town. We seem to have warped into another time where all the inhabitants have been transported elsewhere. Even though I didn't expect everything to be normal, I did expect to see people. After all, we're in another country. My heart races as if it will jump from my chest. Frank's jaw tics.

A white wooden shack, the first building to the right, houses more border patrol personnel. I'm unable to take in any information about the town other than the white shack. We cross the street and look into the windows. They're boarded up. We turn around and start back. From the side of Frank's mouth, "Not exactly my planned first visit into Mexico."

We start back across the border, thinking we have to get into line with the cars. We expect a long wait. Guards check inside and underneath all vehicles. Have we landed in one of those old escape Nazi Germany movies?

Chapter 13

A guard motions us to an enclosed glass walkway. We cross the border without incident.

We exhale.

Deprived of the benefit of radio signals and television, we remain aware, but detached from what has happened. The impenetrable shell of feelings around our relationship keeps me removed from the attack.

Since there is no reason to remain in New Mexico, we set out for Colorado the next day. Frank stops at various places looking for trailers or campers to put on his property. The property he has yet to buy because of the water question. When I ask about the feasibility of buying a camper so far away, he turns red in the face and punches the steering wheel, "Now you're trying to control whether I buy something to put on my property!"

His property? Why would you buy a camper for land that you haven't bought yet, and don't know if the site has water? Seems pragmatic to me, but he calls it control. "One of your blind spots," he assures me.

After words about my blind spots, I seem to be no longer in the seat beside him. He refuses to look at me. He refuses to speak to me.

He stops to buy a snack. He climbs from the truck. He goes into the store. He comes back with his snacks. Not a word to me. No offer to share. He twists the cap on a cold Coke, and the gas escapes with a loud hiss.

I'm thirsty, too, but will he leave without me if I go inside for something? We're in an unpopulated area. I have no chance of calling for a rental car to take me to the airport. I'm trapped in a truck with a crazy man with no foreseeable escape and this, after I vowed I'd never put myself in a situation like this again.

Am I being paranoid? In a similar situation, Todd would have left me. What's about Frank and what's about Todd? Can't seem to separate their behaviors right now. I don't go inside for a drink.

Frank's driving becomes reckless. He speeds up, tailgates, takes curves like he's driving my old Supra, not a dually truck with a camper perched on its bed. There is snow and ice on the road as we come closer to Colorado. My muscles clench for hours. Frank's thumb and forefinger rub together on the steering wheel making a dry sound. It grates on my mood. I want to tell him to stop. Stop it right now. I stare out at the empty landscape and listen to the rub.

We make it to some barren town and stop overnight at a truck stop. He goes running. I open my journal.

September 15, 2001

Why didn't I get a drink and a snack? I was afraid Frank would leave me. Just because alcoholic Todd would have, I have no reason to think Frank would do the same thing. Once the fear takes hold, I'm on the monkey path of stinking thinking. What's my fear of his driving? A familiar heart-racing feeling. When have I felt this before? The time Mother left my brothers and me in the car, parked on a hill. It began to roll backwards toward the edge of a cliff. A man came from nowhere, opened the door, and slammed on the emergency brake before the car gained speed. I thought I had worked through the belief: If you say you love me, you will try to kill me. Hadn't Alex and I worked this out when we were mountain driving in North Carolina? Apparently not, but then I always knew I was safe with Alex. Does my fear increase my hip pain? It's almost constant in the truck.

Is this paranoia? I'm feeling crazy again. My obsessing is a signal that an addict is in the vicinity. So what's Frank's addiction? He must have one.

A dyadic, two-person relationship is the most unstable relationship form. Bicycles are less stable than tricycles or four-wheeled wagons. That's why we use a third person, an illness, or a philosophy on which to focus rather than on our partner or spouse. Right now, I'm focusing on Frank's possible addiction, while he must be focusing on my slights and control. Am I also focusing on his slights towards me? Maybe. I need to ponder this.

I stuff the journal in my backpack as Frank returns from running with a different attitude. What changed? Running? Phone calls?

The next day as we continue toward Colorado, Frank stops often to use the restroom. It seems to happen soon after he checks his cell phone. "You trying to control when I take a leak?" after I mention it. "For god's sake, I had prostate surgery."

Yeah and you've not worn mini pads since before your six-month check-up. "You seem to take a long time, too," I push.

"There was a long line." Yeah, thirty minutes worth. Is he calling someone? Why is it that every time he looks at his phone, we must get off at the next rest stop for him to go to the bathroom? When there is a bathroom in the camper? Which end of him has the diarrhea?

We're on the twelfth day, and my patience has fallen over one of the cliffs along our route. Okay, this time I don't start anything when he says we need to pull in for the night. There's no point in contradicting his opinion that I think I'm too good to stay in a truck stop.

Staying at truck stops might be a good idea since he won't get himself worked up over finding a proper campground before dark. Maybe we can work something out that will benefit us both. I'll have to be careful how I broach the subject.

First, I need to get over my envy of his being able to run while I can't. What I can do about eating late is to eat something now and then eat lightly when he returns. Good idea.

"Why don't we stop at a rest stop a little earlier so you can run?" He usually runs around four or five. "Then we can find a truck stop to spend the night."

Frank's knuckles turn white as he grips the wheel. "What do you mean by that?"

"Just a suggestion." I turn and look out the window.

"I'll stop at a truck stop and then run."

"Fine." What do I care when he runs?

Frank drives until *he* wants to stop. We pull into a truck stop close to the interstate. There are people around. Frank changes and goes running. I eat half a sandwich. When Frank returns an hour later, I'm fine.

"Hi, Hon. I'm back," as he opens the door. "Think I'll have a beer to cool down and then we can eat." He pries one shoe off with the other. "That okay with you?"

Running is certainly good for his attitude, or did he have a phone conversation? "Sure, I had a snack." I hand him a beer. "How does chili and a salad sound to you?" I can make a big salad and use chili as dressing for mine. This gives him more chili. Has my change of attitude affected his or has running done it? Or? Whatever the cause, the change is good.

Later, after I do the dishes, I sit on the hard ledge below the bed rather than at the table. I pluck my current book from my backpack.

Frank puts down the magazine he's reading. "Why are you sitting over there?"

"The way the seat has been overused, it's uncomfortable on my back." The person who sat there must have been obese. "The cushion is squashed, so I thought I'd try this for a while. There isn't enough room to stretch out on the long bench behind the table. There's too much stuff on it, and it's easier to sit here than move my stuff."

"Hell of a long answer for a simple question." He pauses with his beer halfway to his lips. "What's wrong with you now?"

"What do you mean?"

"You sound pissed off."

"Might sound that way, but I'm not." Well, damn. That must have sounded like the whiney girl from nowhere. My stomach knots and the muscles in my neck tighten. I've had enough of this eggshell-walk-relationship. Damn, I can't even carry on a neutral conversation with this person without being accused of something. I go back to reading my book.

"Can't stand your attitude. Going out for a while." He stomps out, slamming the door behind him.

This is getting old. What did I do now? Has he gone to call a woman? Wouldn't surprise me. At this point, nothing would. Whatever keeps him quiet. Time to journal:

September 15 cont'd

Another upset this evening. What did I do this time? Did he take my explanation as a complaint? Perhaps I should have said, "I thought I'd try this for a while," and left it at that. Remember: Don't complain. Don't explain. Oh well, think I'll just get ready for bed and hope I'm asleep before he gets back. We can't get home soon enough for me; and we've just begun the trip back.

Thirty minutes later, I finish my shower as Frank returns. "The stars are beautiful out tonight."

Smile. "I know. I noticed them when I opened the top over the bed. In fact, I was headed there to star gaze."

"Would you make us a Coke float while I shower?"

Hey, there is an elephant in this camper. Do you not see it? The tension is overwhelming. How can you ignore it?

I think grocery list to keep my voice level. "Sure." Assured I'd kept a neutral countenance and tone. Good.

Nothing more is said as we resume our journey home. Frank continues to check his phone for the time, and then to find the nearest rest stop. I say nothing.

We're somewhere in Tennessee when the sky begins to darken. Frank touches my arm. "Hey, what would you think about stopping in north Georgia to see where I was conceived and then head to the cabin before we go home?" His tone is friendlier than it's been for days.

Could be fun. He'd told me about how his parents had lived in a tent during the time his father developed the land. His dad had sent his mother to Atlanta to have him because they were so far from medical services.

"Sounds good to me."

"We can visit the Clayton's. Their property is near there."

They are people we know from Tallahassee through one of Frank's entrepreneurial schemes. "Great."

This is my lesson in being flexible. Since we left the ranch, we seem to have no real itinerary but go from place to place at Frank's will. There is no way I'm going to confront him when I have no other transportation. At least I'm getting closer to civilization, even if he does take us through the worst parts of cities and towns.

Frank had planned on visiting a friend in Memphis, but for some reason he seems to have cancelled it. However, we spend the night in a campground between Memphis and Knoxville. The next morning Frank makes plans to drive to Blue Ridge, Georgia, spend the night, and spend the first part of the following day at the courthouse. He calls the couple and tells them we'll stop by day after tomorrow sometime in the late afternoon.

We drive to Murphy, North Carolina and spend the night. Murphy is no longer the combination gas station-convenience store it was when I was in college near there. I point to the building. "That store sold the cheapest cigarettes in the state."

Frank slows. "It still advertises the cheapest cigarettes."

Early the following morning, we're at the courthouse in Blue Ridge looking at deeds. Frank takes a last slug of iced tea and wipes his mouth. "I'd like to find Dad's property before we go see the Claytons."

"Fine with me. Are they expecting us at any particular time?"

He shakes his head.

As I climb into the truck, I slip over to the middle. While we drive toward the property, Frank gives me two maps: a county map and one he's copied from public records.

I drape a map over my knees and run a finger along a pale blue line. "It looks like the Anderson's house is close to where we're heading now."

"The old Islip property is the next road down from the one we turn on to go to the Anderson's." He stabs a spot on the map.

I'm almost certain that both properties are down the first turn-off. I say nothing, and second- guess myself. I'm directionally dyslexic. However, with a map, I have no problem.

We take the second turnoff, more like a dirt path than a road. Within fifty feet, the road narrows and becomes more rock than dirt. We can still back out. As we move ahead the length of the attached camper, a rocky cliff appears on the driver's side. My neck muscles tighten. The passenger window overlooks a drop-off that has no bottom from where I sit. Because the camper is on the back of the truck, Frank can no longer see to back out. I don't have room to get out and direct him.

Frank must stay as close to the cliff as possible without hitting the rocky edges. The additional width of the camper allows little room for error. The rocks in the road hit the underside of the truck and skitter over the edge of the drop-off. I go into tendon guard reflex, paralysis. I barely breathe. I look straight ahead. Fear fills the truck with mephitic, fetid air. I say nothing.

"Stop it! Stop being afraid!" His jaw tics.

As if I can regulate my fear. I don't respond. I look down at my hands and am surprised to see my fists clenched. I force them open. I won't let Frank know I'm terrified. Not now.

I look over the precipice at the brilliant sunlight on the trees in the distance. As I turn back to Frank, I see where the cliff has blotted-out the sun, creating a malevolent shadow hovering over our impending death.

When I glance out of the corner of my eye at Frank, his knuckles are white from gripping the wheel. I breathe in to the count of four, hold for four, and release counting backwards from eight. I try to think of other things. Hard to do while I'm envisioning my rapidly approaching demise as we roll over and crash down the mountainside into only the gods know what.

I hate living on the edge, fearing for my life. Frank's knuckles exacerbate my fear. The tense silence between us increases my awareness that much of our time together on this trip has been more disagreeable than agreeable, beginning with the second day on the road. An unfriendly branch bangs on the truck roof and then the camper, like the cone—days earlier. I jump, restrained by the seatbelt. Thank the gods, Frank doesn't seem to notice.

As we slowly make our way up and around, then down and around the edge of the mountain a red pick-up heads toward us. I dig my nails into my sweaty palms. Now what are we going to do?

Chapter 14

My full attention is on the road. We stop. The red truck backs down the mountain until it comes to a small turnout. Frank creeps down the mountain toward the truck. I roll down the window. Frank stops and leans over me. "Is there any place to turn around on this road?"

"Go on down the road a ways. You'll come to the end where you'll see double-iron gates. Thar's a narrow strip of land wide enough for you to turn around. Back toward the rocky cliff, so you'll face the drop-off. Then you can head back out. About five more miles."

I let out my breath. We again begin to wiggle down the curvy, rocky path. We've driven all the way in first gear. At least I know there is a way out of here. That is, if Frank doesn't kill us both. I begin to question why I'm here. I didn't trust my instincts. I knew not to take this rocky path. We should've taken the first turn-off. Why do I sublimate my instincts to a man? Because I've been taught that men know better than women. Good job, Mom. Old teachings die hard.

Frank has the same belief, or at least he acts as if he does. My dyslexia is about turning right or left on instinct, not about taking two rights or reading a map.

Here I am, in the same place I was before I began this path of self-discovery. All the changes I've made over the years pushed aside so I can have a healthy relationship with Frank.

Okay, forget healthy.

Maybe forget relationship since all the strange cellphone behaviors.

Forty-five minutes later, we're at the bottom and turning around. Frank's hands relax on the steering wheel. The twitch in his jaw disappears. The ride back seems easier. I don't have to look at the drop-off. Frank can see how far he is from the edge. An hour and fifteen minutes later, we're back on the main highway.

Frank lets out a sigh, "We made it." Relief? I smile and say nothing. We turn left on the highway and drive to the next left. Frank doesn't mention further searches for the property.

I remain silent, contemplating my current situation and where I want to go from here. I know this area. If I can hang on long enough for us to get to Franklin, North Carolina, I'll find a way to Asheville and the airport.

This road is wider but slippery, muddy. Even though it isn't paved, the road is smoother, no rocks. There are a few scary places, but we make it to the Anderson's in about twenty minutes.

As we look at the view from their deck, Frank points, "I was conceived here. Where we're standing. See how the lake curves in right there?" He tells me that as a child, he'd been shown pictures of the lake "from this very spot."

Our worlds readjust. Frank's sudden relaxed, easy manner tells me he's content. I am not. I see the last few hours as a metaphor for our relationship.

After a short, but pleasant, visit we leave. We take Highway 64 out of Murphy, a road I've driven so many times I know it by heart. Once with Todd and my mother to spend Thanksgiving with my youngest brother and his family in a nearby town. That trip was not a pleasant one, as Todd spent more time looking around than at the road.

Later, when I attended Western Carolina University in Cullowhee, on Alex's last trip through the Nantahala Gorge, he was at the wheel on the twisty, winding road, while I threw up in a garbage bag, courtesy of my sister-in-law—the garbage bag, not the illness. Every turn caused my stomach to heave. By the end of the drive, my stomach was empty, but I kept right on heaving. Later, after Alex died, I made the trip, sometimes with a heavy heart and sometimes with the joy of driving this road, windows down, sunroof open, singing along with my favorite CD, *The Soundtrack from Twin Peaks* by Julee Cruse.

When I worked on the psychiatric unit in Franklin after Alex died, I drove to Murphy once a week to see sexually abused clients, some of whom had been my patients. As Frank takes a turnoff to drive through the mountains into Franklin, I remember another hairy evening coming over this mountain, when the melting snow was refreezing, leaving patches of black ice.

That drive was a white knuckle one like the one today, just not as scary because even though I couldn't see the black ice, I could shift gears to slow down and not slide.

We drive on into the night, stopping only in Franklin for fast food. I mention I would like to see some friends in the area while we're here. Friends who knew Alex and were my support group once he died. For some reason, I feel the need to connect with them right now.

Frank doesn't respond.

I'm disappointed in his lack of interest, and I'm not certain I want my friends to meet this man. Perhaps he'd let me take his truck into Cullowhee. Alone. Won't mention this while he's at the wheel. The result could be scary.

We reach his cabin in the early hours of the morning. When we turn onto the road that intersects with the cabin road, Frank points to a house. "The woman who lived there was a friend of my parents. She was an author who wrote romance novels. Every couple of years, she would leave her husband for several months and go off to find romance and write about it."

"This is the third time you've mentioned this. What exactly are you saying?" I suspect he wants me to do the same. "Are you telling me to go off for months at a time, or that you want me to have romantic flings?" He knows I have no intention of writing novels. I'm a therapist, for God's sake.

"That's your perception."

No point in pressing the point. I'd like to get a good night's sleep. Besides cell coverage is too iffy out here, and I'd have no way to get to the airport.

When we arrive at the cabin, I unload what we'll need for the night while Frank turns on water and gas.

I don't get to see my friends, but in between making repairs on the cabin, Frank takes me hiking and otherwise roaming the mountains. On our way back to the cabin from a hardware store run, Frank pulls onto a golfing community road and then makes a turn towards someone's house. "Have something to show you."

The farther up the road we go, the more my tension mounts. I have visions of being arrested for trespassing. Frank seems to have no problem as he presses on towards the house. He stops a few feet from the side of the house and opens the truck door.

A powerful roar greets me. When I climb out, Frank takes my hand and leads me behind the house.

I stop. I'm so close to a huge waterfall that it sprays me. I try to imagine what it would be like to live with a waterfall spraying within a few feet of my screened porch.

I lean into Frank. "Standing here in front of all this power, I can easily see how the Tennessee Valley Authority works."

He squeezes my waist. "Thought you'd like this. When we were kids, we had a path through the woods. We'd come here every day. That was before there was a road and the land was developed."

Ah, maybe he doesn't feel like he's trespassing. Squatters' rights? Experiencing the waterfall makes me forget the hellish part of our trip.

We have no more flare-ups, no more stony silences. Still, as we pull into my drive, I can't wait to get out of that truck and be alone. I'm pretty sure Frank will head home as soon as we unpack.

When we walk inside, the cats are gone. They don't greet us as we move my things into the apartment and Frank's into the truck cabin, nor when Frank takes the camper off the truck. Even though I keep calling them, I'm not particularly worried. They can come in the cat door, but mostly they're letting me know they don't like my being gone so long. Frank seems concerned. "Hey, Hon. Let's go out to eat tonight. You must be too tired to cook and I know you're worried about Yin and Yang."

After dinner, he stays the night. As I set up the coffeemaker for auto start, I see a note from George, mostly hidden under the dry cat food. "Can't find cats. Think they got out when I left yesterday." It's dated today.

Following breakfast in the morning, with his hands in his pockets, "I'm gonna ease on outta here. I'll call you," as he walks out the door. "Need to go through all my mail and do laundry."

Relieved, I call George. While his phone rings, the cat door bangs, once, and then twice. When his phone goes to voice mail, I leave a message: "The cats are home." I wasn't nearly as concerned this time as I was months ago when Frank made me leave them at the beach. After all, they know where home is.

Wait a minute. He wasn't concerned then. Today he is. He's never asked about their return. Did he know they were snuggled in the pillowcase? Nah. Way too cruel. Not as cruel as leaving them outside to fend for themselves in a hostile environment.

Chapter 15

I return to work on my dissertation. Megan's suggestions improve the entire piece. I'm in the process of double-checking every citation, which leaves little time for Frank. We've been back less than a week when Frank goes to visit his daughter. George and I continue our work together, either at his office, the townhouse, or the lake.

Two weeks later, Frank returns. He arrives wearing a new Marine tee shirt and khakis. This is something new. He grabs me and pulls me tight against him. "Missed you," his voice low, his tone seductive. "Dinner smells good. How about we eat and then take a trip to the bedroom?" We are having our coffee after dinner when he gets a call. "It's Blythe. I need to pick her up from the airport." He gulps his last swallow of coffee, grabs his keys, and leaves. "See you soon."

Soon is three hours later. When we get in bed, he pulls me to him. "Thank you for putting up with me." He kisses my neck and begins to move down when his phone buzzes. He checks the number and ignores it. Instead of continuing what he'd started, he builds a barrier with his pillow and moans into it. I turn over and ignore him.

The following day, George and I sit in the small international restaurant, near the lake, that serves Persian food. "I think I've finally resigned myself to the fact that I must ride the rapids of feeling instead of using work or school to avoid an emotional freak out."

George laughs. "You? An emotional freak out? Really?" He puts his elbows on the table and rests his chin in his hands. "Tell me more. This should be good."

"Frank came back last night. Everything was going fine…"

"How long was he gone?"

"Two weeks. Why?"

"When you two have an argument, or rather Frank has an argument with you, and he storms out, how long is he usually gone?"

"Two weeks."

At that moment, the owner brings our food, and cocks his head towards George, "You must be a new acquaintance, because this person has no friends. You know, you are going to ruin your reputation if you keep hanging around her."

I give him my evil eye. "You'd better be nice to me or I'll tell everyone you poison the food with vitriol."

He turns to the two couples sitting at nearby tables, and shrugs, "We try not to serve her, but sometimes she sneaks in under the radar. What can I do?" A raised finger at a nearby table catches his attention and off he goes.

I laugh, and then turn back to George. "Where was I?"

"You'd told me Frank was gone two weeks."

"I'd realized that he's always gone two weeks when it's a sudden thing."

He gives me a high-five. "Then what happened?"

"As we're finishing dinner, his wife calls. He says she asked him to pick her up from the airport." Could he have lied? "Three hours to pick up someone who was waiting outside and deliver her to her house? At that hour, probably fifteen minutes to the airport, maybe fifteen to her house. Drop her off and back to my place another twenty. At the very most an hour and fifteen minutes."

I take a bite of rice and feta. "I'm a little annoyed at first but then let it go. However, before we go to sleep, he gets another call. After he checks the number, instead of snuggling like we usually do, he builds a barrier with his pillow and then proceeds to moan into it like he's making love to the pillow." This feels way too familiar. "That was when I started to catch on to his timing."

George scratches his head, "What did you do about it?"

"What could I do? If I made a big deal of it, which I think he wanted, he would have either gone to sleep on the sofa or left. Either way," He'd have won. "I'd have been even more upset."

George pushes his lentils onto his fork with a piece of pita.

My temples tighten as I talk about Frank. I'm not so caught up in the story that I don't notice the look of surprise on George's face. "Anyway, that's over." For now. "He brought me coffee in bed the next morning. Perhaps a conciliatory gesture." Sounds lame, even to me.

"He's getting bolder, isn't he?" He takes a bite.

Good point, George. "You know, I've come to the conclusion that Frank is going to do what Frank is going to do. At this point, I think looking into my past relationships is a better use of my time. They may give me insight into why I put up with him." He must have more lessons to teach me. Otherwise, I'd have kicked him to the curb long ago.

"How're you going to do that?"

"I'll start with journaling about them," I wrap a strand of hair around my finger and pull it tight. "I've gone back to look at some of my old journals, journals that began while I was married to Todd, continued through Alex, and on into grad school and Frank."

"You've kept your old journals? I'd have to burn mine."

"You've already seen the ones with self-discovery exercises and rants. Many are more insightful than I imagined at the time." A crow caws three times. Should I pay attention to what I'm saying? How did I hear the crow inside with all the conversation around me? Aah, perhaps a message.

George, who doesn't seem to have heard a thing, takes a slug of water. "Where are you going to start, and how will you organize it?"

"I'll start with Alex, the most recent marriage. And the most soulful."

"Soulful? Is that what made the marriage so good?" George drops a forkful of food on the table. "I'm trying to figure out what I'm missing here."

I hand him a couple of napkins. "Alex brought out the best in me, and maybe I brought out the best in him," Keys clank to the floor from the next table. "While journaling, I rediscovered I was self-centered and focused on my student life. Something I'm doing now. When I wasn't my best, it wasn't because of Alex."

"Your marriage sounds so different from my idea of marriage as drudgery. I'm not sure how you managed that."

"Is that why you've never married?" I stab a tomato. "Because marriage is a drudgery?" As I talk with my hand, I sling the tomato onto the table.

He nods.

"Could I have one of those napkins, please?"

"You stayed with him during his cancer unlike any woman I've ever known." He reaches across and picks up the tomato with a napkin, and sets it by his plate. "How did you handle his cancer?"

"Until we went to Emory a week after the cancer was diagnosed at our local hospital, I held out for a misdiagnosis," something I later learned is not uncommon. "At Emory, after two days of testing and retesting, Alex was diagnosed with squamous cell cancer of the larynx. I was in the second semester of my master's program."

"Damn," George stretched out the word into two syllables.

"When the surgeon ran the laryngoscope speculum with a light down Alex's throat, he called me over for a look. There it was. A tumor of the most beautiful shade of rose, coloring a smooth, shiny nodule on Alex's larynx." How could something so beautiful be so treacherous?

"And, you stayed in school?" His voice faltered.

"Alex continued work and I continued school." I can't seem to keep my hand away from my mouth. "Looking back, it was the only way we could maintain some semblance of normalcy. You might question that when I tell you what I put together after he died."

George props one elbow on the table and leans forward, "Tell."

"Four odd things happened around his cancer. The first happened before we were married. I regularly talked to a woman who called to ask if she was crazy. She received messages from a spirit guide. Even though she was terrified that she was crazy, the advice she received was always helpful to me. One day she called to tell me that her guide had passed on a message from my guide." I take a deep breath and a slug of water. "She was to tell me I'd learn something about Alex that would devastate me. And, to let me know I'd make it through this and come out on the other side." This helped me so readily accept the message from the burning sweater.

"Because the woman I worked with had sexual abuse issues, the worst thing I could think of was that I would find out Alex was a child molester. I even asked him about it. He told me he didn't think so."

I stare at George's drink can, sitting in a puddle of condensation. "I realized why the guide had her tell me rather than communicating directly. I would have hounded my guide to tell me what I was about to face."

Besides, it was okay for her to talk to spirits, but not me. Did communing with spirits make me crazy or was I not ready to go there, yet? I shift in my seat.

"You have a guide that talked to you through her? Not that I'm surprised."

"I think I wasn't open to getting information directly from my guide. When he talked through her, he had a dry wit. I liked his touch of sarcasm. He'd even allowed me to argue with him that day." Still, I appreciate his sense of humor.

"You've always been open to those messages outside the physical realm."

I'd forgotten that. "The second occurrence happened the day following our wedding. I have an antique clock that requires daily winding. After Alex wound it the day after we were married, it forever stopped at eleven fifteen, Alex's time of death a little over four years later."

George's smile encourages me to continue.

"The third event occurred a short time after his wisdom tooth extraction."

"What extraction?"

"We'd been in North Carolina only a couple of months when Alex developed a persistent toothache. He found a dentist who pulled his wisdom teeth without curing the infection first. We later thought the extraction activated the cancer cells."

George winces and then squirms on the bench as I continue.

I wipe my sweaty palms on my pants. "And here comes number four. Alex was determined to learn to watercolor, so I'd begun to teach him. When he called me to look at two paintings he'd done, I told him his paintings were horrible; they were the ugliest paintings I'd ever seen, and I never wanted him to pick up a watercolor brush in my presence again."

My shoulders tighten. "Alex didn't react. He stopped painting. I left the room. We never discussed what happened." Normally, we would have talked about it. "I think he understood on some subtle level." Neither of us wanted to face our fear.

George touches my shoulder.

"After his death, I began to understand that his death was the devastating information predicted by the spirit guide. The week after he died, I found the watercolors tucked away in a drawer. One was a cancer cell. The other showed the path the cancer took in his body. Both were beautiful and neither of us saw the information hidden within the paintings." Had he been afraid to see, too?

"I thought he might have been leery of my behavior. If I look at my behavior objectively, I was irrational in the moment. I sounded like a crazy woman."

George grins. "I can see why he might feel that way." Thank you, George, for lightening up my confession. Otherwise, this would be too painful.

"My daughter Claire now has both paintings. I kept them in my office for several years as a reminder that the clients or patients always know what's wrong with them on some level. My job is to tap into—"

George interrupts, "What a gift that must be for you. Keeps you from needing to control the therapy."

As my cheeks crinkle into a smile, my shoulders drop. "Yes it is, and for my clients, too." I take a bite of rice.

"Three years after the painting session, we were at the Asheville Mall eating lunch at our favorite restaurant. Alex bit down on something hard that brought tears to his eyes. He began to shake. With my psychology background, I could see he was losing control. I told him that if he didn't pull himself together, I'd have him committed. That worked. We got out of there and hightailed it back to Cullowhee."

George's eyebrows rise, but he says nothing.

How was that for compassionate therapist? Not! How could I have been so hateful, with never a thought of behaving badly? My motives may have been good, but the message was far from acceptable. How could Alex continue to love me to the end? What if the situation had been reversed? Would I have been so forgiving?

"Alex made a doctor's appointment the next day." I break off a bit of pita. "This was during Christmas break, either the end of December or the beginning of January. The first diagnosis was TMJ, Temporomandibular Joint Disorder. The protocol called for relaxation exercises and eliminating caffeine." I take a drink of water, and then a deep breath. I must get through this.

"In late February, Alex had another episode which sent him back to the doctor. This time Blackshear made the connection between the current symptoms and the fact that the socket from Alex's wisdom tooth hadn't healed. He scheduled a biopsy to take place in the middle of March. You already know the diagnosis story."

Tears begin to collect behind my eyelids. "I remember thinking: This can't be happening. I don't do cancer. I do heart conditions. I do alcoholism. All my previous fears from birth onward seemed to flood my mind in that one moment. Every nerve and synapse fired at once, as if I might explode from so much fearful energy. I wanted everything to return to normal. Cancer becomes the new norm."

I stand and stretch my arms skyward and then behind my back. George gathers our utensils and dumps them in the trash. Once at the counter, I spot Greek feta in the case. I point to the cheese. "I'll have a pound of that, please."

"I can't sell you that." The owner's eyes sparkle with laughter. "I only sell to nice people." I silently thank him for breaking through my darkness.

"Okay, sell it to George."

He reaches for the plastic bag, "Can't sell it to friends of not-nice people," and cuts a pound. He then covers the cheese in brine before sealing the bag.

I pay for my lunch and cheese. "Let's walk some more. I need to shake off reliving the worst period in my life." It feels like I've been placed face-down under a rock. Smothering in my own emotions, I can barely breathe.

As we walk out the door, "And don't hurry back."

I turn around, hike and lower my eyebrows. In a singsong voice, "Oh, I'll be back. You can count on it, sooner rather than later. Have a miserable day." I flip my wrist as if to say, ta da.

Before we get into our cars, George takes my hand. "You know you have to write about this, don't you? Relive it."

I follow George to the church parking lot for our walk around the lake. For some reason, I hadn't been here since the trip. I'd opted to walk in my neighborhood.

George points to some debris stuck partway up a tree trunk. "The lake flooded while you were gone. Got some of the businesses in the cottages closest to the lake."

We walk and talk a couple of times around. On our third circle, George points to a shadow figure standing by a tree up ahead. "A stalker, if ever I saw one."

I look over. "I know that woman. She's the one who tore up the beach house. She was stalking the owner." Wonder whom Joy's stalking now.

"I've noticed her several times when we've walked around here. Be careful."

"She can't be stalking me. I'm the wrong gender."

"Just saying," his tone serious. "Better get to my class. Talk with you later."

On the way home, I buy two pints of Ben and Jerry's Phish Food. I finish one pint before dinner. When Frank calls to touch base, I tell him about my walk with George.

"I'm sorry, Hon. Would you like some company?"

Before I have time to think about it, "Actually, I would." I put the phone on speaker, slip off my blouse, and into a periwinkle tee. Turning off the speaker, I put the receiver to my ear. "I could sure use one of your hugs right now. Thanks."

"I'll be over in an hour. Can't stay long because I'm meeting the guys for a beer."

"That's perfect. I'm sure I won't be good company anyway. See you then. Love you." Another reason why I love this man. He seems to know when I'm in need of his support, and he comes through.

Several days pass before I pick up the ruby pen and red silk journal. I know I must re-experience this. To do this, I will use present tense. I stall. I get coffee. I turn on the light from the green lamp over the desk before I begin to write. Yang comes in and puts his paw on my hand. "You know I don't want to do this, don't you, little fellow?" As I stroke his fur, I'm grateful for the respite. When I write the date, I realize I haven't heard from Frank all weekend. It's Monday already. Where has the time gone? Oh, I'd spent the weekend checking references against the bibliography without a thought for what day it was.

I know I'm supposed to re-experience this, but I cheat and copy from an old journal.

> January 31, 1990
>
> I sort through the information from the American Cancer Society and find that his cancer is deadly and that his stage is the final one before death. My heart and my head are no longer in sync. I can't wrap my

mind around the fact that I may lose this man who has become my whole life. How am I going to live without him? Even now, ten years later, I have tears in my eyes while writing.

Alex begins chemotherapy in April. We drive to Atlanta on Sunday mornings and stop at our favorite Sunday-brunch restaurant before checking into Emory. He decides he will be too sick for me to stay in town with him. I return to Cullowhee to an independent-study class and to begin the prospectus for my master's thesis. I'll drive back to Atlanta on Saturday, pick up Alex, and return home. We made the decision that he'd call me when he felt like talking. He calls once, doesn't talk long. He's too sick.

My journaling is interrupted by a call from a classmate. Thank you, whoever you are. I need a break. When I answer, "Can you help with my stats?" says the voice on the line.

Are you kidding me? Surely you jest? "Apparently, you haven't heard about my battle with stats. Stats won." I sat through statistics twice before I passed. "You might try John. He's really good at it." After we chat a few minutes because I extend the conversation, I hang up and do yoga stretches before I return to my journal. I hear George reminding me to stay in present tense. "You've got to relive it and feel it."

Okay, I'll rewrite this in today.

March 25, 2002

The first treatment period leaves Alex sick. Within moments of settling into my Supra, his eyes glaze over. I can tell that all he wants is to sleep. If he can. We stop in Gainesville, Georgia, to pick up anti-nausea medication. He climbs into bed the minute we get home and stays there for almost a week.

No sooner is Alex settled in bed than our minister calls. He's coming over to bring a loaf of cinnamon bread that his wife baked this morning.

I tell him Alex is too sick to see anyone and the smell of food makes him nauseous.

He ignores me and shows up with a loaf of frozen cinnamon bread. Alex has never been able to tolerate cinnamon. I stopped using it when he was home because it bothered him so.

I refuse to let him in the house as Alex is sleeping. I physically block him from pushing his way in. I put the bread in the freezer, so Alex won't smell it.

By the end of his first week home, he is able to get out of bed but doesn't go back to work until the fourth week. He returns to Emory the next week.

The second round is worse than the first. Alex's follow-up blood count is so low that the docs decide he can't take another round. He's given six weeks to recuperate before he starts radiation therapy in July.

Sometime that month while Alex and I sit in the living room, I notice he's gotten a haircut. When I mention it, he looks at me in his you-must-be-kidding way. "Look again. I have no hair." I wonder about my ability to accept such changes without notice. Had I become Thomas Hardy's *Dead Man Walking*?

By June, Alex feels well enough for us to leave for New York and Claire's college graduation. We make a fun trip of it. We stop in Hershey, Pennsylvania, and stay in the Hershey resort. Alex feels well enough to eat which lets us take advantage of the excellent food and all the chocolate. Mother had talked about the wonderful food at the hotel after she and my dad visited there when I was a child. Her influence must have rubbed off on me as I remember the food when I take a trip.

Memories saw through me like a dull knife. Can't continue. Must stop and clear my head. I put down the pen, check the temperature, and walk out the door. Once I reach the lake, I close off so I'm unapproachable. I want to focus on nature, place myself in another realm. I've had too much realism for one day.

Ahh, the eight geese born at the lake last year have returned. Haven't seen the big guys for a while. How long will they stay this year? The gray heron has also returned. The turtles sun themselves, some on the grass, some on the turtle condo in the middle of the lake. Their delight in the sun as they stretch their heads out toward the golden circle in the sky mirrors the cats soaking up rays by the French doors.

As I continue to walk, I run into a former client, a young woman who was so depressed she was unable to hold down the most menial job. Gone are the sloppy sweats and grungy tennis shoes. She is neatly dressed in warm gray slacks and a red sweater. She walks towards me with a smile that lights up her face. "Hi, Lee."

"Well, hello there." I'm careful about using clients' names in public. "How are you?"

"Doing great. I'm going to school. I have my own apartment, and I even have a boyfriend now."

"You are doing well. That's terrific. I'm so glad." She doesn't even look like the same person I saw three years ago.

"My last therapy session, where I confronted my issues with my brother, changed my life. Thank you." At last, I'm validated for doing mind/body therapy, which caused a stir in my practicum. My supervisor that night, "I don't like what you did with this client, but I have to say it worked." It saved the client and me six months of talk therapy, which may or may not have been effective.

"You're welcome, but you did the work. It took a lot of courage to do what you did. I simply facilitated your process."

"Well, gotta go. Meeting my boyfriend at the coffee shop." The soles of her shoes flash as she jogs off in the direction of Starbucks. She's still unable to own her positive assets. Will that come to her at some point? I need to remember it took me a long time to own mine.

Thoughts of my sessions with this client bring back my struggles to fit into the expected mold of the marriage and family program. Like much of my life so far, I swim upstream. Am I willing to live with the professional consequences of providing therapy that works for each client but doesn't fall into the traditional method espoused in my program?

I finish my walk. When I get to the car, Frank has called. He is supposed to be working today. I return his call. "I'm heading to the coast in about an hour to see about a trailer for the truck. Want to go?"

"I'd love to, but I have too much work to do today. Maybe next time." As I drive home, my energy levels increase with the awareness of a renewed sense of purpose. I do make a difference in peoples' lives.

After showering, I return to journaling. I'd rather go to the coast than journal, but it needs to be done.

>March 26, 2002
>
>Alex is scheduled to start radiation the middle of July. It's to be six weeks, five days a week. I stay with him alternate weeks at the motel used by Emory. The weeks I stay in Cullowhee, I work on my thesis. During this time, I defend my prospectus and start my thesis with the literature review and the vignettes I'll use. The weeks I'm in Atlanta, we play early in the day. Alex's treatment is always scheduled for late afternoon so he won't have an entire day of nausea. Instead, it comes at night when he can sleep through it. Evenings, I work on the vignettes while he watches television or reads.
>
>I come to look upon our times in Atlanta as some of the best in our marriage, because, until then, we'd never had a chance just to be together for long stretches during the day. We do our Hotlanta walks early in the morning and then explore the city. When I mention this to the radiologist on our last day, he turns red in the face. "How dare you? You have no idea how difficult this is for him." Alex hasn't complained, so how would I know?

I feel so slimy that I have to take another shower. If only I could scrub away the memories of those final months. After my shower, I lie down for a few minutes to clear my mind. The energy I put out must signal my need for solace because Yang hops up on the bed and over to my stomach. Yin follows suit and butts my elbow. "Are you here to offer comfort, too, Little Girl?" I swear she rolls her eyes.

I now have one on each side of me, purring. The sound of their purrs and the softness of their fur against my arms settle me. After a few minutes, I get up and make some coffee. I am determined to finish this journaling today.

I take my coffee out on the deck. Banana leaves sway in the breeze. Behind them, a squirrel climbs out on a pine branch and rolls on its back where the branch meets the trunk. Within seconds, its little paws make dream jerks. My world shifts from one full of pain to one full of blue skies, soft breezes, and trusting animals. I breathe in this new energy.

The dog next door begins its afternoon barking that turns into yelps. I get up and find the dog whistle that doesn't work very well. After an hour of frustrating myself trying to get the dog to stop, I remember that I can sit quietly and see the dog calm down—a technique I learned from a spiritual book.

When I return to the chair, the cats have disappeared. I no longer need their comfort.

Two days pass before I pick up the journal again.

March 28, 2002

After Alex finishes radiation, we begin to travel to Atlanta once a month for checkups. Alex is pronounced in remission. During his second checkup in October, the treatment team wants to do exploratory surgery. They're looking for the source site of his cancer. My gut, in its knotted up, twisted way, lets me know this is not a good thing. Somehow, I know this may cause the cancer to return and run rampant. I express concern to Alex and then tell him that I'm sure he knows what's best for him. The decision is his to make, not mine. The surgery goes well. He's sent home the next day. The doctors release him from care for six months.

Regardless of his status, Alex still has his shunt inserted for his chemotherapy, which must be cleaned once a month, so Dr. Blackshear keeps check on him. I never question the shunt. The doctors are expecting to use it again. I don't understand the why of the shunt.

Life gets back to normal. We're beginning to relax. I've finished the fall semester of my second year. As Christmas comes, we continue our daily three-mile walks on the WCU campus track. One morning, as we walk and talk, Alex brings up the fact that something doesn't feel right, an intuitive something. "Me, too. I've been asking myself why, when on the surface everything appears to be perfect, I have this feeling that something is terribly wrong."

Must take a break. I get up and move around. I stare out the French doors. The pale blue sky is filmy with thin white clouds. When I look over at the table outside the screened portion of the deck, a small black snake suns itself. I can count on nature to restore my energy and calm my spirit.

I don't journal for another three days.

March 31, 2002

By the end of February, we're told the cancer has metastasized to his lungs, bones, and entire body. He has no more than six months to live unless he undergoes a bone marrow transplant, a very painful procedure. There is no guarantee the transplant will extend his life. Alex opts out of the transplant. I can't blame him. I'd rather lose him earlier than make his final days so miserable.

As soon as we return to Cullowhee, we set up the hospice protocol. I'm to attend weekly family treatment team meetings. Because I'm doing my internship and seeing clients, I'm not always available to attend. I'm aware that I'm speeding through this period, particularly the day Alex receives his death sentence. I call it the death-sentence-day, for years afterward. I make myself go back to that day. Neither of us reacted openly while we were at Emory. We stayed overnight at our regular motel. I watch the ink run on the paper as the tears drip. We spent the night; our arms wrapped around each other and vacillated between sobs and whimpers.

Following his prognosis, I think he might benefit from psychotherapy to deal with his impending death, although he's dealing with it spiritually. Looking back, I believe I was insistent, rather than encouraging. He sees my therapist. Today, I wonder about my control issues around his cancer. I know not to take on the responsibility of doling out his drugs, Percodan and Oxycontin. I know if I get involved, I will surely try to control everything, not just his medication. He does just fine, thank you very much, without my help. I think my therapist benefits as much or more than Alex from their relationship. What an exaggerated sense of self-importance I have. Talk about superiority. Grandiosity too. Who do I think I am to purport to know what is best for him? Yet, in other ways, I stay out of his decision-making about the needless exploratory surgery to find the source site. I don't take control of his medication. Am I justifying here?

Easter weekend is coming up. Alex tells me he is probably going to die on Good Friday. His brother and sister-in-law come up from Florida along with a couple of friends we made in Atlanta. I have a workshop in Asheville, so I'm an hour away.

I put down the pen and shake my right hand as I flash back to the weekend following his death sentence. To me, there was no nice, prettified way to put it. Alex was going to die. Sooner rather than later. I go to the kitchen, reheat my coffee, and then pick up my pen:

Two weeks later, I pack my overnight bag with the essentials for a two-night stay in Asheville. I had signed up two months ago for a mind-body workshop called Hakomi. I'm not sure what it's about, but I'm curious. I've made reservations to spend Friday and Saturday nights in a nearby motel. No way I can get up and drive to Asheville for an eight o'clock check-in.

I don't want to leave, but the hospital where I work is paying for the workshop. "Will you be okay?" I ask, knowing his answer.

"I'll have plenty of company tomorrow and Sunday," his voice soothes.

I try to keep concern out of mine. "What about tonight?"

He hugs me in the way only he can. I am enfolded in a protective cocoon waiting to emerge and fly. "Honey, I'll be fine." His voice upbeat. "The hospice volunteer will call me around ten and again in the morning...and I have his number. My parents' only son will be here in the morning. Early. You can count on it."

I pull away just enough to look him in the eye, swallow my tears, and laugh. "I swear our mothers are clones."

Each time Alex reassures me, I have the same sense of being cared for as I did when he hugged me through my cousin's cancer death. An everything-will-be-all-right hug. I already begin to feel my loss as the heat leaves my body. I'll have no one who will love me like Alex.

He envelops me once again. In his arms, the world is safe. "Everything is going to be okay." I don't have to keep up my guard.

I know he speaks the truth, for in this moment, my world is good. Alex holds me. We have a roof over our heads, clothes on our backs, and food in our bellies. Well, maybe not Alex. The cancer is filling his abdomen. I hold on to that moment, which is all we ever have.

"Go, before you have to drive in the dark. Call me when you get to your room."

"I love you." I let go while my whole being cries out, stay. I hesitate at the door.

"You know I love you," his tone as soothing as a parent rocking a fussy baby. "I can take care of myself."

I turn, pick up my bag, and go to my car. When I look up at our deck, Alex watches me. I start the motor. He waves, and as I back out, he goes inside.

The workshop is exactly where I need to be. I'm in a room full of therapists who are able to sit with my grief. Indeed, encourage me to feel it, all of it, even that which is stored in my cells. I find myself being supported by a woman who puts her hand on my back behind my heart while another person sits in front and has me scan inside my body to see what I notice. "I feel a swoosh of energy." My hands indicate it's rushing up.

"If it was a bumper sticker, what would it say?"

Like a fountain spewing water, "DON'T GO" accompanied by a rush of tears. I've found, besides Alex, another safe place to cry.

For the first time in months, when I drive back over the mountains to Cullowhee, I notice green starting to pop up here and there. The clear North Carolina blue sky is cloudless, a perfect background to the gray and tan mountain stone. The air is clear and sweet. I fall in love with my mountains all over again.

Alex did not die.

I arrive home Sunday afternoon, complete with swollen red eyes. Alex's face registers pain when he looks at me.

"I'm much better now. I've been holding back the tears so you don't have to worry about me."

"Oh, Honey. You don't have to do that. Maybe we both need to express our grief openly."

He does not die Easter weekend. Six weeks, not six months, from the prognosis, Alex dies.

I put down the fountain pen and run to the bathroom. I throw up. The accumulation of tears has no place to go but down my cheeks. As they spill over my lashes, my body shudders with sobs. I thought I was finished with grieving. This present tense stuff sucks. It's time to get out of here and go for a walk. Wish I could just run off this energy. Not going to happen with the hip injury.

I straighten, and then after checking the temperature, I enter the bedroom where I find a pair of navy shorts and a navy and white striped tee.

When I get to the lake, I run. Damn the consequences, I run and run until the pain in my hip weakens my legs. I stop and limp back to the car. Physical pain is easier than emotional pain. I call home to remind myself to add to my journal: I will not go crazy, and I will not die from this. It just feels that way.

When I return, I shower, put on clean clothes, and head to the kitchen for something to drink. The answering machine flashes. Two messages. The one I'd sent. I'd already forgotten about adding to my journal.

"Hi, Babe. It's just me. Frank Islip here, touching base. Sorry I missed you. Hope you're having a great day." I return the call and leave him a message. When I turn to go back to my work, I dump the cup of coffee on my clothes.

As I start to change, the phone rings. "Hi. Hon. It's just me. Frank Islip here. How about dinner tonight?" How does he know when I need support?

"I'd love it. Your place or mine?"

"How about yours?" He uses his charming voice. "Mine is a mess. I'll bring the food."

"You're so thoughtful." I need to get out of these sticky clothes. "You always seem to know when I need a change of pace."

"See you after I close the park. Shouldn't be too late."

"Great. See you then."

I welcome the interruption. Even though I have a couple of hours before Frank is due, I store the journal and pen in the desk, done for now, drained. The hair on the back of my neck rises when I think of Frank's timing. This is one of those times when my gratitude for him grows like the fern in my window. How does he pick up on those times when I need his caring and concern around Alex's death? How does he know the right things to say? How does he know to show up fully present during those times? Is it my vulnerability that softens him? I'm usually so careful to hide that from him—or anyone, for that matter. It's a mother thing. "Don't cry. You're a crybaby." So you learned to avoid crying. If you learned it, you can unlearn it.

I ignore my uncomfortable clothes as I pick up piles of dissertation papers and perch them on the edge of the desk in the office. But I know better. With cats around, they're likely to end up on the floor. I shove them in a drawer.

After a quick shower, and before dressing, I lie down to meditate for twenty minutes. It's amazing what meditation can do for my attitude. I should do this more often.

Yin jumps on my stomach. "Hi, Sweetie Cat. Did you come to get some of this good calming energy? You did?" I can tell when I'm in the calm zone because the cats draw near.

When Frank arrives, we have a quiet dinner. As I clear the table, Frank tells me he'll be leaving over the weekend to go back to New Mexico for at least a month, maybe two. I'm almost grateful he'll be gone a while. This will give me time to work on my dissertation without interruption. The formatting is almost as time consuming as writing it.

I look over at him, sitting in his chair at the table, sipping his wine. What is the difference this time? I'm not in the least bothered by the information. Oh, he came over to support me, and he was relaxed when he told me he was leaving. I don't sense a hidden agenda. This is new. Is it me? Is it his attitude? Both?

I lean on the counter behind the table. "Will I see you before you leave?"

"Sure. If you don't mind, I'll leave from your house Saturday morning."

"I'd like that very much," as I walk over to him, put my arms around him, squeeze him and then kiss him. He leaves.

We seem to get along much better when I'm otherwise occupied and not concerned with what he's doing. Last night, Frank was very loving. We slept snuggled up all night, either he to my back or me to his. An anticipatory reaction to knowing we will miss each other? A possibility.

Chapter 16

George and I have settled into a weekly Friday meeting to go over my history. Today, a waiter shows us to a table by the window of the dimly lit restaurant. Because we've scheduled lunch after the noon rush, we have privacy.

"How's the hip?" George watches me sink deep into the booth's soft sofa cushion.

I straighten my skirt. "It's okay today."

"Really?" He scrutinizes my face. "You're limping and one breast is an inch lower than the other. Don't you think you should take care of it?"

He's comparing the altitude of my breasts? Brothers don't do that. "It's not that bad. And quit checking out my breasts."

"You're out of balance and you said your hip hurt on the New Mexico trip."

Must have done some real damage on my run the other day. Guess I'll go. Might want to quit telling George so much. "Okay, you win. I'll make an appointment tomorrow." He doesn't know about the run. "Will that satisfy you? Come on, George. Get that self-satisfied look off your face."

"Try happy, not self-satisfied."

His eyes home in on mine. "I seem to remember that one of your professors asked if it is possible that your injuries might have something to do with guilt?"

Yeah. Professor George. "Probably." Hadn't thought about it.

The waiter brings the food. George's Reuben makes me wish I'd ordered one. Instead I have a chef's salad.

"I'm…not sure. Thinking back, last injury—before Todd threw me out of bed…I was fifteen or so. No…take that back…burned and cut myself in the kitchen…wasn't focusing on what I was doing. Hmm…injured myself when I went back to school…happened while married to Todd."

George signals the waiter to refill his water. "Do you see a pattern?"

"Maybe. Not paying attention?"

George leans towards me. "What else do your injuries have in common besides not paying attention?"

I search my memory. "They've occurred when I was stressed. Cuts and burns cooking at premenstrual times."

The waiter fills his glass. "You've mentioned that Todd was abusive. I don't see you as someone who would allow it. What's with that?"

I pour dressing on my salad and take a bite. I shift my memory to Todd. "When Todd drank, he got drunk, and then he'd wake me by hitting me about the head with his fists."

"Present tense."

"Apparently, I kick him to stop because I wake up kicking. Next thing I know, I'm on the floor. The only memory is of shaking and my heart racing." I shift in my seat. "His story was that I kicked him and then he hit me. Once I'm asleep, I never move, don't even turn over. I've watched him flail when I've not been in bed, only when he's drunk." I reach for my coffee. "You know, for someone who was asleep when he hit me, he was careful to leave no marks."

George's eyes widen. "You allowed him to get away with that?" He over-salts his fries.

"I know. My brother never believed Todd was abusive because he couldn't fathom that I wouldn't have retaliated or called the police. Now, I can't believe it either. After several years, I realized that it only happened when he'd been drinking. Those nights, I slept on the living room floor. What a relief! Problem solved. I still prefer sleeping on hard floors."

The clinking of silverware and tinkling of glasses from the busboys provide background noise. I look around to see if we're the only ones left. Three other couples and a party of women remain.

"Was he an occasional drinker?" He bends his elbow to bring the water glass to his mouth. He takes a gulp.

"If he'd been an occasional drinker, I probably wouldn't have noticed his alcoholism. I'd had a hard enough time recognizing it as it was." I butter my roll. "When he drank, he drank every day, so I wouldn't have described him as an occasional drinker, even though he could sober up for a month or two. He called himself a binge drinker. First threw me out of bed on our wedding night. Landed on a terrazzo floor." I tear off a piece of the roll and bite down on it.

George winces. "Didn't you live together before then? Your wedding night was the first time he did that?"

I finish chewing and swallow. "Damn." This is like returning to seventh and eighth grades, only our content was different then. "He was able to contain himself before we were legally shackled. Is that some ownership thing married men get into?"

"I wouldn't know from experience, but I know men who think like that."

"I do, too." I push the salad around with a fork. "Then again, I'd begun to see that he must have been flailing in his sleep. Those violent exchanges occurred when we were both asleep." I drop my fork. It clatters to the glass top. "I take that back. My insights didn't happen until much later in our marriage." Have I begun to rewrite the history of our marriage? I pick up my fork.

"That's a change in perspective."

Had I already told him this? "Why didn't I see that before?" The change just occurred.

"New insight, right? One of the things you've taught me," he wipes his forehead, "we cannot see things while we're in the middle of them."

"George, that was a rhetorical question."

"Rhetorical or not, it's true."

"Well, thanks for the reminder. Sometimes I forget." I shrug. "What can I say?"

For the next few minutes, we concentrate on our food. When I finish my salad, I drain my cup and lean back, satiated.

George's interest in alcoholism and the family has driven so many of our conversations that when he stops to wipe his mouth, I make a decision.

"This might be a good time to tell you about my introduction to alcoholism and how it affected my marriage. Might even give you some insight with your clients."

I signal the waiter for more coffee. "I didn't know anything about alcoholism when I met Todd. My only experience with alcoholics happened when I was a child, before we moved to Bradenton. I heard a drunken mother and her equally drunken son raging at each other." I rest my elbows on the cool glass covering the wooden table, put my chin in my hands and I become nine years old. My stomach turns into a series of knots as I slide into the present tense George requires.

"The summer night is hot. The windows are open in both houses. My parents never raise their voices to each other so I've never heard adults scream and yell at one another. I'm so scared I call Mother." A chameleon on the restaurant window blows its red-bubbled throat.

"Where did you go?" George shifts his gaze from me to the chameleon and back again.

"I'm back in the bedroom I share with my two brothers. My parents have a drape across the middle of the room so we have some privacy. I can see into the kitchen window of the house next door. People look like they're going to hurt each other. 'MOMMY!' I cry." My voice sounds so young, my stomach tightens as I remember.

"Mom comes in, closes the window, and holds me while she tells me not to worry. 'They can't hurt you.' She tucks me in bed."

George pulls on his earlobe. "That was your only exposure to alcoholism until Todd?"

"Guess I didn't know enough about addiction to recognize it. When I started to write about addiction in my life, I recognized how early it had begun to affect me. Not until Mother acted so crazy about getting and taking her iron supplements did I begin to suspect her addictive nature. Even now, I sometimes wonder if I'm wrong."

"Tell me more about Todd, how you met, your marriage, his addiction." George dumps ketchup on his fries and shoves two in his mouth.

I'm not sure where to start. "When I met him, Todd owned an architectural firm and was in the process of buying a fixed-base operation with a flight school."

"Fixed-base operation?"

"You've seen those little out-buildings at the Tallahassee airport with small private planes tied down?"

He nods.

"They're called fixed-base operations or FBOs. Besides renting hangar and tie-down spaces to airplane owners, they sell fuel. Some offer charter or repair services. Some offer both. A few have flight schools connected with them."

George picks up his dripping Reuben, "How did you meet Todd?" He takes a large bite and the sauce squishes onto his hands.

"I was the Girl Friday at a small FBO on Craig Field. The day was unusually warm for December. My door, which overlooked the parking area, was open. I watched an intriguing looking man get out of his car and stride towards my office. He walked with purpose, a man who was going somewhere. He wasn't particularly handsome, with his balding head, but his warm, brown eyes and neatly trimmed black beard flecked with gray made him striking. What I didn't know: Todd was a man of importance with a fatal flaw and a can full of worms about to crawl out on the pavement under him."

"How do you remember all these details?"

"I don't know, but when I think of meeting Todd, I see him in vivid detail. And I feel the same excitement I felt then."

George wipes his mouth on the napkin and holds out his hands. "Reuben disaster. Be right back."

When he returns from washing his hands, "Okay, tell me more about his fatal flaw thing, and remember present tense."

I roll my eyes and go on. "Imagine this, my boss comes out of his office to greet this man. He never leaves his office to greet anyone. He then introduces me to Mr. Cameron. They tour the hanger and repair shop in our building. It's when they move across the field to the larger FBO with a connecting flight school that I realize he's looking to buy the business." Even as we talk, I see Todd swagger across the field as if he owns the world. "His carriage belies his financial condition. I wonder now if he was aware of his financial picture."

"How could he not be aware?" George drinks the remainder of his water and sets the glass on the table. "It was his company, wasn't it?"

"I found out later he had a trusted friend who was a sorta-business manager. I'm pretty sure he tried to warn Todd, but Todd wouldn't listen. He was one of those people who wanted what he wanted when he wanted it. And that day, he wanted a flight school and charter service."

"An addict."

I hope George won't notice as I shift my weight to my right hip, "My boss tells me Mr. Cameron is a prominent architect who wants to buy both a charter service and a flight school. I learn that he recently bought several new airplanes: a twin engine Seneca, a Cherokee Six, a Cherokee Arrow, and a Cherokee Warrior. He'd also added two smaller, slower planes from Piper to use in teaching students. He had gotten a deal."

I turn to look when the wait staff presents a cake and sings "Happy Birthday" to someone at the next table. "Within the last few months, he's learned to fly, going from single-engine, private to multi-engine, commercial license, and is now currently working on his instrument rating. He plans to use these airplanes in his business to travel from job site to job site all over Florida, Georgia, and Alabama. However, since he can't justify the purchase of all the planes for his architectural business, he wants to buy into the aviation business. He learned to fly at the flight school across the field, so I hadn't seen him before."

"He sounds crazy."

When I put myself back into that time, I see a different man than the one I saw then. "If he had been the least bit muscular, I would swear he was on steroids and they were turning his brain into Swiss cheese."

George sounds puzzled when he asks, "Alcohol can do that, can't it?"

"Yeah. Long-term use."

Laughter breaks out at the next table. When I look, everyone is wearing pointy paper hats.

"When Mr. Cameron and my boss return, Mr. Cameron stops by my desk to chat a minute. After he leaves, I learn that he's a millionaire in a bad marriage, and that even Mr. Cameron's attorney complains about the nastiness of his wife Elaine."

"You called him Mr. Cameron?"

"Odd, isn't it? I don't know why. I guess because he was going to be my boss." I signal the waiter for more coffee. Could use a piece of that birthday cake, too.

"Your whole countenance changed. What happened?"

"As I was telling you about it, the insanity of a four-person architectural firm with six planes hit me." A waiter walks by with a piece of decadent-looking chocolate cake and takes it into the other room. When I point to my cup, he indicates the coffee is coming. "I suddenly understood his former wife's complaints. She must not have expressed her reasons for calling him insane. Or perhaps she did, and the guys making money off Todd either didn't see or didn't want to see."

I take a deep breath and lean back. Putting all that into words helps me see the grandiosity of his decision-making. This is exhausting. Getting into the chaotic quality of his energy during that period gives me an adrenalin rush. "My god, he got a rush from gambling with his business."

George's face turns quizzical.

"No wonder a psychiatrist unfamiliar with addiction diagnosed him with bipolar disorder. Why didn't he prescribe lithium if he thought Todd was manic?" The clinical psychologist kicks in. "Or Todd was prescribed lithium and didn't take it. Why hadn't I seen this before? Maybe I didn't want to see. I haven't thought of Todd's behavior in years, before I got my master's degree. I didn't understand what I was seeing."

A burst of laughter comes from the next table. Oh my god, who gave the birthday girl a dildo? With a straight face, I point to the next table. "He supposedly stopped drinking at the psychiatric hospital. If you give up one addiction, you find another, unless you address the underlying problem. Hence, the gambling."

George runs his fingers through his hair as he turns to look, and then he sees the gift. He laughs and turns back to me. "Gambling? I'm beginning to see why you are so insistent about the bipolar diagnosis versus addiction. You've lived it, haven't you?"

I pick up my napkin and pretend to cough so I'm not laughing out loud. "Pretty much." I shift in the seat to keep from stiffening, slip off my low-heeled black sandals, and then fold my legs up under me. A rush of energy runs through me. "You know that feeling you get when you confront a crisis? I lived like that for thirteen long years with Todd. I don't know how I did it."

I stop and breathe a few deep breaths. "Later that week, I'm invited, along with my boss, to the Cameron annual Christmas party for friends and business associates. I meet Elaine, who within minutes asks about boyfriends. She advises me to ditch my current single, thirty-eight-year-old boyfriend as 'not marriage material.' I wondered what made her such an expert since she was so unhappy in her marriage."

George's attempt to suppress a smile fails. "Go on. Keep it in the present, okay? You need to feel it."

I twirl the ring on my finger. "Mr. Cameron intrigues me, but I don't think of him again until close to midnight on New Year's Eve, when he calls to wish me a Happy New Year as the clock strikes twelve. His gesture brings tears to my eyes. I'm alone for the first time on New Year's Eve. I miss Claire, who is with her father. My dad has had a stroke and I'm feeling the loss of him. I am having a pity party all by myself. I'm so vulnerable to Todd's kindness that I'll believe anything he says. Had he not called me that night and had I not been in the throes of loneliness when I answered, he would have remained Mr. Cameron. Talk about being needy."

"He picked up on it, didn't he?"

The waiter tops off my coffee and hands George the check.

"On New Year's Day, I go with several pilot friends to test fly a newly acquired Aztec, owned by a company that hangars its plane where I work. But we're unable to fly because of rime ice."

"Rime ice?"

"A white ice that forms when the water droplets in fog freeze to airplane wings. The ice can cause the plane to pitch and roll uncontrollably. If the carburetor ices, the plane can no longer fly."

"I take it that's not a good situation." He pulls out a credit card. "Then what happened?"

I start to get my card when he motions no. "You're doing me a favor. I invited you. I buy lunch. Back to your story."

"As I leave the airport to go home, my boss offers to take me to lunch at AnnieTiques in Regency Square," a restaurant known for its good drinks and expensive hamburgers. The pub-like setting with its low lighting and heavy, dark mahogany tables and chairs provides a decadent atmosphere for the business lunch. Not terribly unlike where we're sitting.

I pull out my lipstick. "When I arrive, Mr. Cameron is already there. This feels like a set-up. I thank him for last night's call. A self-acclaimed recovering alcoholic, a fact, I don't know, he orders a round of Harvey's Bristol Cream. Because my only knowledge of alcoholism is my terrifying childhood incident, I don't know he can never drink. The next day, one of Mr. Cameron's flight instructors gives me a ten-second-crash-course in alcoholism. She tells me he can never have one drop of alcohol. I must have filed that tidbit away, not to be explored until I went to a twelve-step meeting." I return the lipstick to my purse.

"The next seven years are filled with drama, beginning with Todd's first heart attack and open-heart surgery, followed by two car wrecks. He wrecks his car. He wrecks mine. Each results in his being jailed and charged with driving under the influence. When he loses his license for six months, I become his chauffeur."

George leans forward and puts his elbows on the table, as if to say continue.

"So many wasted years worrying about Todd. I was raised that if you love someone, you worry about him. Strange how I never figured out my worrying had no effect on the outcome. I worried. Todd drank."

A tray clatters to a tiled floor. I jump.

"Oh, and add his divorce from Elaine and bankruptcy. All this occurs before we are married."

George's head jerks, "Really? He divorced before you married?" He laughs and then his face turns serious, "So back to Todd getting arrested. Did you bail him out?"

The waiter places the bill on the table. George signs.

A flush of embarrassment burns across my face. "Yeah, but the second time I didn't. Somehow, I knew not to do it."

A little girl in pink walks to the window and puts her face to the glass. Her mother pulls her along.

"That was an improvement." He reaches for his wallet and puts in his credit card and receipt.

"I know. I can't believe how many mistakes I made in trying to be a good wife and help my husband, including trying to control his drinking, all of which helped him maintain the pattern."

"Remember, present tense."

"I hide his bottles. I pour the booze down the drain. I cry. I beg. I get angry. I threaten to leave. It's worse after we're married. The drinking continues. He switches from Ron Rico rum to Jack Daniels, but always a fifth of vodka hidden in reserve. I think he'll stop if only…I'm a better wife. I'm prettier. That's a trophy wife for you."

George laughs. There's a burst of laughter from the banquet room.

"When I think about it now, I wonder where Todd got the money to pay for all his alcohol. Today, I have so many questions. How did he get bail money? We'd each had a limited allowance for spending on non-necessities. Had he filed for bankruptcy yet? Had he held out money for booze?"

He signals the waiter for more water.

"My 'if onlys' include being a better housekeeper, cook, lover. Nothing works. I'm so caught up in his drinking that I live on coffee and cigarettes during those years. I think I became addicted to the adrenalin rush."

George touches his cheek. "Addicted to adrenalin?"

"Yeah. If a behavior doesn't work, I amp it up. I keep trying. And without knowing it, I'm insane. Each time I expect different results. How sane is that? I'm emotionally out of control. My life is unmanageable. I'm a Seligman rat participating in his learned helplessness experiments. I learn that nothing I do has any effect on his drinking."

My gaze flits around the restaurant, trying to find a place to land where I won't feel so helpless. Nothing, not even looking out the window at the bright red cardinal perched on a branch, nor the clear blue sky mottled with puffy white clouds, provides relief. A cloud passes overhead; a shadow moves across the window. The waiter returns with water for George.

"I reach my limit the day I go to my flight surgeon and medical doctor complaining about my two-year bout with diarrhea. 'You're healthy. I can't find a thing wrong. Now tell me what's really going on with you.' He then tells me Todd loves me so much, I should just make him stop. For once, I recognize bad advice. I can't make Todd stop drinking." I take a deep breath and let it out as I feel the emptiness of desperation.

Dishes bang in the background. When I look, there is another couple in the restaurant.

"I'm willing to try anything. Within hours, I'm given a gift. Someone puts me in touch with a woman who has twenty years in recovery. She still lives with her alcoholic husband and is happy today. I have hope. Two days later, I go to my first meeting. Now I know. I didn't cause it. I can't cure it. I can't control it."

Even George's eyes smile with that last statement. He leans forward and puts his wallet in his pocket.

"There is such freedom in knowing his alcoholism is not my problem." I take the last sip of coffee.

"After I'd lived with his drinking for seven years, he goes into treatment. I'd been in recovery two months. I learned how to let go of his drinking and became willing to watch him die. Not an easy decision to make. Encouraging him to buy a million-dollar life insurance policy didn't hurt my chances that he would get sober, either."

"You didn't!"

The waiter comes by, "More coffee?"

I put my hand over my cup. "None for me. Are you ready for us to leave?"

"Oh, no. Sit here as long as you like."

George leans in. "The life insurance policy?"

"Todd's old friend and insurance agent came to the house to sell him the policy, and then tried to get him to stop drinking. After the man left, we talked about it. I suggested that he might want to purchase such a policy.'

I shift positions, readjust my legs, and continue. "With the encouragement of—"

George's alarm goes off. "Hold that thought. Time to leave for my class."

I gather my things, "Thanks for lunch," and walk towards the door.

"My pleasure."

As soon as I arrive home, I change into walking clothes and head to Lake Ella. I walk two laps. The lake and trees receive my undivided attention. I avoid eye contact with other walkers.

Once I clear my mind, I allow myself to go back to the night Todd moved in, the latter part of January. Going back is like watching a movie of my past.

I heard a knock on the door. Todd stood, unannounced and uninvited. He walked in with a few clothes.

"I've left Elaine."

Because I was so happy to see him, I didn't think through the ramifications of his move, including the effects on his wife and children. I never realized I heard only one side of the marriage. I couldn't conceive the long-term effects on me. To be honest, I wouldn't know those effects until six years later. I believed I needed a man to be complete, and after all, a new love was exciting and full of surprises. Todd was my knight in shining armor. How naïve I was.

Todd had been to my apartment once before, also without warning. That time he walked through inspecting my closets and pantry. He knew my apartment well. He'd designed it.

The sky darkens and a black cloud rushes toward the lake. A few drops splatter. I run to the car. Once home, a bit wetter than when I left, I grasp my red silk book. I need to look at this. If I don't, I'll not uncover the old beliefs that keep me repeating old situations.

April 5, 2002

Todd puts down his things, heads to the dining room, and pulls out an unopened bottle of Cherry Heering from my pantry. My favorite liqueur, a Christmas gift I'd been saving. He'd spotted the bottle the first time he was here. I pour a small amount in the liqueur glasses. Todd gulps his down and grabs more. I regret letting him near my gift, not that I had a choice. Todd consumes half the bottle before I finish my half-filled glass.

Something is wrong. I've never met anyone who drinks like him. Perhaps the stress he's under causes the drinking. He wants to celebrate, the first excuse I make for his drinking during our life together. By the time I finish my glass, Todd is drunk, sloppy, slurring drunk. When he passes out on the bed, I believe he's asleep. I learn the difference between going to sleep and passing out in a stupor.

I'd been warned about his alcoholism, but I don't understand. This is the first time I see him drunk.

I don't grasp the power of his addiction when I walk into my apartment several weeks later to find he's destroyed a drawing of a kitchen chair, one of which I was particularly proud. I feel my hand move as I draw the yellow chair in the Novato house where Richard and I lived before our marriage ended. The drawing sits face down on my desk. I read: FUCK YOU! AND FUCK THE WORLD YOU LIVE IN! How could he do this? I turn the paper over. The black smudges from the block letters made with a black felt tip pen have destroyed my drawing. I cry.

Discovery Statements:

I learned: From the beginning I gave my power away to Todd. I relearned: I was naïve. I discovered: Giving away my power is a pattern. I was surprised: Unknowingly, I encouraged Todd's drinking. I wonder: What would have been different if I'd gotten Elaine's perspective before I married Todd? I was saddened: by my lost years. I was happy: I'd gone to twelve-step meetings and had the chance to learn what a good marriage was like after Todd.

I close the journal and pour a cup of coffee.

Chapter 17

At the lake, a steel sky sets off the white spire of a nearby church. The wind whips off the water and sways branches. Gray turns black. People rush to their cars. After threatening all day, the weather has taken a turn for the worse. The weekly vegetable vendors start to pack up. A white goose nips at a young child's heels. The child screams until her father picks her up. In an instant, the sky turns bright and the wind becomes a breeze.

The weekly vendors stay put. I stop at my car for bags and return to the organic market. I halt at my favorite stand, which sits in a corner near the Green Frog. Today the vendor has dark green kale, zucchini, yellow squash, bright red tomatoes, and other vegetables. I buy what I notice first. I pull a twenty from my pocket. "Can you break this?"

He smiles and nods his head as he places the tomatoes in my cloth bag. "Picked 'em this morning." He takes my money, gives me change, and then turns to wait on the person behind me.

I move to the woman with eggplants. While I make my choice, more people arrive. I point to the black-purple colored one. "I'll take this one." It will be good baked with a sliced tomato round, topped with mozzarella. I run into several people I know, all of us in a rush to avoid the possible storm.

I carry my purchases to my car as I think of all the people who have crossed my path here, mostly at this lake. These are people connected to the earth who have taught me the value of spending time in nature. Even Frank has had a part in my nature connection. At the car, I open the trunk, move two bags for Goodwill, and place my purchases between the soft bags. I straighten and stretch to the sky. All is right with my world in this moment.

Because I want to keep my serenity, several days pass before I sit, pen in hand and begin to write:

> April 11, 2002
>
> I don't want to relive those years with Todd. I don't want to think about the insanity of living with a practicing alcoholic. Not present tense—not willing to go there. Life was unmanageable. I couldn't—maybe didn't would be a better word—control my emotions. I hit inanimate objects. I screamed. I yelled like a common washerwoman, Mother's words. I gritted my teeth. I tensed my neck and shoulders. My abdominal and lower back muscles just above my kidneys stayed tight and tense. If I didn't clamp and lock my feelings, I would have released my anger. When that happened, a tsunami of rage flew out in all directions. I didn't care who was around to hear or see it. The aftermath was not pretty. Cleanup was difficult, and it never made me feel better. I found no relief until I walked into my first twelve-step meeting.

Focusing on my emotional crash breeds more questions than it answers. I'm coming up on a recovery anniversary. Of course. My nose itches. I need to shift into another position before I continue. I stand and stretch. I twist to my left and to my right. I yawn. Coffee. I tap my upper chest, immediately below the collarbone, to replenish my energy. This discomfort and sleepiness is about avoiding. Even though I know the games I play with myself, especially when self-examination is involved, I get more and more subtle with them. Am I making a searching and fearless inventory of myself?

Because trees have meaning for me, the view from the French doors comforts me. Because of my psychology background, I'm more intrigued by bare trees than those full of their many shades of green. Because I paint trees without leaves, a psychologist friend equates this with being willing to be emotionally naked to the world. Not feeling willing right now. A few touches of green sprout from branches cut in January. The landscaper assured me I would have plenty of green before summer. Soon blooms will appear and cover my view of the chain link fence at the back of my property. I take a few steps back. The fence disappears, and a forest appears. The line of trees and foliage is not wide, but it covers the buildings beyond, leaving the illusion of forest.

Light flashes. Thunder booms. Is a storm arriving? So many these last few weeks. Overhead, black clouds smudge the sky. I watch as rain deluges the earth. Puddles become streams as the water rushes to a holding pond. The storm ends as quickly as it began.

I return to the desk and continue journaling: I wish this storm to end before it begins. I remember to stay in present tense.

> April 11 (cont'd)
>
> Within six weeks, Todd makes the decision to go into treatment. Must be the life insurance policy, but could be the decision that I am willing to stay and watch him die—he later told me he knew I would no longer save him from himself.
>
> His youngest son and I take him to treatment, along with a bottle of wine to sedate him. I don't want him trying to get out of the car or physically fighting us. I don't want him to change his mind. We leave him at the treatment center and drive home.
>
> When I walk in the house, I crave a drink. I never had an intense desire for alcohol before this day. I begin to understand Todd's craving. I don't take that drink.
>
> In hindsight and years of recovery self-searching, I believe proving I'm better than you has driven me to jump on the sobriety wagon. What a crazy, cunning bitch. I never recognized that part of myself. Okay, not present tense. Not going to happen.
>
> I spend the month Todd was in treatment running his business and doing a Fourth Step—Made a searching and fearless moral inventory of ourselves. A recovery friend told me I could do a Fifth Step— Admitted to God, to ourselves and to another human being the exact nature of our wrongs—with one of the counselors at the treatment center. That was my first

experience with any sort of counseling. By the time I returned to pick up Todd, I had written thirty pages. I read them aloud, at her suggestion, and then burned them in a bucket. Gone was the past. Erased. We will not regret the past, nor wish to shut the door on it.

I have been shutting the door on it. I stop writing when Yang jumps into my lap and nudges my writing arm. "Hey, little fellow. Did you come to help?" I scratch his ears. When he bites my wrist, "Hey, that hurts." I put him on the floor and return to the journal.

Cont'd

When Todd drank, he passed out. I then had a habit of doing what I wanted when I wanted. Once I had adjusted to the change in our relationship, Todd's first year sober was the best period of our marriage. We talked about everything. We attended the same meetings since I decided that I might have a problem with alcohol, too. Looking back, I realize that was a way to control the alcohol in the house, so many hidden agendas.

We celebrated Todd's first year of sobriety while on a business trip at an old plantation between Tallahassee and Thomasville, Georgia. The owners served a six-course meal with wine to match. We did without the alcohol. Our meal of Beef Wellington, asparagus with hollandaise, and crème brûlée waltzed about on my tongue in a perfect chorus of tastes. We retired to our room afterwards. I climbed up on the high double bed and settled in to read.

The next day, we drove to Madison, a small town between Tallahassee and Jacksonville, for an inspection, and then returned to Jacksonville. That last day of our trip was the perfect build-up for the thud that occurred the night we returned home.

As I journal that last line, I am pitched back in time to relive our first night back home.

"Call an ambulance. I'm having a heart attack."

Without warning, my adrenalin pumps and I'm back in the house experiencing his heart attack. I call the ambulance. Within five minutes, help arrives while I'm still slinging on clothes and gathering my purse and keys. This is Todd's second, so I know the drill, but sitting in the emergency room waiting area, I smoke and shake and smoke some more. After what seems like hours of testing, the doctor comes out. "We're sending him to the coronary care unit. You may see him briefly before he goes up."

He's sedated when I walk into the cubical. I lean over the gurney and place my hand on his forehead then lean down and kiss him. "I'm being sent home. I will see you in the morning the minute I'm allowed in. I love you."

Exhausted, I fall into bed. I'm wide-awake. I tell myself he's in better shape than when he had the first one. Doesn't help. I can still see the fear in his eyes when he awakened me. Even now my heart trembles.

I lie awake thinking of Todd and then my mind travels to things I have to do in the morning. My mental list includes all those important phone calls plus keeping the office running with our one draftsman. As soon as the draftsman arrives, I'll head to the hospital. Probably won't see Todd until later, after the angiogram and whatever. Call the hospital before going. No sense in sitting in the waiting room all day. Back and forth, my mind paces. I get up and have a cigarette. Then, I try to sleep.

I call at eight, after staff report. "The doctor will be in sometime around ten or eleven." I get there at nine-thirty. I need to see him to know that he'll survive. I'm allowed to see Todd before ten because I couldn't spend time with him last night. He's still groggy from the medication.

The surgeon breezes into the cubicle as I prepare to leave for the waiting room. I expect to be reamed out for Todd's poor health. Instead, he says, "We'll be testing all day. Go home and take care of the office. He's in much better shape than after the first heart attack."

Thank the gods he's not blaming me for his heart attack. I return to the hospital around four-thirty knowing the doctor won't make rounds until six or after. When I get to his cubicle, Todd's color has returned, but he's still sedated from the tests. I return to the waiting room.

When the surgeon arrives, "He's blown out a large portion of his heart. We'll go in and make the repair by stitching a Teflon liner—

like bias tape—to reinforce that portion of his heart. This will be a much easier surgery since he's in better shape this time." My mother has arrived from Tampa to sit with me during his surgery. She reminds me to pray for the surgeon's hands, that they will perform a miracle.

The surgeon doesn't tell me this surgery has only been done twice before. One died. He's never performed the surgery. He will stay up half the night studying the reinforcement.

The surgery is a success. Todd is discharged within two weeks. Once he's home, he has to wean himself off the pain medication. Even though I know depression will follow his heart attack and surgery, I'm not prepared for the verbal attacks directed at me. The smallest thing becomes a major problem, like mentioning the number of sponges used during surgery. Todd's rants last on and off for the duration of our marriage.

Meanwhile, I work both my recovery programs. I look at my part in the flare-ups and check out my motives before I act, most of the time.

Need a break from memories of Todd. Time for a wind-down walk. The journal goes in the drawer across the room. Yin jumps on the vacated spot. "Like those warm spots, huh?"

I take a quick, wet walk on the road by the apartment. Even with speed-bumps, drivers speed by, some testing my courage by coming as close as possible to the road's edge as if they want to clip me with a mirror. Carrying my walking stick might be a good idea. If nothing else, banging on a fender might get their attention. When I return and enter the foyer, I glance to the right into the living room. The late afternoon sun shines on the table by the French door, exactly as it did the afternoon in my dream house when a drunken Todd broke a glass and scraped a shard into the wood—even the way the sun shines through the crystal chimney of the candleholder, and the way it streaks the wood with golden light, broken only by the deep gouge. I miss my house.

It was the first house built in Jacksonville's new suburb Avondale. In nineteen twenty-seven, it was a showplace with its traditional brick exterior and Tara entryway. The house's five thousand square feet included six bedrooms, five baths, two sleeping porches, library, sewing room, sunroom, thirty-eight-foot-long living room, and thirty-foot-long dining room. Servants were quartered over the garage, now home to my stepson. All sit on three-quarters of an acre, flanked by two large oak trees.

My eyes are drawn to the gash on the table and I'm thrown back to another time.

Six months later in an early spring afternoon, I stand at the edge of the counter dividing the kitchen and breakfast room. I look out the narrow, white, French doors, across the drive to the large oak, with its blackened knothole, about twenty feet away. A momma raccoon checks out the landscape below, to see if it's safe to make her evening trek to the neighbor's pool house for cat food. This momma knows where to find food for her kits. The setting sun variegates golden flecks amidst the shadows across the narrow drive and into the breakfast room, leaving an echo of gold on the candle's crystal chimney to reflect back on the warm brown table.

While I watch the birds, they chirp as they look for a place to settle for the night. New birds. I don't recognize their language. I do, however, identify a controversial conference among the crows, agitated by the interlopers. A car, spitting and coughing, intrudes upon the chirps. Must be an adolescent boy driving. Todd, who's surprisingly agile for a large man, walks silently up from behind and pushes me out of the way with his bully stomach, for no reason I can think of.

It's a reminder of his drinking days when such an incident would have escalated into an argument, providing him with an excuse to get drunk. Not reacting to his ploys to fight increases my sense of power. It's been four years since his last open-heart surgery. You'd think he would be over his meanness. Could he have other problems?

I check on dinner when the mixture of onions, beef, carrots, and potatoes grabs my attention. The melding of aromas brings back childhood memories. "Dinner's ready." Todd and I sit down to a dinner filled with pleasant conversation. What a difference five years of sobriety makes. Before sobriety and recovery, Todd would already be in his cups. I would eat alone.

At the time Todd went into treatment, I was sure I was an alcoholic because of the craving I had when I left him in the treatment center. I prefer spending my calories on good food. I see now that thinking I had a problem with alcohol was really an excuse for not allowing alcohol in the house. It has taken Alex's death, and a doctor friend insisting I show no signs of alcoholism, for me to test the waters again.

I notice the clock and realize I'm to meet Megan in twenty minutes to go over what I've done so far with formatting the appendix. I'd better change clothes, gather up my things, and head to the lake. How did I lose track of time?

I sit by the window at The Green Frog. A pair of geese circling the lake on the sidewalk intrigues me. They appear to be arguing. As I see one pair of wings lift a little, I imagine it's the female scolding her mate. The other goose appears to listen—she's luckier than most females. Since I'm inside with closed windows, I don't really know if either is making noise, but the gestures look like an argument.

With my nose pressed on the glass, I barely notice Megan walk up. "I see that all your committee members are back in town." She pulls out a chair and drops her briefcase on it. "Why don't you disseminate your dissertation and set the defense for the day after Labor Day?" She returns with coffee and a bowl of soup.

As she sits, "Your appendices and citations look good. I doubt you'll have to change any of them."

We chat for the next half hour while Megan has her lunch. As we're about to leave I say, "I'll recheck that the date we set for my defense is amenable to everyone, and I'll put the entire dissertation on a new flash drive and take it to a copy place. I should have them on everyone's desk within two days since classes are a couple of weeks away."

Megan searches her purse for her car keys. "Sounds good. Let me know when it's set up. I've reserved the conference room for that morning."

Before she turns to leave, I give her a hug. "The best thing Simon did for me was to fire me. I appreciate how easy you are to work with."

She laughs. "We make a good team."

I drive home and put my dissertation on a thumb drive then take it to the local copier. "We can have your order for you by four tomorrow." Perfect. I'll pick them up and distribute them the following morning.

With my dissertation out of my hands, I have time to get my apartment in order. George comes over to help me put together an office chair. He studies the directions on the floor. He positions the seat upside down and connects the swivel thingy. He points to a packet of screws. "Can you hand me those? The whole packet. I need the hex key."

He places the connector plate on the seat and puts the screws in the holes. He picks up the hex key. "What was Richard like?"

The best way to describe Richard is to see him in action. "I met him the summer we moved to Tampa. He was twelve going on thirty. He walked me home from the Sunday night church group. Three blocks. As we cut behind the Winn Dixie, he pulled me to him and forced a wet, tongue-darting kiss down my throat. 'Yuk! You kiss like a plunger.' Turns my stomach even today."

George's shoulders shake as if he's trying to suppress laughter. "You said that?"

"Yep." I sit cross-legged and look out the open, slatted, vertical blinds. A brilliant red cardinal lands on a branch. "He told me I was a snob. That about sums up our relationship. He may not have been having sex at twelve, but it wasn't because he didn't try." I'd lay odds he did.

George tightens the first screw. "Why did he call you a snob?"

"I guess because I told him he kissed like a plunger." How strange. "I've never thought about it."

George scrunches his face and tightens another screw. "Doesn't make sense, Lee."

I'd always assumed that was the reason. What other reason could he have? "My parents, his grandparents, and his mother all belonged to the same church. I wonder if he heard something negative from his grandparents about Mother. She was a snob." But you already know that. "I was to be the perfect little lady." Didn't happen.

George nods and turns the last screw. He picks up the legs to attach them to the seat.

I hold the seat in place. "We went our separate ways for six years. He moved to the Orlando area, and I didn't see him again until I was twenty. He was nineteen, attending the University of South Florida, and separated from his wife. According to him, she claimed she was pregnant. He married her against the advice of the veterinarian mentoring him who suggested a pregnancy test. For good reason, I might add. He refused to have her tested. She wasn't pregnant." I hand George the chair back to attach. "According to Richard, his mother raised him to believe he could do no wrong." A belief I witnessed. "I guess he thought he and his girlfriend could have unprotected sex for months without getting her pregnant." Could that explain his later behaviors?

"When I saw him again, he looked like a clean-cut college guy." Very different from the pimple-faced, obnoxious adolescent I'd known six years earlier. "We dated about four months. Meanwhile, he got divorced." No reason to tell George I paid for it, is there?

"He proposed and chose a date three weeks hence. Looking back, when he set our wedding date should have been a warning sign of things to come." But a girl's gotta do what a girl's gotta do to get away from home.

For someone who hates to be told what to do, how did I miss this one?

"Because our families went to the same church, he wasn't an unknown. In retrospect, he might have fared better with my mother had he been someone new."

George turns the chair upright. "How so?" Done.

I try out the chair. "Well, his mother had a reputation. Gossip was that she seemed to want to make babies, not raise them. She even pitched a good old-fashioned-southern-hissy fit when we didn't postpone our wedding for her convenience." Strange, no one acknowledged her crazy behavior.

"Perfect, George." He takes the chair into my office.

I stand and stretch. I settle on the couch looking out at the blooming pink crepe myrtles that watercolor my balcony. The deep blue sky is the perfect foil for the puffs of white clouds turned golden by the sun. A hint of onion and garlic from last night's dinner remains in the air. I prop my feet on the trunk and admire my world.

When George returns, he sits across from me in the tub chair by the French doors. "She wanted you to postpone your wedding?"

"She was living in Kansas City, with her second husband, going to school for her undergraduate degree. She acted as if there could not possibly be a wedding without her presence. Somehow, she'd managed to make our wedding about her. Richard refused. We were married as planned, and the world didn't shatter."

I'm thirsty. "The wedding was small." I stand and walk to the door. "Because Dad had had a heart attack six months earlier, only my immediate family, Richard's grandparents, the best man, and maid of honor were there. After learning years later that Nana never liked Richard, I understood why she made a quick exit from Tampa before the wedding."

George nods with his I-know-why-she-didn't-like-him look. He'd met Richard early in our marriage when Richard expanded like a puffer fish and took the floor with his pompousness. It was not a pretty scene.

"As my dad prepared to walk me down the aisle, he reminded me that I didn't have to go through with it. I could still back out." The very same thought had tiptoed across my mind.

"I told him I couldn't." I didn't hear myself. "I never mentioned desire, only a have to." Damn, I'd even clenched my teeth as I approached the altar.

George turns to me, props his elbows on his knees, "Why would you do that?"

"Remember, this is the early sixties. Women got married and had children. The average age was nineteen then. I'd already told people I was getting married. I thought I was getting old, so I needed to marry. I wanted to get out of the house. I wanted to be free to have sex."

His eyes search my face. "How old were you?"

I guess you don't know. "Twenty. Just weeks away from twenty-one," I laugh. "Doesn't sound like I was the epitome of maturity, does it?"

He shakes his head.

About as mature as any of us, George, but you didn't marry. Smart man.

215

"We'd had six pre-marital counseling sessions and the night we were married, I believed my duty as a wife was to perform sex whenever he wanted. I believed I had to support my husband in his chosen profession, which was being a student. I believed I had to be the perfect cook and housekeeper, and to work full time. Prescriptions on how to be a slave were what they were."

George scratches his jaw.

"We were back from our one-night honeymoon by mid-afternoon Saturday. Richard was to start his work-study program the following Monday. That meant white shirts: one clean shirt every day, starched and ironed. From the first Sunday after our marriage, I cried every night as I ironed his shirt." My fists clench. "I hated being married. Hated being a slave." I was a spoiled brat.

"After the second week of listening to me cry, Richard somehow found the money to pay for sending his shirts to the laundry. No more white shirts. Ever. I guess he did try to please me. He gets one point in the plus column."

George rolls his eyes. "It would seem so."

I laugh. "Two years later, after Richard entered graduate school, when I ran for Mrs. University of Florida, I chose speed rather than accuracy for the white shirt competition. Won that round. No tears, either."

I need water. Now. "Want some water?" as I duck into the kitchen.

George sighs, "Yes, please." He stands and stretches as he watches me across the bar. He takes the glass from me. "What is your most vivid memory of this period in your marriage?"

I wipe my upper lip on my sleeve. "We'd been married about six months when we went to visit Richard's friends in a trailer park near Shands, where Richard had lived during his first marriage. We were there for a football weekend, and Gainesville had just gone wet. After the game, we'd gone back to their place and had a pitcher of daiquiris among the four of us after which we went out to dinner at the Primrose Inn near the University."

"Present tense, Lee."

My stomach knots. "After dinner and another round of drinks, Richard and the wife go off into the bedroom and screw. We can hear their moans and groans in the living room. We attempt to retaliate but neither of us can."

Tears form for the person I was back then. "The next day when Richard and I are at the pool, I want to talk about it, but he blows it off as being drunk."

George touches my shoulder. "Stung deep?"

His words bring tears to my eyes. "I should have left him right then. I didn't."

"What kept you there?"

I have to think a minute. "I didn't want to admit I had made a mistake. I must have used my wedding vows as an excuse."

"Were there others?" He keeps his hand on my shoulder.

"Lots more than I probably know."

"Is this what eventually broke up your marriage?"

"Not this incident, but a similar one with a lot more shame at its core." No more. "George, can we continue this next week? I can't go there right now."

"What do you need from me?" His arm continues to rest on my shoulder.

"What I need is to walk this off. Are you up for walking with me?"

We head to the lake.

When I return home, I feel the powerlessness of my situation with Richard. I had not been raised to confront the person I married. I learned to keep my mouth shut and make the best of a situation. I'm not sure I learned that from Mother or from the culture of the fifties and early sixties.

Chapter 18

A week later, George records the date and place of the interview. I settle in on my sofa. To the right of the paned-glass doors, my French-style easel holds *Reflections*, a watercolor of white flowers in a negative space background begun in a workshop several years ago. Something about it soothes me.

George sits to my left, his knees above his waist on my low narrow sofa. Without preamble, "Back to Richard. Why did your marriage break up?"

I take a deep breath and slowly let it out. A pain pricks the side of my throat. "It all began to unravel on my thirtieth birthday. We were living in a small community outside of San Francisco. I'd cooked dinner for Richard's previous secretary and her new husband. Richard opened a couple of bottles of champagne during dinner, but I don't remember why we stood on the white marble entryway waiting for Richard to return. He stopped on the second step of three coming from our bedroom, a Polaroid of nude me poised in his hand," my stomach turns, "taken the week before. He showed—"

"Present tense."

"—it to the husband, 'How would you like to have this for the evening?' I can't move. I can't speak." Even now, my mind goes blank when I try to remember the earlier part of the evening. "The couple must have been leaving."

George's eyes turn black. His fists clench.

I enclose my chest as I cross my arms. "I wanted to melt into the floor like a salted slug even though the husband merely said, 'No thanks.'"

A cold shiver runs down my spine. "Richard's offerings told me I was nothing more than a piece of meat to be shared with acquaintances. Or strangers." I bend over and clutch my stomach. "How could he do this to me, the mother of his child? Even now, I can see the picture. See the camera take the picture, and see me pose. I still ask myself how I allowed it."

I put my hand over my mouth and run for the bathroom. I pull up the seat and hurl my breakfast remains. I start to get up and more comes until I have the dry heaves. The smell of the soured milk from the oatmeal makes me want to heave again. I turn on the fan. I take the toilet brush and clean the bowl, and pick up the rug where I splashed. I roll it up, and then I take a washcloth from the rack, wet it, and wipe my face. When I look in the mirror, my face is splotchy red. I reach into the cabinet and pull out my mouthwash to get the sour, bitter taste from my mouth.

I drop the rug and washcloth into the washing machine, throw in some soap, and turn it on. I stop and breathe. I go to the kitchen and get a can of ginger ale to settle my stomach, and then return to the sofa. "I'm sorry."

"Are you okay?" with concern in his voice. "You look awful."

"I know," my voice hoarse. Feel worse than I look.

"Can you continue?"

I will finish this today even if it kills me. "I think so."

George's voice is barely a whisper, "What was your relationship like after Richard's offer?" as if lowering the volume will soften the content of the question.

Tears struggle to contain themselves as I try to remember. "I think Richard began working later. At least one night, he and our neighbor stopped at a tavern. He arrived home after the late night news. Drunk. Ugly drunk. I took a bottle of cheap perfume, a Christmas gift from his mother, and sprayed him over and over." I smile at the memory. The perfume smell was worse than the alcohol. Wonder if it ever came out of his suit. I don't recall.

"I banished him from our bedroom. He slept on the pullout sofa bed in the guest room that night."

George breaks out into a grin, and then his face sobers. "What else do you remember from that period?"

"A few nights later, Dale and Karen Baines meet us in San Francisco at a popular steak house for yet another dinner to celebrate my birthday. Karen is a nurse at the hospital where Richard works. Dale is her husband. I met them when Richard and I hosted a Christmas open house for the hospital staff. I didn't spend much time with either of them at the party. I do remember he looked like an English country gentleman in his well-cut wool suit and Italian leather shoes."

George leans forward, hands on his knees.

"Over drinks, the talk turns to boating and sailboats. We make plans to meet in Sausalito on a Saturday two weeks from now to go sailing on the bay. The day is pleasant, and when we stop for drinks afterwards, Richard mentions he'd like to buy a sailboat. A discussion begins on which boats are stable and forgiving and which are not. Richard insists he'd like to look at boats. We agree to meet again two weeks hence midmorning in Alameda for a boat hunt. The day we shop for boats, Richard decides to buy a twenty-six-foot Folkboat." My stomach muscles relax as we move to a safer topic.

"Just like that? No consultation with you?"

"That's Richard."

George frowns, "Go on."

"While Richard fills out the paperwork, I take Claire outside to look at the water." The memory of my beautiful daughter pointing at gulls and trying to say bird brings a smile to my heart. "Afterwards, we stop for lunch and Richard talks about how it should be easy to get a loan from the hospital's bank. I'm not so certain."

George raises his eyebrows in a question.

"Richard never had a problem when it came to running our bank balance to less than a dollar. I did."

Damn, this is my most humiliating experience and he's taking notes, too.

"A little over a week later, Richard came home bubbling with enthusiasm. The loan approval came through."

"Present tense."

Yeah, it makes me relive the memory. "He informs me he's invited the Baines over this weekend to celebrate the new purchase. I cook a dinner that won't require much work once the guests arrive. Hawaiian chicken, always a good choice with its sweet and tangy sauce. We have drinks before dinner, and instead of white wine, Richard pulls out the chilled champagne he'd apparently stashed in the small refrigerator behind the bar in the den. As he pops the cork, he mentions we have a whole case. I don't remind him that we've already been into the case."

George pauses in his note taking, "I have a feeling this isn't going to go well."

My stomach churns as I remember. "We moved to the den after dinner, and by the time we opened the second bottle, I'd begun to dance on Claire's toy chest."

George touches my wrist, "Present tense."

Right. "Within minutes I leave, headed upstairs for the bedroom and adjoining bathroom. I throw up." My stomach gets queasy again as I talk. "I should know better than to drink more than one drink."

George writes on the notepad, and then looks up. "You can't drink more than one?"

I nod. "Dale follows me into the bathroom, wets a washcloth, and places it on my forehead. How thoughtful is that? When I ask about Richard, Dale matter-of-factly tells me he and Karen are in the backyard. Screwing."

I bend over and clutch my stomach. "My mind crashes. No information in. No information out. Dale holds my head while I wretch and mosaic blue tiles on the floor spin out of control."

I wipe my forehead and my eyes on my sleeve. "Damn, George, this is a repeat of that first time in Gainesville when Richard screwed his friend's wife."

"Back to the break-up."

I want to stall. "Sometime in the next week or so, Dale calls to see how I'm doing. I find out Richard's late night two nights ago was spent with Karen, not in a meeting. When he returns home, I confront. He admits it. I insist on my night out. I call Dale the next day and arrange a meeting on his boat in Sausalito. We talk. We have revenge sex."

George jerks backward. Is he judging me? "You've got to remember, George. This happened in the seventies in San Francisco, the time of free love and open marriages—accompanied by free-flowing alcohol, and for a lot more people, pot and acid. You remember what it was like then, don't you?"

His lips part as if he wants to say something. I shake my head assuming he's questioning if I had been into drugs.

I have to get through this as quickly as possible. "With the revenge sex out of the way, we find we actually like each other. After a few weeks of this, Dale tells me I must decide what I want to do. If I stay with Richard, he will back out of the picture. He puts the decision in terms of concern for me, as I'm being torn between wanting my marriage to work and what I now know was really the survival of what little self-esteem I still had."

In hindsight, the only way I could manage any self-esteem would have been to run, not walk away from that marriage long before I did.

My hands rush to my mouth. "My god. My decision affected Dale, too. How could I have been so self-absorbed?"

George gives me a thumbs up.

"I tell him I'll stay. I have too much invested in my marriage to leave."

George crosses a leg over his knee and leans back, kicking his foot up and down.

"More time goes by. I have no idea how long." A sharp pain crosses the back of my neck. At the time, I don't realize this will be my last day of indecision in the House-of-King-Richard. "As we sit down to a meatloaf dinner in our sunny kitchen, a doe munches on the red geraniums outside the floor-to-ceiling window. Richard licks his lips, 'Meatloaf. It's one of my favorites. You never fix it anymore. All we eat around here is Mexican or French.'"

I need to shift. I put my feet up on the trunk. "He's never mentioned it before. Could have saved me a lot of time and a lot of trouble. Not really," I realize I cooked what I like to eat. "I tried to cook things that were healthy for him."

"Meatloaf's not healthy?" I can almost see George salivating.

"Not the way we liked it, which kept it off his cholesterol-reducing diet. Bacon on top of well-marbled ground beef was not on the menu for him."

"He had high cholesterol? Wasn't he younger than you?"

I think a minute. "Yeah, he was probably twenty-five or six when he was told to reduce it."

"Sorry for the interruption," he says. "Back to the break-up."

"In the middle of dinner, Richard asks what he should do." A smile breaks out as I remember. "I ask what he's talking about. He wants to know what he should do about Karen."

George's head startles back.

"Stunned? Me, too. Why would he ask me what to do? That's as bad as Mother asking me, a three-year-old, if she should call the doctor. For once, I tell him I don't give a flying flip what he does. Nor with whom. Enough is enough. Besides, I know he's not going to give up what he can maintain on the side. If I've learned nothing else from my marriage, it is that Richard is unable to keep his pants zipped. I say, 'I'm leaving you,' in my most matter-of-fact voice." My neck and shoulder muscles let go.

"Just like that?" He picks at a cuticle. "You made the decision just like that?"

"I did." I press my fingers to my lips. "Oh my god, I did the same thing with Todd. When enough is enough, I go."

George gives me another thumbs up. I point towards the bedroom. He stands while I shoot through the bedroom into the bathroom. False alarm. Dry heaves.

When I return, he asks if I'm okay.

I take another sip of ginger ale. "Pretty much." Can I do this?

"Richard informs me he has more resources than I do. As if I needed that reminder. The Voice of Reason also reminds me that I will be a single parent, that I have no education, and that my earning power is limited."

George writes in his notebook. "You shrank down as if you were a child. How old are you?"

I take a deep breath and feel my age inside my body. "Five," when I had no education.

He signals me to continue. "I reminded him how he got his two degrees."

"That's right. You put him through school."

"Not according to Richard, whose tone of voice signaled an increase in his blood pressure. I simply paid my living expenses." My forehead tightens. "Guess you would have to believe that if your father cut you off from funds because you married again so soon after leaving your first wife."

George's face turns red. "How did you know his blood pressure was high?"

"He'd been diagnosed with high blood pressure, and his face couldn't have gotten any redder without capillaries bursting."

"You're doing good. Know this is hard. Can you hang in here a little longer?"

"Think so." I'm not so sure.

"…Pay your living expenses…," he prompts, looking almost as haggard as I feel.

"I remind him we lived in the same apartment and shared the same utilities. Ones I paid for."

"Present tense."

"I remind him that Claire is still my daughter."

I put my hand over my mouth and sneeze. "In his I-know-what-is-best-for-all voice, he predicts my future: no man will want to be saddled with our daughter and—here's the clincher to his argument—I need a husband to support me. Then he reminds me Claire will have two parents instead of one if she goes with him."

"Damn," he stretches the word into three syllables.

"I know."

I'm back in that kitchen. "Paralysis sets in. I can't think. I feel the wood's coolness as I run my finger along the top of the yellow kitchen chair. My eyes trace the seat's basket weave. I want to run; my legs glue themselves in place. I want to fight back. No words come." The knot in my stomach increases. I can do this. I will do this. "A vise squeezes the breath from my chest. I am powerless."

Where did the strength come from? "'NO!' I walk away. Movement opens my mind. I weigh my options. I want to talk to Dale about it. After all, Richard will marry his wife if I leave."

My leg vibrates. "Even after all these years, I still can't shake off the helplessness. I know Richard has a point. I can't give Claire all the things Richard can. She needs two parents." I get up and pace.

"I also know Richard won't stop me from seeing Claire. As angry as I am, I'm afraid I would prevent him from seeing his daughter. Not fair to Claire. I don't know what to do." As I sit down, tears stream down my cheeks and drip on my shirt. "I don't know how to be a mother. I'm afraid I'm a bad mother." Terrified is more like it.

George reaches over and puts his hand on my back behind my heart. "Cry it out." I sob until there are no tears left. He shifts position and cradles me.

"Why would you think you're a bad mother?"

"Because. Because." I sniffle. "Because I have no way to compare my mothering to a good mother. I don't know how to be a mother."

"I think you've had enough for now." His eyes tear up. "Is there anything you want to add before we stop?"

"Richard informs me we are going with Dale and Karen to pick up our boat from Alameda and move it to our new dockage in San Rafael on Friday night." My stomach churns as I remember that night. "They will meet us in San Rafael and drive us to Alameda to pick up the boat. We'll have a car in both places." My crossed leg begins to swing back and forth, faster and faster. "That's it."

"Lunch?"

"Not sure how much I'll be able to eat, but rice and feta should stay down." I sit up. "A walk around the lake afterwards?"

On the ride to the little international restaurant, I readjust my attitude and put on my smiley face. When we walk in the door, we're the only customers. The owner starts by crossing his arms into an X.

I point a finger at him. "Don't you start with me," as I check out today's special. "If you do, I will tell everyone you serve rats for the chicken on your menu." His face turns into a replica of The Scream.

By the time I've ordered my usual comfort food, rice and feta, his eyes twinkle. "If you tell people I serve rats, I will lock you in the storage room without food or water until you recant."

"Took you all that time to think of a retort?" I laugh again, and take my cup to the water cooler to fill it before I go to my usual table. George soon follows. He's laughing. "He said he'd pay me big bucks to pick you up and carry you out of here right now. And make sure you don't come back."

"He *was* laughing, wasn't he?"

George shakes his head, no. My face must have registered shock because they both start to laugh. I shake my fist at the owner, and he laughs harder.

George picks up a piece of pita and uses it to push the lentil onto his fork. He takes a bite and swallows. "What was San Francisco like when you were there? Sounds like a lot of drinking."

"There was. At one of the places I worked, we'd often have drinks at lunch. I soon discovered that was not something I wanted to indulge in."

"Why not?"

I take a swallow of water from the paper cup. "I worked in places where I handled money. It was too easy to lose concentration. We did go out for drinks on Friday night after work. All get-togethers, regardless of the reason, revolved around alcohol. It was simply a way of life out there."

I gather a forkful of rice and feta. Some falls onto my plate. "When I think about it, I suspect the drinking was more about the times, because even in Jacksonville, we'd go to a bar after we'd fly. Open containers were a way of life. Remember the drive-in liquor stores?" I take a bite.

"When you worked at the airport?"

All at once, customers start piling into the restaurant. The noise level rises. "Yeah. Had a lot of pilot friends who would take me up. There were three or four of us who flew and then partied. I don't remember any of us having more than one drink before we dispersed to our respective homes."

George leans in and props his chin in his cupped hands. "Have you always hung out with guys?"

I finish chewing my salad and swallow. "Hadn't thought of it that way, but pretty much. I'd mostly had boys to play with as a child. There was just you in the Bradenton neighborhood."

"And now, your two best friends are male."

"No wonder my neighbor calls me a slut. She thinks I sleep with my friends, all of them. She doesn't realize you guys are like brothers." I sip some water. "That's about her. Not me."

George shrugs as if to say what's new.

I gather my dirty plate and plastic-ware together. George takes his and comes back for mine.

When we pay our bills, the owner says, "Don't forget about the storage room," in his most serious parental tone.

I mumble, "Rats," and then laugh.

He grins, and as we walk out the door, "Don't hurry back!"

George opens my car door and then gets in his car. We drive the short distance to the lake. It's one of those rare Florida days with a cloudless baby blue sky, bright sun, and a cool breeze. Perfect for a walk.

Chapter 19

When I pull into my usual parking space at the lake, I look at my phone before placing my purse in the trunk. There is a call from Frank. No message. I return the call but it goes straight to voicemail. I turn off the phone, place it in my purse, and close the trunk.

As I walk toward the Frog, George finds a shady spot near the coffee shop. The organic market people set up as we begin our walk. I wave to the man in the corner with fresh greens, potatoes, onions, and peppers. Might have to stop by before I go home.

George greets me with a hug, and then we circle the lake. I reopen the Claire conversation because I must get this out, and I'm in a safe place. A place where I won't break down and sob uncontrollably. Can't afford to go back to that mental state. I have to have been through the worst of it when Alex died. I did not drink through that. I keep reminding myself that my feelings will not kill me; nor will they cause me to go crazy, but it feels like they will.

"George, are you okay with finishing up my Claire story while we walk? I'm calmer now, and maybe walking will help work off the feelings of inadequacy and helplessness before they swamp me."

"Sure. It's a big piece of who you are now." He points to a family of geese. There are eight of them. I recognize them from last year when they left one behind. It hadn't learned to fly yet.

For some reason, seeing all eight together gives me a feeling of security. "We'd pulled into the San Rafael dock. Once the boat was secure, Karen picked up Claire and set her on the dock, less than a foot away from her dad. I stepped off the boat, an almost empty cooler in my hands. A large dog ran by me, brushing my leg. Before I could call out, Claire was in the water." A pain digs into my throat.

"Present tense."

"Black water appears between the dock's slits. I can't see Claire." I clutch my stomach.

George places his hand on my back as we walk.

"A man jumps into the black water." The pain creeps down to my shoulder.

"He has her. She is back on the dock, coughing and wailing. The kind of cry that only a terrified child can make." Tears drip from my eyes and the sweaty salt on my face combines with the memory of the fishy air of San Francisco Bay.

Even though the temperature is in the eighties, I wrap my arms around me to warm myself. "I am frozen in place, cold. Chilled to the bone, into-my-very-cells cold. Every muscle in my body strains to reach out, take my baby girl in my arms. I leave my body. She has another mother now. Through the self-created veil between my mind and my body, I hear Richard shouting at me to go with Karen, and take care of my daughter because she needs me."

I stumble. George catches my arm, "I follow Karen. I don't take care of Claire."

He leads me to a bench.

"I leave that up to Karen. I know if I hold her, I'll never let her go. Emotionally, I feel nothing. I throw up." I will not. I will not. I will not vomit.

George reaches over and touches my shoulder. "How could you stop yourself from feeling?"

My leg bounces, up and down. Up and down. Years of practice living with an unfaithful husband. "We had wine with dinner, the feelings balm." Egad!

"Your whole body just shifted," George says, "What happened?"

"I realized that was the moment I began to use alcohol to snuff out my feelings. Months and even two years afterwards, I used to sit in my chair and look out at the Golden Gate at sunset with a glass of wine or two or three. Can you believe that I even drew a curled-up young woman in a wine glass? I drew it on paper and never made the connection."

My laugh is a nervous one. George laughs with me.

"I have no memory of how we got to my house, but I must have bathed and put Claire to bed. I remember Dale pulling out his guitar and singing *The First Time Ever I Saw Your Face*. Not since my mother sang lullabies had anyone sung to me. I don't know where Richard and Karen had gone, but they weren't at the house." Why can't I remember? "I think that is the night I left. I don't remember when I packed my clothes and books. That whole week is a blur." The whole six months after my birthday is a blur.

From my birthday until the divorce is final, almost a year later, I have no recollection. My life is a jumbled mess. "I think I stayed with Richard until sometime in July. I have snatches of memory of Richard and me during that time. Like taking dinner to the boat and eating while it remained at the dock. We must have tried to keep the marriage together."

"We, Lee?"

"Okay, I tried. I don't have whole memories, just flashbacks. Pieces of a memory, here and there." I'd never understood how people couldn't remember their childhoods. So this is what post-traumatic stress disorder is like. I put my arm through George's. "After I move out of the house, I see Claire every other weekend from July through the middle of December. We pack the weekends with trips to the zoo—Claire is fascinated with the orangutans. We watch sea otters from the Cliff House. We take walks in Golden Gate Park, first to watch buffalo wandering around in their habitat, followed by tea and almond cookies at the Japanese Tea House. We even take her to Sausalito to see the replica of San Francisco Bay and watch the tides." Claire is a curious child and wants to see everything.

"Richard and Karen plan to spend Christmas with Karen's family." I will not spend Christmas with my child. "The weekend before she's to leave, Dale and I take her to FAO Schwartz to pick out her Christmas present. Funny how I remember, for her birthday, she picks out a doll's suitcase, patent leather, shaped like a hatbox, and makes it her own. I don't remember what she chooses for Christmas."

As George and I walk along the concrete walk, I stumble. "I'm confused, George."

He grabs me and leads me to a nearby bench.

I flashback to a walk with Claire in Golden Gate Park. Dale remains in the background.

Claire, dressed in her blue and white dress and shiny patent leather shoes, becomes a fairy princess as we spend the afternoon at the park, ending with almond cookies and tea. She reminds me while we drink tea that she's, "a big girl now, Mommy."

We drop off Dale and my then three-year-old packs the rest of her things in her suitcase, one for a big girl like her. Once her bag is packed, she crawls into her car seat, with a box of raisins, for her ride back to Marin County. She's subdued on the trip. I am too.

When we pull into the drive, she begins to cry as I release her from the car seat and gather her things. By the time we get to the front door, she sobs. She screams. "Mommy, Mommy, don't go. P'ease, Mommy, don't go." I cough to suppress my sobs.

George reaches into his back pocket and pulls out a handkerchief. I dab my eyes as the picture returns.

I grab her, hold her tight, and with tears streaming down my face, I tell her I have to go. And to "remember that I love you and that I'll always love you, no matter what. I'll see you soon, my darling daughter." With that, I walk out of a house filled with memories of my old life.

When I get to the car, I let go. My tears flow freely as I drive down the hill towards the freeway that takes me back to the City.

Two days later, I call Richard. I tell him that our weekend goodbyes have become more traumatic for both Claire and me every time I take her back to him. I tell him I'm not going to see her for six months. He yells and yells at me. He yells that I can't do that. Not to his daughter.

I tell him six months will give her time to adjust to her new family and provide some distance for me to come to terms with this. Again, he tells me I can't do that. That she's my daughter. I pour a glass of wine.

My body shakes and trembles like aftershock as wave upon wave of grief rock my body. George leans in and places his hand on my back, but says nothing.

When I look up, the bamboo cage by the American Legion building catches my eye. I am a prisoner whose memories keep me in that cage. Time to let go.

George's hand behind my heart supports me. "Where did you go?"

I describe the flashback. "I did what was best for both of us. I tried to explain that the bond we had would loosen some and she'd become used to Karen as her mother. I hung up and threw up." The dappled shadows sway across the concrete walk as a breeze picks up. "Where did he get off trying to make me feel guilty for doing what was best for Claire and for me? He's the one who threatened me with a custody battle. He's the one who told his family and mine that I had left him for another man. He's the one who instigated the divorce. How could my mother have taken his side?"

George clears his throat, his hand still on my back. "Stop and think a minute. For her, who was that about?"

I take three, slow, deep breaths. "Of course! She was afraid of losing her granddaughter, her only grandchild. Still doesn't make it any easier to take."

I lean back on the bench and process what I have told George. For some reason, I begin to understand that Richard was reliving his own parents' divorce and his subsequent loss. His reaction was coming from that six-year-old child whose father disappeared.

I turn and look at George. "Five months later, when I pick up Claire, Richard and Karen are living in an apartment in San Rafael. So much for Richard's insisting that Claire needed to stay in our house for continuity."

I take a deep breath. "I'd signed the quit claim deed within a week of leaving."

George exhales, "Whew!"

"The first five years after our divorce were the hardest. There wasn't a day that I didn't plot some sort of revenge. It got easier…. Let me back up. Todd and I had promised Claire I'd regain custody once she turned twelve, the age children can choose. That year, we asked her if she still wanted us to do that." I shift to my other hip.

"My mature child told us her dad needed her more than I did. She recognized that I had remained happy without clinging to her. Even I knew he would be devastated if she lived with me. Like my daughter, I couldn't do that to him either."

I learned why I was comfortable letting Karen raise her. "Several years ago, I did a past life regression to see why even as a child, I felt such a connection to India. In the process, I discovered that I had been born in India at some point, but the more interesting piece was when I moved forward into the eighteen hundreds. I saw myself getting married in London at a cathedral." A crow caws. Another one answers. "My mother was helping me dress and giving me advice on being a wife. That mother was Claire's stepmother, Karen. Somehow I had known that my daughter would have a good mother. So that's why I could give up Claire and not resent Karen."

"You don't seem to have much animosity towards Richard, even though you lost everything in the divorce."

"You're right. Losing Claire to the divorce and Alex's death taught me the value of relationships versus material things. I've always maintained a relationship with Claire. Besides, I didn't lose my sanity."

His face quizzical, "Didn't you have to struggle to pay your bills?"

"Not really. I knew what I could afford and I didn't exceed that."

"Tell me about your job."

I have an urge to push on. "Teller for Bank of America in a small branch."

"Your demeanor changed right before you spoke."

"I was remembering—"

George's alarm goes off. "Time to go to class."

"Your last question brought up an incident at the bank where I worked. It's important. Do you mind if I write it out and email you?"

"Please do. See you later."

As George hurries off to class, I circle the lake two more times. Now I'm ready to write about what turned out to be a life-changing event.

Yin and Yang greet me as I walk in the door. When I leave my shoes at the door, Yin rubs all over them. Yang tugs on my leg. When I stroll into the den and place my purse and keys on my desk, the babies follow. I lie on the floor and play with them until they get bored, and saunter away. What was chaos and tumult, metamorphoses into the calmness of a sheltered lake.

After a few minutes, I'm ready to pull down my journal from my cubbyhole and write my experience to George:

June 7, 2002

I was remembering what, at the time, I considered a minor blip that caused me to leave Bank of America where I worked as a teller and safe deposit person. Last year when I was learning to do TIR, trauma incident reduction, I picked out the bank robbery as my traumatic incident.

Yeah, George. I hear. Present tense.

Three gunmen, dressed in black, stockings covering their faces, storm the bank. Guns drawn. I'm sitting at the safe deposit desk, and automatically do what I'd been told for years. I size each man up against the wall, noting where he's standing from my point of view so that I can give accurate descriptions.

The nearest one points his gun toward me and tells me to go to the vault and get him the money. I have no way of doing this without the key to the money. I look at the head teller to give me the keys as I tell him I can't. She turns her back on me. He lines me up in his gun sight. His voice is low. Threatening. "Go. To. The. Vault." I go, knowing I cannot get to the money. Instead of following, they leave. I walk out as the police enter the bank. Guns drawn.

The police take my statement. Later that afternoon, someone from the main office calls and congratulates me on arguing with the gunmen. I should have been reamed out for arguing, not congratulated.

Not until the TIR training did I realize the importance of the decision I made that day. In the TIR protocol, you project the incident on a visual screen in your head and repeat the scene out loud. At the end of the description, the facilitator asks if you feel lighter or heavier until you get clarity about how the incident changed your belief system.

I chose the bank robbery because it was easiest and the least traumatic, but significant, incident in my life. Now I know I was guided to choose this particular occurrence. At the end, I realized I made the decision that my life wasn't worth twenty-five hundred dollars, the amount that was stolen. And lived my life as if that were true.

Explains a lot, doesn't it?

Later, when I learned Richard was making a million dollars a year with a two hundred fifty thousand dollar expense account, I was happy for him. Without him and his money, my life flows along in the stream with as few crashing waves as possible. Even better, he has no say in how I live my life.

I walked away from even more money and from my dream house in my second divorce. Gratefully. When Todd began making money again, he thought he could use it to control me.

Hmm, I think this explains my need to be financially independent.

I scan my journal pages and fax them to George. I collapse on my bed, mentally exhausted. This process consumes energy like a fire consumes dried grass. Instead of relaxing, I think about the changes I should make to my dissertation.

A week later, I'm at Frank's house, editing, when he comes in from the park. As I'm about to gather up my things, he invites me to return for dinner.

"Great. I'm going to go do my run and then clean up. What time do you want me back?"

"How about six-thirty?"

"Works for me," I say as I give him a quick kiss on the lips. I settle into my car, open the sunroof, back out, and cruise home.

When I return to Frank's, his shower is running. I choose one of the books I left on the floor and thumb through it.

Frank walks naked into the living room. "Hey, I didn't hear you come in. Have you been here long?"

"Just long enough to find my place in this book. And, to hear you sing "Strangers in the Night" off-key. Anything you want me to do while you're naked?"

"No, Hon. I'll cook if you'll clean up."

Okay, he either didn't hear me or he used a shot last night. "Want me to set the table while you do dinner?"

"Wait until I clear it off."

There is no way I would tackle the table: layers upon layers of papers, junk mail and bills mixed together cover the surface. He knows where everything goes. I don't. "Okay." I return to the book.

Once dressed, Frank microwaves three pieces of chicken, a thigh and drumstick for him, and a thigh for me. While the chicken cooks, he clears off the table by stacking everything in a heap and putting it on the floor, amongst his many other piles. When the chicken is done, he microwaves two small potatoes and a mug full of frozen mixed vegetables. He dumps mixed salad into bowls and adds grape tomatoes. The bottled dressing is on the table. I pour the wine. To Frank's, I add two ice cubes and then fill his glass with water.

I rarely eat at Frank's. My mother, who never met Frank, would have described his cooking as "boiled, no seasoning, plain food." The meal is a corpse lying on the plate. The beige-gray chicken is without spices to walk across the tongue. I say nothing and fill up on salad. Hold the dressing. I'll get some nutrition from the raw vegetables.

The dinner conversation is light and easy. I talk about the dissertation, Frank talks about what he'd done that day to avoid painting the park's restroom. To buy paint, he took the most circuitous route to the farthest paint store that mixed the color he needed. I laugh at his antics, particularly when he tells me, "I thought I would call in tomorrow and tell them I'm having eye trouble. Can't see why I should show up." Why do I encourage his bad behavior? Because. I might say the same thing, but I wouldn't act on it. That's why.

With dinner over, I start the dishes, and Frank goes to the back of the house. I'm thinking about an editing change when Frank stalks into the kitchen and says, "You need to go. Now!"

Chapter 20

I shudder at his tone. I turn, a plate in hand. "How about when I finish the dishes?"

"I said now," his face in a snarl. "Quit trying to control me. You have to have everything your way," says this man, who seems to make it his life's purpose to avoid being controlled. This is a repeat of the beach. For God's sake, what set him off this time?

The evidence of his fear of being controlled is over his shoulder, on the floor and on the sagging bookcase crowded with old magazines and junk newspapers. His need to collect everything has now accumulated into a mound of paper spread halfway across his living room. The junk he removed tonight will remain on the floor, soon to receive yet another layer. No one is going to make Frank toss anything. He doesn't even know he's controlled by all that stuff he keeps, so much of it that he can't find what he needs. He buys more to replace what is buried deep.

"After five years," I place the plate in the drainer, "you should know what happens when you order me to do something." It has been a running joke that I'll refuse to do it, even if it's something I'd planned to do all along. A childhood reaction to my mother's demands.

I soften my tone. "You're right. In some areas, I control. That's why I have two computers and a back-up hard drive for my dissertation. As for trying to control you, I don't think so." Frank is a product of his family, too.

He is an only child, born when his parents were in their thirties. According to a woman I recently met who has known him since he was a child, his father was an alcoholic and his mother a compulsive

Christian. They abided by the unspoken rule in alcoholic families: Don't talk. Don't trust. Don't feel. Written in marble by the time I met him. Parents deny what the child sees and experiences. Does Frank worry about being crazy like I do? Did he think he was just a little kid, so, what did he know?

"You need to leave right now," his face as red as the ripe tomato sitting on the counter. "This minute!" The vein on his temple pulses.

"And. Lock the gate behind you." He says through clamped teeth. Whoa. What's this? His cheek tics. Why does he want me to lock the gate? What would happen if I don't? The rebellious child is out tonight.

I put my hands on my hips and spread my feet. The powerful woman stance, the one I learned from Frank. Oh yeah, and Mother, too. "I'll leave when I finish the dishes. I have my own work to do." Okay, this is a conscious choice. "On second thought, I think I'll stay. I refuse to be ordered around. I had enough of that as a child. You are NOT my mother!" I rub my eyes and shake my head to clear my thoughts. Why do I allow him to bait me into acting like a child? I have no need to finish the dishes. They're his dishes. On second thought, screw the dishes.

I slowly dry my hands.

I mosey over to my things.

I put on hand lotion.

I pick up my pens with deliberation.

I put them in the backpack.

I gather my papers.

I place them, one by one, in my burgundy briefcase.

I place one book at a time in the briefcase.

I pick up the laptop.

I slowly zip it into its case, and place it in the backpack.

I pick up my purse, briefcase, backpack, and finally, the laptop.

I slip into my sandals.

I'm ready to go.

"Is the show about over?" Frank's face is the color of the wine we had for dinner. "Just leave. Now," he says as he lightly shoves my shoulder.

Acting as if I don't feel the shove, I saunter, with an attitude, towards the door.

He follows me to the door and slams it behind him.

"I don't know who you think you are, but you aren't." I say as I stroll to the car. He returns to his house. I start the motor as he closes his window. Then, the curtain. When I get through the gate, I lock it behind me. Once outside, I stop, my back against the gate. Why do I react to him the way I do? Even when I recognize I'm doing something childish, I either seem unable to stop myself, or I choose to continue. Am I being paranoid or is my gut telling me something important?

I pull the cell from my purse and call to apologize for my part in the argument. I've learned that if I take responsibility for my own actions, I clear my conscience and leave no unfinished business to muddy up my life but Frank's line is busy and he's not answering his cell.

Wonder who he's talking to. A woman? A woman I could watch drive up if I sit here? What would cause him to act like this? A woman? I will not sink that low, and I will not resort to spying. This is not who I am.

When I get through to Frank's voicemail, "I'm sorry for my part in this. Wish you'd pick up."

The light on the gas gauge blinks yellow. I stop at my regular station. My mind on the confrontation with Frank as I reflect back to our first year together and my original purpose for being with Frank: personal growth, and fun. How much fun is this? Not. Personal growth? Yep. I pull up to the pump, insert credit card, and just before I start to pump the gas, I notice I've lifted the *regular* unleaded lever. I reinsert my credit card and start over. This time, the pump tells me to go inside.

I wonder what made Frank so aggressive as I get in the car to pull up to the pump closest to the little store. As I pull away, I hear a strange noise. When I get to the new pump, the cover for my tank is twisted. I walk back to the other pump and see I must have pulled away with the nozzle still attached to my tank. My legs start to shake. Now the hose is disconnected from the pump. I tell the station manager and then pump premium gas from the new pump. I can't close the cover over my cap. I cannot let Frank's behavior affect me like this. Otherwise I might do even more serious damage.

When I walk into my townhouse, the light on the answering machine blinks red. I push play.

"Just who the hell do you think you are?" Did he slam his fist on the table? "You need to grow up! You act like a spoiled child!"

I picture him in a playpen, dressed only in a diaper. He lies on his back kicking his feet, tears streaming down his red face. In spite of myself, laughter erupts. Yeah, I'd been childish, but his rants and raves are perfect examples of his own maturity level. I don't respond.

I look out the window behind my chair. So much for working on the dissertation. The starry night and the cool light from the nearly full moon wash over me while I attempt to regain my equanimity.

What is wrong with that man? His mood jumps from the calm, rational person I fell in love with to this angry, aggressive stranger who wants me out of his house in a matter of seconds. How can he go from calm and relaxed to full-blown fury in sixty seconds or less? That's faster than my Supra from zero to eighty on a downhill run.

I cross to the desk and pick up my journal. The red silk cover reminds me of a sari. I need to journal more than work on my dissertation. I can't concentrate on the dissertation now anyway.

As I sit in my chair, lumps in the cushion's padding intrude upon my thoughts. Was Mother right about my being the princess who feels the pea under every mattress? To the left, beyond the antique chest used to store table linens and placemats, the kitchen calls. Coffee. Coffee. Coffee.

No. Instead, I open the journal and write:

June 15, 2002

How did a quiet dinner turn so vitriolic without a look or word from me? What's not right? I can't get a handle on it. Is there another woman? Did I say something wrong? No. I wasn't even talking, just thinking about what I had to do later. Okay, it's not me; at least not until I chose to engage with him. That's my part in the fight.

Oh yeah. George reminded me to get a plan. This is the second time Frank's been a little aggressive. I did get out, but I could have moved faster. I may need to rethink this. Time to problem-solve.

The problem: Frank's "You need to leave. NOW." Shoved me, gently, but still shoved me. How do I feel? Angry, hurt, disrespected, conflicted. What do I think?

Better pay attention to his mood swings. How do I want to see this problem resolved? Our time together should be pleasant. This is not pleasant.

I can choose to get sick, throw myself into my work, confront him, accept my powerlessness over the situation, and/or let it go and get on with life.

Right now, I can accept my powerlessness and let go. Forget the healthy way to do it. Just throw myself into my work. Since I allow him to treat me this way, I can stop.

The last two sentences are engraved into the paper two pages down. I put down my pen as Yin and Yang vie for attention by racing across the top of the footstool and then my feet, one after the other. I reach to scoop them up, but they're having none of it. When I get up from the chair to collect my earned coffee, they run and hide. Silly cats. Who needs cable with such entertainment?

The next day, I call George and explain what happened last night. After I finish reading him my journal entry, "Sounds like you can't let go of it. Did his behavior remind you of your mother?" His dog barks.

Yin turns and stares at the phone. "Do I need to let you go?"

"Nah, she just spotted a rabbit. About your mother?"

"Maybe. I'm pretty sure it was the demand that set me off. You know how Mother demanded rather than requested."

A mosquito buzzes around my ear. "When I hit my teens and experienced my runaway hormones, my mouth ran full throttle." I swat at my ear. "That's when I began baiting her."

"I remember. Was your engagement part of the bait?"

I rub my fingers through my hair and push it off my face. "I'm pretty certain she thought we were having sex." I rap my nails on my coffee cup. "The engagement must have confirmed it in her mind."

"Were you?" Curiosity tinges his question.

"God, no. Sex made babies and I wasn't going there."

"Smart, if simplistic. So what did you do?"

"Threatened marriage. I even got her to buy me a plain pale, gray-blue wool sheath, and then told her it was my wedding dress. Lots of threats to run off to Jessup, Georgia, where we could get married at sixteen."

George sighs, "What stopped you?"

"That's an interesting story in itself."

"I have plenty of time."

"It was a sweet night." The scent of gardenias and orange blossoms permeated the air. "And the first time I met my fiancé's twenty-three-year-old best friend. We double-dated to a Jai-alai game. Even used his friend's date's driver's license to get in."

"How'd you get away with that?"

"Remember, no photos then." I roll my neck from side to side before continuing. "On the way home that night, my so-called fiancé's friend said, 'Do you have a cousin Belinda? I dated a girl named Belinda Lawrence. She looks just like you, only five years older, and she talks like you, too.'" I take a breath. "Now comes the amazing part."

I walk to the kitchen. I pour a cup of coffee and microwave it. "When I got home, I diddly-bopped in the front door and…" I pause for effect. "…Both my parents are sitting in the living room. They'd never done that before."

"Was she a relative?" George asks.

"Well, when I asked, 'Do I have a cousin named Belinda?' Silence. Silence so filled with tension it was electric.

'No!' Mother answered while Dad sat there. I remember putting up my hands and backing out of the room, wondering what I'd said wrong this time." My stomach tightens.

George clears his throat, "Did you ever learn what you said wrong?"

"Yeah. When Mother went to church the next night, Dad sat me down in my bedroom and explained he'd gotten drunk at a frat party, while he was pinned to my mother, and got his high school girlfriend pregnant. He'd married her and then divorced her after Belinda was born." Bet you didn't know that about my family.

"That is a shock."

"I later learned he'd spent a lot of time in Venice, I presume with her and her mother. My dad must have known who the friend was. That's why they were waiting in the living room."

George's intake of breath comes through the phone. "God, Lee. That must have been a shock. I thought you came from the perfect family."

"You would. It was Mother's public persona. After he related the story of Belinda, he told me that if I were so hell-bent on getting married, he'd sign for me, but that he would not let me come between my mother and him. Three days later, I broke the engagement." I take a deep breath and let it out. "We broke up because I was going to your Christmas party at the Manatee Hotel. After all, the idea of marriage was no longer fun."

Silence.

"You had no idea, did you?"

George lets out a breath, "Whew! Did your relationship change before she died?"

I heat up my coffee. "Yeah."

While he thinks it over, I stick my coffee in the microwave for another thirty seconds. "Years later, after Alex died, I said something to bait her, and she calmly said, 'I'm not going there.' That's when I realized my part in our problems thanks to my years in recovery."

He chuckles. "You haven't changed. You still study yourself, don't you?"

"Pretty much." I take my coffee back into the den and sit in my chair. "I made my peace with her before she died. She was grateful to me for helping her through her guilt after Dad died. Then she was supportive after Alex died, not during the process, but afterwards." I swallow a sip of coffee. "While Alex became weaker and weaker, she changed the subject whenever I brought it up. It became so comical that Alex and I took bets on how quickly she'd make the subject about something innocuous. I guess people do weird things when death pounds on the door. At least Alex and I did."

"Do I remember something about her going into an assisted living apartment? That didn't happen?"

"It did. My brothers put her into a facility about three months before she died. I was able to stay out of the fray because I was moving here for school around the same time. Mom's threat was always that she would die within a month of going into a nursing home." She didn't. But she came damned close.

A door slams and shakes my townhouse. I jump. "Did my mother keep in close contact with your mom over the years?"

"After my dad died. Didn't yours die first?"

I nod. "I think so."

"Do you see any correlation between your balking at Frank and your relationship with your mother?"

"Well, yeah. Haven't you heard me say I married my mother three times?" Maybe not. "Richard was the controlling mother, Todd the addicted mother, and Alex the nurturing mother. Guess Alex could also fit into the addicted label, too, even though he was sober. One of the first things I noticed about Frank was that he often says things in my mother's tone and with her mannerisms. When both of us are relaxed and that happens, I can tell him no and laughingly say he sounds like my mother. He knows that's one of my buttons."

"Whose choice is it to react?"

You sound like Alex. "Mine," I take a drink of the hot coffee. "I know."

"I have to ask, did Frank get aggressive again? Sure sounded like he might have."

Oh George, I know you're having difficulty staying detached, and I know you won't tell me what to do. "You mean the push?"

"Yeah," his tone expectant.

I don't want to answer. To be honest, I hadn't thought about his pushing me out the door as aggressive, but it was.

"Lee? Where'd you go, Lee?"

"Thinking about last night. I guess he was a little aggressive. He only lightly pushed my shoulder to get me out the door.

"A little aggressive?"

Didn't we already have this conversation? "I did it again, didn't I? I make molehills out of mountains around events that should be taken seriously and I exaggerate the insignificant ones."

"C'mon, most people do at one time or another. As for you, why do you think that is?"

"When I took Hakomi professional training in Asheville, that came up a lot. Those of us who grew up in families where we were told to believe one thing and we saw something entirely different, grew up unable to discern toxic behavior from nurturing behavior." I take a swallow of coffee and think about the lecture I gave my cats.

"Mother spanked me often and harder than necessary to get my attention, while at the same time telling me it hurt her worse than it did me." My eye tics. "Ha, she never spanked me unless she was angry. Even as a little kid, I knew that was pure bullshit."

I look at the time. "I'm sorry, George, I shouldn't have taken up so much of your time on my relationship problems."

"That's what friends are for. If I were in a relationship, I'm sure I'd call you."

"I bet you would." I smile, hardly believing how easily we've picked up where we left off in our teens. "Well, I owe you a home-cooked dinner for this one. You available anytime this week?"

"I'm staying in town this weekend. How about Friday or Saturday evening?"

"Let's make it Saturday. I'll call you tomorrow and we can set the time."

Two days later, George calls and asks if I can meet him at the Lake Ella Vietnam memorial helicopter by the American Legion at nine the next morning. I assume it has to do with the journal piece I sent him.

The next morning, I arrive a few minutes early and take a turn around the lake. The air is clear with a soft breeze off the water. It seems more like spring than mid-August. The cooling rain last night has broken the heat. Mallards and geese stop by their summer resort on their way to somewhere else. Besides the waterfowl, the lake area is a stopover for the many vagabonds wandering through here.

By the time I complete my round, George waits on the bench by the helicopter. He stands as I run up to give him a hug. He is the one stable person in my life right now.

We cut across the grass towards the Frog's deck. The high table for two overlooking the lake is perfect. I wait while George goes for the coffee. Behind me, I hear a familiar voice from my past. Is that Joy behind me? On her cell?

"Yes, I'm talking about the Frank Islip." She has my attention. "Seeing two different women. One is that bitch that bought Vinnie's beach house. Needs a lesson in humility. No, she has no idea. You'd think two would be enough but, no, he has three more he sees during the day. What? Of course I'm following him. Don't I always?"

I look toward the lake hoping I can overhear better.

"I heard him tell one of his pilot buddies that when he goes out of town with one of them, he has to use the restroom several times a day to keep in touch with the others. He was laughing when he said, 'Can you believe she swallowed my story about having diarrhea when I spent twenty minutes in the can. Funny how I don't get up at night to go.' Yeah, he said that."

What the—? Is she talking about Frank?

"They both laughed. 'I should weigh practically nothing since I've had diarrhea for the past thirty days.' His buddy asked something I couldn't hear."

Can't be.

"But Frank said, 'Yeah, I even told her I was just checking the time.' He had to be talking about the beach-house bitch."

Must be Frank. I'm sure I'm the bitch.

"Yeah, he did mention mules."

Can't be Frank. He doesn't own mules.

"Does he own mules?"

Or does he?

I'm so engrossed in what I hear that I jump when George arrives with our coffees. "Thanks, George."

He smiles that smile I remember from our youth. "My pleasure."

I try to hear more of the conversation behind me. A strange look crosses George's face. Joy passes by the table. I'm glad she didn't stop.

I lean in toward George. "What brought on your frown?"

"Did you see that woman who just passed us, the one who looks like death warmed over?"

I nod.

"She gave you the strangest look, a self-satisfied smirk."

My skin crawls. Was Joy telling the truth? There has to be some truth in what she said. How else would she know what he did on our trip?

He stirs his coffee. "I see her lurking behind trees a lot when we're here."

"She's the crazy one who tore up the beach house before I bought it." My stomach sinks. "She was just talking about Frank on her cell."

George leans across the table and takes my hand. "How do you know that for sure?"

"She described Frank's behavior on our trip." Sweat forms on my forehead. "And she mentioned the beach bitch, which I assume is me, who bought Vinnie's house."

George squeezes my hand. "Guess that's the answer to your question the other day."

I give him my everything-is-fine smile. "I was going to dump Frank as soon as I knew for sure he was cheating on me. Well, now I know. Time to make a move."

Concern spreads across his face. "You going to be okay?"

"Yeah, once I figure out whether I'm sad or hurt or angry or all three together." I still can't understand why he remains married.

George winks. "And probably many, many more feelings underneath those first few." He gives me a hug before he tucks me in my car, and I realize just how much I'm going to miss my friend for the next week or so. Between grading exams, posting grades, and graduation, he'll stay busy until time to leave for Bradenton. He turns back towards me. "You might want to Google him. Just a thought."

I hadn't thought of that. When I began dating Frank, it seemed like an invasion of his privacy but then if it's on Google, the world has access. "Thanks, I will."

When I arrive home, I go straight to the computer and turn it on. Yin jumps up on the desk and Yang winds himself around my ankle. I reach down, pick him up, and hold him close. "You're such a lover, little one."

I fire up the computer and type, Frank Islip. I keep searching through pages until I've found his name. It's connected with a lawsuit. Oh, my god. There it is: The reason Frank remains married— a wife is not required to testify against her husband. The plaintiff is Simon Dimsley. My committee head Simon. Simon was the plaintiff in a lawsuit against the Islips! I knew Simon had settled out of court. So that's the reason his son no longer speaks to him. Won't visit. Won't allow Simon to visit him in his Alaskan wilderness home. From the few sentences Simon has dropped over the years, his son's attitude slices into Simon's heart. No hope that he won't remember.

I spend another hour looking for more records. None. That was twenty years ago. No newspaper articles, nothing.

Did Simon connect my lover with the lawsuit? Will he find a way to destroy my chances of getting my doctorate? What can I do? My trembling hands can barely tap the keys. Breathe. Make a plan.

I get up and shake. I start with my head and neck, then my shoulders and arms, and finally my legs and feet. I shake and shake and shake. Finally, I can begin to think again. What would I do right now if I hadn't seen this?

I continue to prepare for my defense, trusting that I will know what to do before I go into the defense. Over the weekend, I talk with two friends in recovery. I know what to do, have known it all along. Just needed a reminder. I make an appointment with Simon for this afternoon. Tomorrow is the last day I have to see him before my defense.

As I prepare for my meeting with Simon, the phone rings. "Hi. It's just me. Frank Islip here." Damn, that's annoying.

"Just wanted to let you know my Ocala aunt just died. The funeral is Tuesday, so I'll miss your defense."

"Oh." Good. I won't have to deal with him. I'd forgotten that once I had the date, the first thing I did was invite Frank. No need to say anything to him now. I must do the dirty deed in person.

"Can't help it." His tone has a bite to it. "Have to go support my cousin and my other aunt. Know they'll want to go out to eat after. Gotta go pack my things. Talk to you later."

When I hang up, I search my crowded closet for my black top, one hanger at a time. I'll be so glad to get rid of Frank's few clothes in here. I separate two hangers. I gasp. That blue sweater, a mixture of cobalt lightened with cerulean, a color popular back in the sixties or even earlier—my dad had a golfing sweater that color when I was young. I've seen this sweater in Tallahassee before. The spring before I moved here. Before I knew I'd soon live here. I stood in church singing a hymn when the hairs on the back of my neck came to attention like soldiers preparing for battle. I shifted just enough to glance behind me and see a man wearing that blue sweater staring at me. He's here to pick up women. I will *not* be one of them.

My friend with whom I'm visiting elbowed me. "Predator," she mouthed.

I nodded. Oh, my god. Frank was that man. And I brought him to me with my vehement no!

I want to rip the sweater off the hanger and toss it in the garbage. Soon, both the sweater and the man will be gone.

I knock on Simon's door.

"Come in."

Two of my watercolor Christmas cards perch on the window ledge. He swivels to face me and points to the chair next to his desk. He leans back, elbows on the arms, fingers steepled. "What is so urgent, Lee, that you had to see me today?"

My insides quake. "I, I…" My face grows hot. "I need to tell you something." I can hardly breathe.

My words tumble over the cliff. "I Googled the man I've been dating and discovered he was responsible for—" His phone rings.

"Yes. No. Can we discuss this later?" with an edge in his voice. "Yes." He hangs up. "Sorry. Now where were you?"

"I was telling you I discovered—" There's a knock on the door.

"Come in."

A young student opens the door. "I'm sorry. I didn't know you had someone with you. I'll come back later." She shuts the door.

Simon peers over his glasses with an expectant look.

"I discovered that the man I've been dating is the one who was responsible for your son's injury." There. Now it's out. My muscles let go. Can't do anything about it now. "I didn't know."

His steepled fingers tap against each other. He looks up at me but doesn't seem to see me. Has he gone somewhere else? I can't read his face. Is this the end of my doctorate? I wipe my upper lip on my shirtsleeve.

Tears begin to form. I cough them away. I will not use tears to manipulate this man. He's already told me he's susceptible to women's tears.

It seems like hours have passed. "Lee, I—"

No, not the phone again.

Chapter 21

He picks it up. "I'll call you back." He dials four numbers, "Hold all my calls, please. Thank you."

At last, he checks his calendar and leans towards me. "I've known for months. You didn't seem to know."

"How long?" I take a deep breath. "How long have you known?"

He sighs. "Around the time of your prospectus."

My neck tightens. Stay calm. Don't let him see how you feel. "So you knew when you were moving that section from one chapter to the other?"

"I wasn't sure how much you knew, and I had to do some soul searching about it."

I bite my tongue to keep from saying the wrong thing. I breathe in peace and out my jumbled emotions. He's not making me a victim. He owns his part in this. Breathe.

"I knew that as your major professor I had the ability to keep you from graduating by stalling at each stage of the process, or by making certain your dissertation would never pass." The start of a smile crosses his face. "You are too good a student for the latter to happen."

He squirms in his seat. "I talked to a couple of people out of the department about the ethical thing to do. The stalling was my way of postponing my decision until I was clear about what I needed to do."

Suddenly, I know. "You fired me." I whisper. He did it for me. To protect me from him.

He nods. "I no longer have the power to prevent you from completing the program."

There's a knock at the door. He rises. "I have another appointment." He smiles. "Good luck Tuesday."

Instead of relaxing now that I know Simon won't prevent me from graduating, I go to the required party Friday night, but don't stay long. I want to go over my notes and my dissertation again and again and again. Labor Day is a day of labor for me.

The following morning, I dress in a navy knit suit and white blouse. I carry my heels in my briefcase along with the dissertation. Before I leave the parking lot, I take five deep breaths.

In the conference room, I wait with Megan for the committee to arrive. As we go over a few last minute details, I realize I am surprisingly calm. All my biofeedback has paid off.

George walks in next. Who told him where I'm defending? I forget he still has ties over here. He is exactly the person I need this morning.

Errol walks in. What's he doing here? "How's Atlanta?" He and Sara moved there following his graduation. How had he known about my defense?

He hugs me and grins. "Hot."

I rarely hear from him these days. When I do, it's to harangue me about finishing my program. I'm confused as to why he's here. "When did you get in?"

"Two days ago. We came to see Sara's mom." Joe must have told him.

My defense starts before we can say more.

Within fifteen minutes, Errol turns my defense into his bragging session. In the middle of a pontification, I say, "Errol, this is my defense. Please let me finish."

The committee members ask questions because they genuinely want to know the answers, not to see if they can trip me up. Suddenly, *I'm* the expert. The defense turns into a give and take exchange of information, nothing that feels like pressure. The most negative thing said in the room comes from the member from another school. He insists I'll never get a publication from my research because I have no statistics in the study. Even though I know I've done well, I'm nervous when I'm sent out of the room—Errol and George stay—while my life is in the hands of those four people.

Megan leaves the door open as she walks out. "Congratulations, Dr. Lindsey." Laughter.

My shoulders feel ten pounds lighter.

When I return to the conference room, I have a request for a journal article submission. So much for never.

Before he leaves, Errol congratulates me and gives me another hug. "I'm off to meet Sara."

"Thanks for coming. Will you be in town a while?"

Errol shakes his head, "We're heading home later this afternoon."

"Give Sara my best and tell her I miss her."

Once the conference room clears, Megan gives me a high-five and a big hug, and then we return to her office to discuss the requested changes. "Here are my notes. I will email you the suggestions from the other committee members tomorrow."

George waits outside Megan's office. "We are going to celebrate!" He grabs me and wraps me in a bear hug. "How does it feel to be Dr. Lindsey?"

"Strange. For the last seven years, my entire focus has been on this day. Now what'll I do?"

"You'll spend your time making corrections and preparing your dissertation for the university archives."

"Forgot about that."

"I have reservations at Chez Pierre for one-thirty."

I kiss him on the cheek. "Wow. Thank you."

When I arrive at the car, I call Frank and leave a message. George follows me home. Once inside the townhouse, George turns to me, hands on my shoulders, "You handled Errol well this morning. I'm not certain I'd have been as calm."

I must be getting better at being assertive. "Thank you." I hug him.

The weather is so hot when we return to the townhouse that I suggest a swim. George keeps a suit in the car for those times he can catch a quick swim at one of the city pools. I change into my suit in my room while George uses the guest bathroom. When we arrive at the pool, I realize I haven't been in since it reopened. George is a lap swimmer like me. As I swim, the sun beams its benevolent light on me and my heart opens like a leaf unfurling to allow photosynthesis to take place. I complete my laps and when we leave the area, I notice a bright red cardinal perched on a branch to my left. An omen?

Lunch is one of those leisurely, enjoy-the-moment times as we sit on the deck overlooking a small, wooded area. I can almost imagine being in a secluded resort, perhaps in Costa Rica. Afterwards, George drops me off as he heads to his first class of the day. This semester will cut into our Tuesday night dancing. He has a seven-thirty to nine-thirty class. At least he has forty-five minutes between classes.

The next day I drive by a bank on Mahan and see a white Miata convertible sitting out front with a For Sale sign on the windshield. I go inside and check the car out. I test-drive it. A Miata is the perfect fit. I receive permission to take the car to my mechanic for his stamp of approval. When I receive it, I become the owner of a 1994 Mazda Miata. I've wanted one since a friend showed me hers in North Carolina.

I call George. "I just bought myself a graduation present."

I have had to fight myself to keep from ending our relationship long distance. By the time Frank finally gets in touch, I almost regret not ending it over the phone or by email. But those methods are not my style. I want no ties to this man who could have cost me my doctorate.

When I open my door, he rushes in and attempts to enclose me in his arms. "I've missed you."

I push him away. "You stand there, expectant, as if the last three years never happened. What is it you want, Sonny Boy? Me? The numerous other women in your life?"

Another woman's Evening in Paris fragrances his jacket as he paws the floor. I could take his pulse by watching the vein in his neck. If I were so inclined.

He places his hand on my shoulder. "I've missed you."

I move away.

"What's wrong with you now?" His voice alone brings back the stench of rotting flesh and threatening gestures.

"You want to know?" I start with my fingers. I tick off my thumb: "You could have cost me my doctorate. You knew Simon was my major professor."

He jerks away.

Index finger: "All those two-week absences after you started an argument—you spent that time with another woman."

Middle finger: "The predicted trip from hell—the mysterious trips to the bathroom when you checked your cell and had to stop at the restroom, you talked twenty minutes."

Ring finger: "You refused to acknowledge my presence as you went into a convenience store to buy a drink and a snack."

Baby finger: "You put my health in jeopardy numerous times—those many women—including your reckless driving."

I start over as I flip up my thumb . . .

His eye twitches. I can almost feel his body jerking from the inside out. "You. You. You're trying to control me." A bead of sweat glistens on his forehead.

Now he's primed that pump. "Yeah. You think?" A surge of energy rushes from my chest to my head. "Let's talk about control."

He sits, his feet pointed towards the door. "You're always trying to control me."

"That line won't work anymore. Do I control what you do? Do I control what you say? Do I try and control what you think?"

His face reddens.

"You are the one with the control issues. You have controlled me by controlling my emotions. If I sensed that you were upset, I backed off. No more."

"When is dinner?"

"Do you think I'm feeding you? What part of this do you not understand?"

"Are you breaking up with me?"

Tears start to form. I cough to cork the tears instead. "Do you think I'm seducing you? No. I'm not. Yes, I want you out of my life." I march into the bedroom and grab all his keys from my nightstand. When I return, I shove the keys in his face. "I'll take my keys now." I hold out my hand.

"You planned this all along didn't you?" his voice strangled.

"Only since I discovered your dirty, little secrets. Even you deserve to be told in person, not by phone or email."

His arms cross his chest. "You invaded my privacy," his voice low and threatening.

"What privacy? How did I invade your privacy? My information came from an overheard conversation out in public. I'm certain the person wanted me to hear it. I Googled you. That gave me the Simon piece. And, by the way, what's this about your having mules?"

His face turns apoplectic. Hit a nerve there.

"I want my keys returned. Any further business we have can be conducted over the phone. Right now, I want you out of here. I will call you in a couple of days to discuss how to get my stored things from your trailer, and we can discuss the camper, but not right now."

He moves to the living room and sits on the sofa. "What can I do to change your mind? The divorce papers are sitting in a drawer in the house I own with her. I could sign them today." He stabs at a tear trickling down his cheek. "Just give me a chance."

I want to reach out, but I stand still.

"You are good for me. You gave me strength through my cancer." His shoulders drop as he folds inward. "You've seen me through some of the scariest moments of my life and been there to share a lot of good ones."

I don't want to think of those shared experiences.

"What will it take?" His voice begs.

Nothing. He's crossed the line. I shake my head.

"Could we at least be friends?"

Not going to happen. Why should I be just another number in his line of old girlfriends?

"Can we talk about this? I'll tell you whatever you want to know."

The hook has been cast. My need to know outweighs my common sense. "Why are you still married?"

He looks down. "The lawsuit." His voice a whisper. "She can be forced to testify against me if we're divorced. We'd lose everything. She has a stake in this marriage also."

That makes more sense than staying married for the adult children.

"The other women?"

"Only one. The others are distractions."

"How long?"

"Several years before I met you."

"I'm the other woman?"

He looks at me through pleading eyes.

As if he reads my facial expression, "I'll do whatever it takes. I need you. You are the best thing that's ever happened to me. I love you."

Words I've longed to hear. Can I be his friend?

He has done a lot for me. When he's kind, he's almost over the top with kindness.

"Tell me about the mule thing."

He stiffens. "No. What you don't know won't hurt you."

I tell myself all the reasons being his friend is not a good idea. He lies. I don't know how much of what he's told today is the truth, if any of it. No. The best prediction of future behavior is past behavior.

A cloud of sadness wraps around me as I shake my head. "I won't do this again."

His cocky demeanor deflates. He turns toward the door. "You know I respect you more than any other woman. Goodbye."

I close the door and relief takes over. I let go of a hundred forty pound albatross. I am free.

I call George. "It's done. I'm done."

The next day I change the locks.

Three days later, Frank picks up his things and drops my clothing and books stored in his trailer in the middle of my living room floor. Memories of leaving the beach house flood my awareness as Yin and Yang decide the mess on the floor makes for a game of hide and seek. Yes, I made a good decision.

George and I continue our meetings, and we spend more time just enjoying our friendship. I spend the next eight months writing the journal article from my dissertation and formatting the dissertation. The middle of April, three weeks before graduation, I meet Megan in her office. She hands me the dissertation. Signed by all the committee members. "Take this over to the graduate office and have the university official reader check it for formatting and sign off on it. With this last hoop, I will complete all my requirements for my degree.

While I walk over to the administrative building, I pray to the gods that my printer is exact on every page. I measured, but I am never certain. When I arrive, I am the only student in the office.

The reader gets out her ruler. I hold my breath while she measures every margin. And, then the exact spacing on every indentation. The longer I stand here, the harder I concentrate to not tap my fingers on the counter or give any sign of anxiety. My hands begin to shake. I keep them low, under the counter, so the reader won't see them. Aah, she's on the appendix now. The last page. She looks up.

"Good job." She signs the page. "Your dissertation is officially accepted."

I break out in a grin. "Thank you." I want to let out a big whoop.

I walk out with a light step and a glad heart. I am officially Dr. Lindsey.

Chapter 22

I apply my make-up with particular attention to detail. Next, I blow out my hair. I spray a quick spray of my precious bottle of Dali perfume. I start to put on pantyhose and change my mind. I'll wear my sandals without stockings. I slip the gown over a naked body and smile. No one will ever know. I attach the hood and I'm ready to go.

George arrives a few minutes early to take me to the ceremony. "Are you ready to make it official, Dr. Lindsey?" He gives me a peck on the cheek. "You do clean up nice."

Make-up is everything. I toss my hair and give him an exaggerated wink. "Why, thank you, kind sir." *If you only knew.* "You're not so bad yourself."

He places a hand on my shoulder. "This has been a long and difficult journey, but you have arrived intact."

Something about his hand on my shoulder…Tears form as I inhale my gratitude for this friend who was in my life when I began my journey to womanhood and will now watch me fulfill my dream of becoming a doctor in the field of marriage and family therapy.

"I have you to thank for the intact part." What would I have done if he'd not gotten me to talk about my secrets? I slide into a hug.

George's hug is the kind that tells me all is right with my world. As long as his arms are around me, I am safe. I am reluctant to move away. "I guess we'd better go," as I leave my safety net. I gather up my purse and briefcase and start for the door.

"Do you have everything?"

"My cap is in the trunk." I have my briefcase with a thank-you card for Megan. And my purse. I can't think of anything else."

George opens the door, and then puts out his hand for my keys. After he locks the door, he returns the keys. When we get to the car, I open the trunk and place my purse and briefcase underneath my cap.

Our drive into town is less congested than I'd anticipated so we have plenty of time to park and head to the Civic Center. I pull my cap from the trunk and head for the line-up place. We are halfway there when I remember the card for Megan. "I need to go back and get Megan's card."

George looks at his watch. "We should have plenty of time if we rush."

At the car, I open the trunk. No briefcase. "Where is my briefcase?"

George takes my cap as I rummage through the nearly empty trunk. My purse is where I left it, in plain sight. I look inside. Nothing is missing. A piece of paper and a CD, labeled "Forgive You" rest in the same spot where the briefcase had been. I look at the paper. It is a poem:

Forgive You

You hurt me for so long,
You treated me so wrong,
What am I gonna do
When I forgive you?
You couldn't make it better,
Your tears couldn't get any wetter,
What will I do
When I forgive you?

The good you did so accidentally,
The life I learned to live alone,
You can't imagine what it's meant to me,
Having this hurt to call my own.

Holding on to you
The only way that I've known how to,
What am I gonna do
When I give up hating you?
You touched my heart,

It wasn't fair,
You reached past like it wasn't there.
What will I do?
How I've loved hating you.

Every step I've taken, I took out of spite,
You made me struggle to grow strong;
My raging heart comforted me at night,
When everything I loved was wrong.
I've never known a passion half as sweet,
A touch on which I could depend,
The perfect circle, endless and complete,
And now I have to start again.

What will I do?
Oh, how I've held on to you.
What will I do?

I hand both to George. After his thorough search of the trunk, "I watched you put the briefcase in here. Let's check inside the car, just in case."

I unlock the car. There are only two places to look: behind the driver's seat and on the floor in front of the passenger's seat. No briefcase.

George shakes his head. "I know it was in this car. If someone had broken in to steal it, the top would have been slashed." He takes back my cap. "Even if you had left the trunk wide open, your purse is intact, and that doesn't explain how the poem and CD arrived." He shrugs. "Beats me." He looks at his watch. We'd better hurry or you'll not march."

We make sure the car is locked and rush back to the line-up. The line is moving out as I approach. George hands me the cap. The designated person in front of me is at the door as I approach. I slip on the cap, and then toss George the car keys. I slide into my place just as I walk through the door and out onto the floor.

I barely listen to the commencement address as I try to figure out what happened to the briefcase and how the poem and CD seems to have replaced it, distracted only by nearby students' texting and emailing. The next thing I know, I'm standing in line to receive my diploma, hats fly, and we're marching out. Where is my briefcase?

How did the poem get in the car? I doubt it came from the author. With only that quick read, I recognized how it described my life. A coincidence? There are none. A gift from the Universe? I can think of no other explanation.

George meets me outside, a big grin on his face. "Well, Dr. Lindsey, we have a signed five-year contract for our study." He pulls out his phone and hands it to me. "The fax came in during graduation."

Excitement winds its way up from my toes to my heart. We'll get to work together for five years. I grab him and do a little dance.

A graveled voice behind me says, "You act like you didn't expect to graduate."

I turn and look. No need to go into depth. "That, too." We walk away.

Later, after all the partying, George and I sit on my sofa and watch the sky color our world while we listen to the song "Forgive You." George scrutinizes my face. "Are you okay? Your briefcase?"

I pause as I sense the profundity of the message I took from this morning's perplexity. "Somehow finding and reading the poem helps me to let go of that burgundy briefcase in which I filed and stored so many memories and issues I had been unable to release."

I take a moment to remember. *Alex, I love you. I forgive you. I release you.*

George squeezes my hand. "Do you feel any differently now that it's official?"

Realization hits. "I returned to graduate school because I trusted that if I could know enough, I would be safe. Instead, I met my enemies, and they are my old beliefs. And the meanings I make under their influence."

About the Author

Roberta Burton began devouring books the day she learned to read. Burton holds a master's in clinical psychology and a doctorate in marriage and family therapy. Both degrees provide her with interesting characters. Before returning to college, she was a bank teller, one of the Navy's first ward clerks, girl Friday for an airport aviation company, and Secretary/Treasurer of an architectural firm. She is currently a member of the Osher Lifelong Learning Institute (OLLI) and continues to take classes to improve her writing. Other interests include award-winning watercolors, martial arts healing, and alternative health medicine. She continues to be a voracious reader.

"For me, writing is not a choice. It is my purpose."
Roberta Burton
Tallahassee, FL 32312
www.askdrlee.com

Roberta Burton

CPSIA information can be obtained
at www.ICGtesting.com
Printed in the USA
FFOW01n0618230215
11194FF